W9-ATT-436

WALL AND **MEAN**

WALL AND MEAN

A Novel

TOM BERNARD

W. W. NORTON & COMPANY New York London

Printed in the United States of America
First Edition

Manufacturing by Quebecor Fairfield
Book design by Dana Sloan
Production manager: Julia Druskin

Library of Congress Cataloging-in-Publication Data

Bernard, Tom.
Wall and Mean : a novel / Tom Bernard. — 1st ed.
p. cm.
ISBN 978-393-06482-7
1. Bond market—Fiction. 2. Brokers—Fiction. 3. New York (N. Y.)—Fiction.
4. Sports betting—Nevada—Las Vegas—Fiction. I. Title.
PS3602.E7595W35 2007
813'.6—dc22

2007002359

W. W. Norton & Company, Inc., 500 Fifth Avenue, New York, N.Y. 10110
www.wwnorton.com

W. W. Norton & Company Ltd., Castle House, 75/76 Wells Street, London W1T 3QT

1 2 3 4 5 6 7 8 9 0

For my wife, Sallie

All of the author's earnings from this book will be donated to Autism Speaks (www.autismspeaks.org) and SafeMinds (www.safeminds.org).

WALL AND MEAN

PROLOGUE

Frank chalked his cue as he studied his shot. The cue ball and the eight ball were in the far right-hand corner. He was too short to lean over the table and too muscle-bound to hold the cue behind his back. Had he been playing for money he would have used the bridge without hesitation, but he played alone. Nobody wanted to risk being assaulted. He glanced at the other hoods and slackers who were passing the afternoon playing pool or slouching against the bar drinking beer. The last time one of them had snickered when Frank used the bridge, Frank had broken a cue over the guy's head and stabbed the splintered handle through his cheek and into the back of his throat.

"Frank, we gotta go into the city. Now." A sturdily built man in his midtwenties had entered the bar. His dark red hair curled over the collar of his leather jacket. He approached Frank directly and squinted as his eyes adjusted to the dim light.

"Yo, Kevin. Let's go." Relieved to quit on the awkward shot, Frank dropped his cue on the table and picked up his New York Jets gym bag. The two men jumped into a red Impala and headed down Flatbush Avenue toward the Manhattan Bridge. At the first traffic light Frank poured powdered methedrine from a vial onto the back of his hand and snorted it noisily. Kevin extended a hand and took his snort at the next light.

"What's up?" asked Frank.

"Henry called. He wants to see us."

"Henry pays on Tuesday. Why can't we see 'im tomorrah?"

"Must be about the other thing." They were quiet for a minute as Kevin sped onto the bridge. The East River appeared beneath them. It was warm for late September, and Frank cracked his window. "I'm a little worried he wants to see us," Kevin said. "Everything should be between us and his client's husband."

"Wha's da worry?" asked Frank.

"What if the husband went to the cops, tol' 'em we're leanin' on him. His wife gives up Henry, and Henry gives us up. We pick Henry up, he could be wearin' a wire."

"Henry'd be afraid to give us up. You're paranoid. Too much meth."

Kevin wiped the sweat from his upper lip. "I don't know. Henry's always sneakin' in places, puttin' tape recorders under beds, whatever. Cops probably got him on a B 'n E or somethin'. It could be part of a plea," said Kevin.

"Henry's a pussy. He'd never risk rattin' us."

"Hey, the guy's a private dick, does some scary shit. If you were humpin' some guy's wife and all of a sudden some P I is pointin' a camera at you, what would you do to him?"

"I wouldn't hump a guy's wife. That's a mortal sin."

"Yeah, right. The point is that Henry pisses people off. Say some guy's got his gun on the dresser, under the pillow—it's gotta be dangerous," said Kevin.

"He's a fuckin' pussy."

"Whatever. We should still check him for a wire."

"Guy's wearin' a wire, he's dead," said Frank.

"We can't whack him."

"Why not?" asked Frank.

"Guy's into TD 30 large."

"Oh yeah."

The Impala jolted its way through Chinatown as Kevin gunned it through each intersection. Traffic was sluggish, and the air smelled like the gutters.

"Hey, stop here." Kevin pulled over to the curb and let the engine idle while Frank ducked into a deli for a six-pack of Colt 45s. Minutes later, with a beer between his thighs, Kevin raced up 1st Avenue, hung a left on 96th Street, and pulled over in front of a coffee shop. A scrawny, middle-aged man in a rumpled black raincoat emerged and approached the car nervously. Frank swung his door open, stepped out, then followed the man into the back-seat. Kevin pulled into traffic.

"Take your clothes off, Henry," ordered Frank.

"You're kiddin', right?"

"No kiddin'. Strip."

"What for?"

"'Cause you my bitch!" Frank leered at him and screeched a maniacal, falsetto laugh. He kept his crazed eyes locked on Henry's as he yanked the raincoat open and grabbed at the smaller man's belt buckle.

"No!" squealed Henry.

"Relax, dude," said Kevin. "Frank just wants to check you for a wire."

"What am I, a fuckin' moron? Like I'm gonna wear a wire on you guys? You think I'm nuts?"

"Just do it. Take 'em off," said Kevin. Henry handed over his shoes and clothes for inspection. He looked even smaller wearing nothing but his socks.

"He's clean," said Frank.

"So, what's up, Henry?" asked Kevin.

"So, I get a call from my client this morning. The wife. She called to terminate my employment, effective immediately." Henry's voice wavered as he struggled to pull on his trousers. "She says her husband confessed to everything last night. Apparently he told her about the blackmail and admitted that he was cheating. She said she didn't see why she needed to pay me to get proof anymore, so I'm fired."

"Why did her husband confess?" asked Kevin.

"Obviously, you guys leaned on the guy too hard. How much did you ask for?"

"What the fuck is it to you? You said this guy is rich," said Kevin.

"Guy works on Wall Street, lives on Park Avenue, summer house in Southampton. He ain't broke, that's for sure."

"I think the guy's a cheapskate scumbag. Cares more about his money than his marriage," replied Kevin.

"Guy's bangin' bimbos three nights a week, you thought he cared about his marriage?" said Henry.

"Whatever. Any idea if our boy went to the cops?"

"No idea. I told you all I know."

"Well, all I know is that you're the only connection between our boy and us. So if the cops come our way, it's your ass." Kevin turned around and glared at Henry. Frank jerked a Browning 9-millimeter automatic from his Jets bag, shoved Henry to the car's floor, and jammed the pistol in his nose.

"One question from da cops on dis t'ing and I'll blow your fuckin' brains out. Un'erstand?" Henry nodded and Frank let him up. Henry pulled out a dirty handkerchief to staunch the flow of blood from his nostril.

"Jesus, Frank. You didn't have to do that. I may be a degenerate gambler, but I'm not a fuckin' rat."

"You got this week's vig?" asked Frank.

Henry handed him an envelope full of cash. "Three grand. Next week will be tougher. I was counting on a check from this client."

"She's stiffin' ya?" asked Frank. He seemed confused.

"Remember the pictures I gave you of your boy screwin' blondie?" said Henry. "You know, the ones he wouldn't pay you for?

The pictures I had to deliver to my client to get paid? Remember?"

Kevin sighed and handed Henry a beer. He popped the tab and guzzled eagerly.

"Good excuse, Henry, but the problem is that TD ain't gonna find out about this fuckup. All he's gonna know is that you're short. Got it?" said Kevin.

Henry nodded. "I got it."

"Where ya want us to drop ya?" asked Frank.

"Here on Lex. Preferably near an express station. I'm takin' the 4 to Yankee Stadium."

"What's da point?" asked Frank. "Blue Jays clinched da pennant."

"Meaningless game, but TD has a line on it. Even money. I bet the Yanks. Just tryin' to keep you guys in business, in case your blackmailing career doesn't improve."

"Fuckin' wiseguy!" growled Frank. He swung the Browning and caught Henry with a glancing blow that tore his earlobe up to the cartilage. Henry dove out of the moving Impala, rolled over once on the curb, stood up, and staggered up Lexington Avenue with blood dripping from his head.

Kevin turned around and grabbed a fistful of Frank's Jets jersey to keep him in the car. "Leave 'im go, ya fuckin' maniac," yelled Kevin.

"Fuckin' wise ass." Frank pulled his legs back in the car, slammed the door, and shoved the automatic to the bottom of his gym bag. At the next traffic light he rejoined Kevin in the front seat and cracked open the last two beers. After a dozen blocks with no police pursuit, they both snorted more meth.

When they stopped to get more beers, Kevin went to a pay phone. He was sweating a bit and his shirt was sticking to his back. He called TD and arranged to drop off the money that afternoon. At least the day wasn't a total waste.

"I ever tell ya about this guy I met in Rikers? Rock Man?" asked Kevin as they drove away.

"Yeah," grunted Frank.

"Rock Man says you get the most from the guys with the most to lose." He paused to wipe his upper lip again. "Forget this adultery stuff, it's small time. What we gotta do is find a rich guy with real problems, somethin' he actually gives a shit about. We play our cards right, we'll be livin' the life of Riley."

"Pat Riley?"

"It's an expression. Means livin' large."

"I was wonderin'." Frank paused to chug his beer. "I was wonderin', dis guy Rock Man's such a fuckin' genius. How come he was hangin' out wit' *you* in the joint?"

Kevin glanced over at Frank, eyes narrowed. "Fuckin' wise guy. I should whack your ear off."

"Try it."

1

The first thing you noticed about the trading floor was the noise. It was a steady, low-pitched roar of men's voices. The room was half the size of a football field. Rows of battleship gray trading desks filled the entire floor. Well-groomed young men wearing blue or gray suit trousers, expensive dress shirts, and colorful silk ties paced frantically at most of the desks. Every fifth or sixth station was occupied by a young woman wearing a business suit or skirt and blouse. Everyone was either on the phone or barking across the desks. Sometimes both. To an outsider, it seemed like chaos.

George Wilhelm felt the knot in his stomach twist as he stared at the trading screens stacked high on the emerging markets desk. Most of the screens displayed numbers representing bids and offers for the loans that George traded; others were television monitors showing current news broadcasts. CNN showed T-72 tanks rumbling through the streets of Moscow. Suddenly, a huge cloud of smoke filled the TV screen as an artillery shell exploded in the Russian parliament building. The prices vanished from the electronic trading screens as Wall Street traders pulled their bids. The numbers reappeared as they reassessed the market for the bond and loan obligations of less-developed countries in the wake of the erupting violence.

George quickly calculated his losses. Ecuador was quoted at 35, down 15 points. Peru was probably down the same amount. He owned $100 million face value of loans owed by the two countries, so he had lost $15 million based on the current prices. On Friday he had been up $15 million for the year. He had traded the defaulted loans adroitly as the emerging markets rallied throughout the year. He figured that in this one morning in October 1993 he had pissed away his earnings for the entire year. It was barely 10:30.

"Bid 25 Russia for Scott!" screamed José, a wiry Argentine salesman whose desk abutted George's back-to-back. José's client, Scott, a hedge fund manager, was demanding the price at which George would purchase $25 million face amount of loans owed by Russia's central bank, Vneshnecommbank.

George pulled one of his phones away from his face and yelled, "Vnesh traded at 22 before the last explosion. Market's lower now. I'll pay 20 for $5 million and take an order on the balance of 20."

"Nobody's going to leave you an order with the market this volatile, asshole!" José spoke into the phone for an instant, then shouted to George. "You bought 5 at 20."

"The bid for 5 only works if I get an order on the balance," replied George.

"It's too late. He's gone. You bought $5 million."

An older trader with collar-length coal black hair sat next to George. He leaned over, put his hand on George's shoulder, spoke to him quietly, then pointed to a trading screen. A trade of $5 million Vnesh was flashing at 19. George had instantly lost a point, or $50,000 on the $5 million block he had bought from Scott. He dove across his desk, grabbed José by the tie, and jerked him forward. George's knees were on top of his desk now and he was nose-to-nose with José. "That scumbag Scott is spraying the Street! Find out what the hell he's doing, shithead! Now!" screamed George. The older trader grabbed George by the arm and jerked his thumb toward two senior executives who stood a few feet behind the desk, observing the action. George glanced at the executives, released José's tie, and sat down.

Philip Gold ran all bond trading at City Trust, and John Peters, his boss, ran all capital markets activities.

"Russia trades at 19. Wow," remarked Peters. "Where was it on Friday?"

"Around 38. Down 50 percent since the tanks rolled."

Peters gestured toward the older trader, the only man with long hair on the trading floor. "Looks like Enrique's got things under control."

"He's seen it all, believe me," replied Gold.

Enrique Guerrero was five foot seven and built like a welterweight who works inside, chopping down his taller opponent with body shots and short uppercuts. His tailored, Ralph Lauren shirt fit him perfectly. The dark complexion, high cheekbones, and severe lips radiated confidence and authority. There was no question who was running the emerging markets desk.

"Who's the hothead?" asked Peters.

"George Wilhelm. Ph.D. in developmental economics from Fletcher, hotshot at the IMF. Smart as hell. He's getting killed today. The more liquid paper, Mexican and Argentine Brady bonds, are down about 5 points, but the illiquid loans that he trades, the exotics, are down a lot more. It's the damnedest thing I've ever seen. Every time they lob another shell into the Russian parliament building the hedge funds come flying in to sell and the market trades down. I think he's doing OK, under the circumstances." Gold leaned closer, speaking out of the corner of his mouth. "Scott is the slipperiest hedgie on Wall Street. He probably has his traders on other phones, tattooing Morgan and Citibank as we speak." Gold pointed to a $5 million sale flashing at 18½ on the screen. "Ten to one those are Scott's loans." Gold's instincts told him that Scott had sold additional Russian loans to other dealers, who were now dumping them, just like George. The market was plummeting.

Peters nodded. "So what's really going on in Moscow?"

"Nobody really knows if the mutiny is gaining traction. The lack of information is frustrating the shit out of Enrique and George. Everyone is trading off of CNN. At least it's a level playing field," answered Gold.

"Sasha? Yuri?"

"Nothing coherent."

"What about Pablo?" Peters gestured toward the only man in sight, other than himself, who was wearing his suit coat. The senior emerging markets economist was standing nearby, speaking urgently into a phone.

"He can't get anyone in Russia. He's spoken to the State Department, Treasury, the IMF, the World Bank, and the Fed. They're all watching CNN, asking Pablo what's really going on," replied Gold. He and Peters returned their attention to the trading desk when they heard José shouting at George again.

"Steinie wants a two-sided market in Ecuador. Size!" Steinie was Lowenstein Partners, one of the largest hedge funds in the world. The hedge fund trader wanted City Trust to simultaneously offer to purchase or sell "size," meaning a large amount, of Ecuadorian loans. By demanding a two-sided market, he hoped to keep City Trust honest, believing that if he asked for a bid *or* an offer, rather than both simultaneously, the City Trust trader would "fade" his price. If asked to buy loans, City Trust might lower the price to lower risk in the brutal market. If asked to sell loans, the bank might raise the price for the same reason.

"I'm not making a market. I'll work an order in the mid-30s," snapped George.

Peters nodded to himself. Wilhelm's offer to buy or sell loans into the market on Lowenstein's behalf, rather than buying or selling with City Trust as principal, was appropriately prudent in the context of the market meltdown. José spoke into the phone, then listened intently.

"Hey, Enrique, David Lowenstein wants to speak to you. On his direct," yelled José. Enrique ended the call he was on and punched the button on his console labeled "Steinie."

"Hello, David."

"Listen, Enrique, I bought $50 million of this Ecuador shit from you on Pablo's recommendation. If you don't make me a market in size, I'm going to pull every fuckin' wire to your goddamned bank."

"Don't you think that's a little harsh, David? I mean, the market's unbelievably tough in here."

"Every wire to every desk. London, Tokyo, bonds, foreign exchange, equities. Every fuckin' wire. Understand?"

"I understand. I need to call you back."

"Make it fast!" barked Lowenstein before slamming down his phone. Enrique marched up to Peters and Gold.

"Steinie says he'll cut off the entire firm if we don't make him a size market in Ecuador. Do you think he's serious?"

"He's serious all right," replied Gold. "Two years ago he put us in the penalty box for six months because we gave him a shitty bid on a mortgage derivative that we sold him."

"We can't afford that again. He's too big now. If we don't see his trading flows, we'll be hamstrung," said Peters.

"Are you sure that he's a seller?" asked Gold. "He probably knows we own a ton of Ecuador. Any chance he wants to make us think he's a seller and then pick us off in here?"

"He's got a billion invested in Russia with probably $800 million borrowed against it. With Russia losing half its value today, he probably owes $400 million on his loans. I think he's forced to sell Ecie to meet margin calls on Russia," explained Enrique.

"How much does he have?" asked Gold.

"He says he bought $50 million from us. Probably about right."

"What do you think?"

"Well. . . ." Enrique rubbed his chin. "The thing is, there's no linkage between Russia and the Latins. I mean, fundamentally, the oil exporters—Venezuela, Mexico, and Ecuador—should do better if the Moscow meltdown disrupts Russian oil exports. It's all about liquidity. Lowenstein isn't the only hedge fund that borrowed heavily to finance Russian positions. I'm sure that's why Scott is selling. He and every other hedgie are dumping anything they can to meet margin calls. Other than the hedge fund traders, there are no natural buyers of exotics." Everyone looked at Peters, a portly, balding man in his late forties.

"My gut tells me that this is an opportunity to buy at distressed prices," said Peters. "Maybe not in Russia, since we don't have a handle on it. But if other stuff is down this dramatically due to margin calls on Russia, it could be a classic capitulation trade."

Another shell exploded in the Russian parliament, precipitating another round of selling. George leaned over and threw up in his wastebasket. Then he wiped his mouth with the back of his hand and resumed his phone conversation.

Peters grinned from ear to ear and hissed "Yessss" between his teeth. Gold and Enrique looked at him quizzically. Peters spoke with authority. "Baron Rothschild once said that the time to buy is when the blood is in the streets. Well, they have that in Moscow. My old boss from Kidder Peabody, who taught me how to trade, said the time to buy is when the trader pukes. It's the purest buy signal in market history. You want to double down on Ecuador?"

"We liked Ecuador at 50 on Friday. We can probably clean Steinie out in the low 30s," answered Enrique eagerly. "If this Russia thing blows over, Ecuador could be back in the 40s tomorrow." He was getting fired up.

"Good luck." Peters patted Gold and Enrique on their backs and walked into his office at the head of the trading floor. It was the only office adjoining the floor that did not have a glass wall and door. The traders called it the blowjob office. Enrique sat down next to George.

"The big kahunas want to double down on Ecie. How should we make 'em?" asked Enrique.

"Jesus," said George. "If we bid below 30, Steinie will probably cut us off and try to sell it away."

"Do you think any swingin' dick out there will buy his Ecie in the 30s? Goldman? Solly?"

"Great question. It looks awfully cheap, but the market is a vacuum. Every exotics trader I know is drowning in his own blood right now. Nobody is making markets."

"How 'bout 31–33?"

"Do we have to be two-sided? I'd hate to let him buy our paper at 33," George replied.

"He's a seller, right?" asked Enrique.

"I sure hope so," replied George. "At these prices I want to buy."

"If you want me to put the trade in my ledger, I will." Enrique was offering to book the trade, if one occurred, in a separate account that would not affect George's year-end bonus calculation.

"No, I'll take it in mine," said George.

David Lowenstein answered his City Trust direct line. "About time. What do you have for me, Enrique?"

"I'm 31–33 on Ecuador, $50 million up." Enrique was offering to buy $50 million face of Ecuador at 31 or sell $50 million at 33, at Lowenstein's option.

"You're way low. Ecie is in the mid-30s!" screamed Lowenstein.

"Then buy 'em at 33." Enrique felt a rush of adrenaline. He knew he had him.

"Meet me in the middle. I'll sell you 50 at 32." Enrique detected a slight crack in Lowenstein's voice. The adrenaline rush became an intense surge.

"I'll repeat the bid once since you're an important client, then I'm out. The markets are crazy in here."

"Fuck you, Enrique! I sell you 50 at 31!" Lowenstein slammed the phone down again. Enrique leaped to his feet and roared.

"AAAARRRGGGHH!" He slapped George high ten and chest bumped him hard against the desk. "AAAARRRGGGHH!" Everyone in the vicinity stared. Enrique was in a zone, and George felt a pang of envy mixed with admiration. The man had brass balls.

2

By 6:30 that evening the activity had died down and most of the salesmen and traders had left for the day. Slouched in his chair with his phone balanced on his shoulder, George Wilhelm spoke to Toshi, City Trust's EM trader in Tokyo, to "pass the exotics book." Enrique and the other traders had already passed the book on the more liquid Latin bonds and loans. George was responsible for risk taking in Latin American loans, and the London team was responsible for Eastern European and African loans. Toshi traded all the loans with the bank's Asian clients after the New York close and before the London open. They discussed the situation in Russia and the rest of the day's events. George cautioned Toshi to stay nimble on Russia until London took over. As the London team had big positions in Poland and Nigeria, they speculated as to how those countries might trade with Russia so volatile. They did not discuss Ecuador. The loans were unlikely to trade until New York opened again the next day. Besides, the bet had already been made.

George wished Toshi luck and turned his attention to the sports section of the *New York Post.* George punched his unrecorded line and placed a call to a 718 number in Brooklyn.

"Yeah."

"York for TD."

"Yeah, York."

"ALCS?"

"Jays are 6."

"Give me the Blue Jays minus the 6, a thousand times."

"Righto. Jays minus 6, a t'ousand times. Anyt'ing else, York?"

"Not on this call." As George was dialing, a tall blond man in a gray pin-striped suit had plopped down in Enrique's chair, next to George. He was clean shaven, handsome, with acetylene blue eyes and a brilliant smile that must have set his parents back thousands for orthodontia. The young man's father was the managing partner of Monroe Brothers. He also served on the boards of the New York Stock Exchange, the New York Public Library, the Metropolitan Opera, and six Fortune 500 companies. Mark Frost Sr. was considered one of the most powerful men on Wall Street. Mark Jr. traded mortgage-backed bonds for City Trust. He was one of George's suitemates at "Club 16B," their Upper East Side apartment.

"Hi, Mark."

"Hey, George. That your bookie?"

"Yeah."

"You're York?"

"Yeah. Because I live on York, he nicknamed me that. We don't use real names on the phone."

"So his real initials aren't TD either."

"Nope."

"So, what does Blue Jays minus the 6 a thousand times mean?"

"In baseball odds the fulcrum is 5. The Blue Jays are favorites in their game with Chicago, even-6. To bet on the Jays you have to lay 6-to-5 odds. If you want to bet the Sox, it's even money. If the Jays were 7–8, you'd lay 8–5 to bet the Jays, and get 7–5 to bet the Sox."

"Say that again. If the Jays are 7–8, you do what?"

"Just put the 5 in the middle. If you bet the Jays, the favorites, you're laying 8–5. If you bet $100 and lose, you lose $160. If you win, you win $100. If you bet $100 on the Sox, the underdog, you get 7–5. You can win $140 or lose $100."

"Got it. What if it's even?" asked Mark.

"Pick 'em. You lay 5.5 to 5. Ten percent vigorish to the bookie if you lose. Same vig as football and basketball. One time is $5."

"So you just bet 5 grand on the Blue Jays. You lose millions of City Trust's money today, and you bet $5,000 of your own money on baseball? Why?"

"Five thousand if I win, $6,000 if I lose. I'm laying 6 to 5. It's a serious underlay—the Jays should be much steeper favorites given Dave Stewart's experience. He's 7–0 in nine playoff starts with a 2.99 ERA. Plus, in Game 2 he beat Alex Fernandez, who's also pitching tonight. Fernandez only gave up one earned run in eight innings last time, but even-6 gives the Sox way too much consideration for home-field advantage at Comiskey."

"Fascinating," offered Mark sarcastically. "But you answered a different question than I asked."

George glanced up from the box scores. "Look, I bet the bank's money on Ecuadorian loans because the market undervalues the prospects for their repayment. I bet the Jays because the market undervalues Stewart's postseason experience. Markets aren't perfect. If they were, there'd be no use for traders."

"So it's your sacred duty to bet on every mispricing in the markets?"

"Only in the markets where I'm an expert," George said.

"You think Vegas doesn't have experts?"

"The oddsmakers don't set the correct spread, they set the spread that attracts an equal amount of action on each team. I don't bet against the professionals, I bet against *Extraordinary Popular Delusions and the Madness of Crowds*. It's all in that tulipmania book. You should read it."

"Yeah, right. Like I have time to read a book." Mark studied a news photo that was taped to one of George's trading screens. It showed a striped-suited convict in a cage in front of a huge crowd. "Why do you have this picture on your desk?"

"You don't know who that is?"

Mark shook his head.

"It's Abimael Guzman, the head of the Shining Path terrorists in Peru. His capture initiated Peru's recent emergence from the dark ages. Huge positive for the market."

"Whatever. You want to go for a drink? You look like you could use one."

"I'm supposed to meet Sue at 7:30 at McNabb's."

"That dump?"

"I want to watch the game. And I suppose you want to hit the meat markets?"

"Look, the Blue Jays will win or lose whether you're watching or not, but the best I'll do at McNabb's is some beast from a softball team who outweighs me and will kick my ass if she doesn't like my performance. That's assuming, of course, that I find one who's not a dyke. How 'bout Stephano's? I'll buy the first two rounds."

"OK. I'll call Sue. Grab a cab and I'll meet you out front."

"Sounds good. I have to make a quick stop on the way. Fifteen minutes max."

"No problem."

It was another trader's misfortune that had brought George and Mark together. With no time for apartment hunting, George had been living at a residential hotel arranged by City Trust when Gold caught a mortgage trader mismarking his positions and fired him. Sam Thorn, a Treasury salesman George knew at Princeton, told him the trader would be leaving town. George immediately introduced himself to Mark and moved in at the end of that month. Mark wasn't George's favorite guy in the world, but George barely knew anyone in the city when he moved, and the bank's relocation subsidy had run out. The guy sure knew a lot of women, though.

Mark stopped the cab on Lexington in the 70s and led George to a steel-and-glass high-rise. Even though he identified himself over the intercom, Mark positioned himself in front of the peephole once they reached the apartment door. A pale, skinny man in his early thirties opened the door and looked George over suspiciously, with lead pellet eyes that were set too close together.

"Morgan, this is my roommate, George Wilhelm. Trades emerging market debt at City Trust."

At the mention of emerging markets, Morgan raised his eyebrows. "EM trader, eh?"

"Yeah. Exotics." George shook hands with Morgan and was ushered into a clean, starkly modern New York apartment. The place reeked of marijuana.

"Excuse us a second, George," said Morgan, as he pulled Mark into an adjoining room. "Where do you get off bringing a stranger here without asking?" Morgan was up in Mark's face, his dark eyes seething. He clenched his fist tighter around Mark's coat collar, pulling the taller man forward until his forearm was pressing against his chest.

"He's not a stranger. Like I said, he's my roommate, and a fellow EM trader."

"Next time ask me. Got it?" Morgan hissed. He was livid, but his rage subsided quickly enough to suggest that he was acting a bit to make his point. Mark straightened his collar.

"Understood. Say, I'm in kind of a hurry, Morgan. George has a lady waiting."

"No problem." Morgan returned to the living room, sat down on a black leather couch behind a glass coffee table, and began chopping cocaine on a small mirror. He scraped out three lines and offered the mirror and a rolled-up twenty to George.

"No thanks." George shook his head. Morgan handed the mirror to Mark, who snorted one and a half lines and handed it back to Morgan.

Mark beamed. "Very nice. How much?"

"A hundred a gram."

"I'll take an eight-ball." Morgan dipped a teaspoon into a baggie full of cocaine, weighed out 3.5 grams, and strained a spoonful into a vial. Mark paid him $350 in cash. They shook hands, and Mark headed out the door with George.

"Don't bring me along on these buys again. Gives me the creeps," scolded George.

"What?"

"What? What if the cops come in to bust the guy and we're sitting there? Or some gang bangers come in with Uzis, knock him over. We're caught in the cross fire."

"Gang bangers? Are you nuts? This guy's clientele is strictly Wall Street. He used to work at Commerce Trust. Traded EM."

"This guy traded at Commerce and now he's a coke dealer?"

"He got busted for fraud. Did a year at the federal prison in Danbury. Can't get a legitimate job with a felony record, so he deals coke."

"Wait a minute. I think I read about this guy. Set up some offshore accounts and ran EM trades through them."

"Right. Big markups. Made a few million before he was caught."

"Jesus, Mark. Thanks for introducing me to your friend."

"He's not my friend. He's my dealer."

At Stephano's, all the furniture was varnished maple. The dining tables in the back were also maple, covered with starched white tablecloths and napkins. The waitresses were young and pretty, and each one claimed she was an actress or a model. Prosperous-looking men and women in business suits, mostly from Wall Street, dominated the after-work crowd. Later on, the "bridge and tunnel crowd," working-class girls from the boroughs, would come in to meet wealthy, eligible men.

George, Mark, and Sue drank beer at a table near the bar. Sue wore a navy blue pin-striped jacket and skirt. She had huge green eyes and an upturned Waspy nose. George thought her lips looked like Julia Roberts's. Her hair was naturally blonde, and she wore it shoulder length, secured in the back with a leather barrette. It had been short when she went to Wellesley, but the combination of her gym-rat reputation and her close-cropped locks had attracted as much attention from her lesbian classmates as from her male professors, so she grew her hair out. Her face was a little too thin and her chin a little too long to consider her a classic beauty. But she was definitely cute. Sue ignored her glass and drank her beer from the bottle like the guys.

George was holding court. "Speaker Khasbulatov and Vice President Rutskoi were leading the communist hard-liners that held out in the parliament building. Rutskoi was an air force general. Apparently he kicked some ass in Afghanistan because in the AP picture I saw, his dress uniform was covered with medals. It looked like fruit salad. In any case, everyone was waiting for his military cronies to rise up against Yeltsin, but the mutiny never happened. The T-72s just kept pounding parliament until everyone was either dead or gave up. When CNN showed the commandos leading Khasbulatov and Rutskoi past the tanks to a paddy wagon, the market gapped up. You couldn't get an offering—"

"What does it mean to 'gap up'?" asked Sue.

"The market was 19 bid, offered at 20. When Khasbulatov surrendered, the guys offering at 20 jacked their offers to 30. The buyers moved their bids up to 26 and the market eventually filled in at 28 bid, offered at 29. No trading took place in the low or mid-20s—that's the gap."

Sue was looking over Mark's shoulder at a guy who looked like an offensive lineman for the New York Giants and a woman who looked like a Ford model. They grabbed the only unoccupied table. The Giant kissed the top of the model's head and lumbered toward the men's room.

"Hey, Mark," Sue piped. "The blonde right over your left shoulder is giving you the big eye." Mark immediately looked over his shoulder and beamed. He pulled two fuzzy golf-ball-sized balls out of his pocket, winked at Sue, and marched over to the model and sat down.

"What's that in your ear?" Mark was smiling broadly. He opened his hand, reached over, and appeared to pull a fuzzy red ball out of the model's ear. Mark was an accomplished barroom magician. He could make the balls disappear and appear at will, and he did various other tricks, but the punch line always boiled down to the girl "holding my fuzzy balls." Mark called it an ice-breaker. Sue thought it was more of a litmus test.

The Giant was standing behind Mark, hands on hips, when, leering, Mark asked the model to hold his balls. Glancing at the Giant, she replied, "I think you better go back to your table."

"I just got here. And I'm really starting to like you." Saying nothing, the Giant lifted Mark from his chair and shoved him toward the door. Mark nearly kept his balance, but then tripped on a chair and crashed into a table full of secretaries. Their happy-hour nachos went flying. The women weren't thrilled. With a grin, Mark strained to maintain a shred of dignity by apologizing quickly and picking up the plates. Then he tried sauntering coolly back to the table, as if nothing had happened. Sue laughed so hard she snorted beer out through her nose. Laughing, but under control, George handed her his handkerchief.

"I can't believe you set me up like that. Trying to get me killed? Fuck both of you." Mark ordered another round of beers and resumed his surveillance of the women in the crowd. He tried to figure out which ones might have witnessed his humiliation. Maybe he could joke about it. Get some sympathy. "Sue, you're the only woman I've ever seen squirt beer out her nose. Very ladylike," said Mark.

"If I wanted to act like a lady, I wouldn't come here." Shaking his head, Mark picked up his beer and left to go mingle with the crowd.

"The Russia stuff is all very interesting, George, but I'm still not sure I fully understand what you do for a living." Sue got serious.

"I trade Latin pre-Brady bank debt for a living. I only trade Russia when London's closed or when they need help because it's really crazy, like today."

"What's pre-Brady bank debt?"

"You're familiar with the Latin debt crisis?"

"The banks lent tons of recycled petrodollars to Latin America in the '70s. When Volker raised rates in the early '80s, commodity prices cratered and they all went bust. The '80s became known as the lost decade in Latin America because economic development stagnated."

"Excellent," exclaimed George. "I'm impressed."

"I went to college, read the *New York Times.* You know I almost joined the Peace Corps, right? I wanted to help the poor in El Salvador."

"You never told me that."

"That's because I got greedy, went to Madison Avenue instead."

"Like I went to Wall Street."

"Yeah, at least you joined the IMF, took a shot at helping the world."

"A brief shot. So anyway, to address the crisis, Nicholas Brady, the Secretary of the Treasury, got together with the major international banks, known as the London Club, the IMF, and the World Bank, and persuaded the debtor countries to consolidate the private-sector and public-sector debt owed to the banks. The London Club agreed to reduce the total amount of debt owed, reduce the interest rates, and extend the principal repayment schedules for up to thirty years."

"So the banks forgave part of the debt. Very unlike bankers. Why?"

"I guess because they can't foreclose on a country like they can on a car or house. Anyway, for their part the debtor countries agreed to resume interest payments on the previously defaulted debt. That's the real reason."

"So these Latin countries had the money to pay, but they refused to pay unless the banks forgave part of the debt?"

"Yes and no. They owed all of the principal and years of past due interest, which they didn't have the money to pay. By forgiving some principal and past-due interest, lowering the interest rates, and allowing them to pay the principal back very gradually, the banks arrived at annual debt-service amounts that the countries could afford. The Latins started paying interest again and the banks made new loans. The logjam was broken."

"I'm with you."

"The banks then exchanged their illiquid, bilateral loans that traded by appointment for liquid bonds—Brady bonds. Mexico, which was—"

"By liquid you mean?"

"Easily tradable. Issue sizes in the billions. Ownership transfers electronically. With the illiquid loans you had hundreds of agreements which had to be carefully documented by the trading counterparties. Very cumbersome."

"Go on."

"Mexico, which was the first to default in 1982, was the first to agree to a Brady deal in 1989. Venezuela, Argentina, and most recently Brazil followed. My boss, Enrique, and the Brady guys trade those countries. I trade the deadbeat countries that haven't achieved a Brady deal yet—Peru, Ecuador, Panama, et cetera. The pre-Brady bank debt."

"That all sounds very sophisticated." Sue mocked George subtly, but he could tell she was impressed. "So, I heard you almost got into a fight today. What's up with that?" She drank her beer.

"This salesman, José, picked me off. Cost me 50 grand."

"This José works for City Trust?"

"This scumbag gets confused. Sometimes he thinks he works for his customers. Enrique's going to have it out with him. I hope he gets fired."

Sue swallowed the last of her Budweiser, leaned back, and

regarded George warmly. He was six feet tall with a lean athletic build. He had pitched for the junior varsity at Princeton but had quickly realized that his 79-mph fastball was not taking his baseball career anywhere. He quit the team after freshman year to focus on his studies. His big, cobalt eyes glistened, suggesting openness and optimism. His chestnut hair was slightly disheveled, his red silk tie was a little crooked, and he had missed a small patch shaving under his nose. He clearly preferred the more casual academic style to the slicked-back, buttoned-down fashion of most of his Wall Street colleagues. He smiled easily and engagingly.

Mark returned with a boisterous, freckle-faced redhead whom he introduced as Noreen. Sam, the government bond salesman from City Trust who had introduced George to Mark, also sat down at the table and greeted everyone.

"What are you doing at the meat market?" asked George. "I thought Joy was coming back from Hong Kong tomorrow?"

"She is. I just stopped for a drink," said Sam.

"How long is her visit?" asked Sue.

"Not a visit. She quit her job and she's moving in with me. She'll be looking for work in the city."

"Are you guys engaged or what?" Sue sounded surprised.

"Not technically, but there's an understanding. You know?"

"Let's celebrate." Mark ordered five shots of tequila. After the tequila, Sam headed out. Mark handed Noreen the vial of coke under the table, and she disappeared to the ladies' room to do a blast. A pattern developed at the table of beer rounds, tequila rounds—which George and Sue started passing on—and alternate trips to the bathroom for Mark and Noreen to snort. Mark entertained with magic tricks and jokes until Sue suggested that they move to a table for dinner. After the four of them ordered, Mark and Noreen went to the ladies' room together. When the food arrived, they had not returned.

"They're screwing in a stall, aren't they?" Sue shook her head. "How romantic."

George shrugged and gave their burgers to the waitress to warm in the kitchen. Mark returned first. He had wiped the sweat from his face, but the hair behind his ears was still wet, and he smelled of sex.

"Noreen will only be a moment. She's fixing her makeup."

"Sit on the toilet, with her on your lap?" asked George. "Or doggie style, she hugs the tank?"

"Every which way. This girl is smokin'."

"Toooo much information," said Sue. "All I want to understand is why you don't just take her back to the Club. Have a modicum of civility."

"You kiddin' me? This girl would keep me up all night. I have to get up at seven and trade all day tomorrow."

"You're a Neanderthal," proclaimed Sue. "Like a sick director, using a bar toilet as your casting couch."

"Well, her audition was spectacular. What if I change my mind, invite her back?"

"You move up the evolutionary scale to Cro-Magnon man."

Club 16B was a four-bedroom suite with a common living area and a small kitchenette. The Sheetrock walls were white and bare. After renting the furniture last year, the men had lost their decorating initiative. Matching, beige plastic couches and chairs were divided by glass-and-steel end tables, which came as a set with the big coffee table in the center. A large TV dominated the room. The mustard-colored acrylic carpet was stained with wine and other cocktails. They could afford to have the maid come twice a week, but sometimes even that wasn't enough.

Nick and Leo, Mark and George's other two suitemates, were drinking beer and watching the ALCS when the party from Stephano's stumbled through the door. The Blue Jays were leading 3–2 in the seventh. Mark laid out lines of coke for himself, Noreen, Nick, and Leo, who snorted eargerly. Sue made a couple of jokes, trying to get Noreen to address the stall sex, but she wouldn't take the bait. When Mark and Noreen adjourned to Mark's bedroom, Sue hugged George and began rubbing his thigh.

"Just two more innings."

Sue ignored him. She began nibbling on his neck. When she stuck her wet tongue in his ear, George leaned forward, elbows on knees.

"OK," she snapped. "How much do you have riding on this game?"

George softened, putting his arm around her. "C'mon, it's only two innings. You can wait two innings, can't you?" George kissed her on the lips. She disengaged and stomped to the kitchen for fresh beers. The Jays scored three in the top of the ninth on a solo homer by Devon White and a two-run triple by Paul Molitor. Warren Newson led off the bottom of the ninth with a homer, but reliever Duane Ward ended the White Sox's season when he got Tim Raines to fly out to Joe Carter in right with the tying run on first. The Blue Jays mobbed each other on the infield to celebrate.

Ignoring the Jays' festivities, Sue led George into his bedroom. They made love slowly and gently, taking care to prolong each other's pleasure. Afterward they lay entwined, stroking each other softly and drifting off to sleep—until they heard a loud banging against the wall and Noreen's rhythmic screaming.

George banged on the wall. "Mark, keep it down, will you!" The noise did not abate, so George slipped on his boxers and banged on Mark's locked door. "Hey, Mark. Noreen. Keep it down. People are trying to sleep." There was no response, and the noise didn't slacken. George went out on the balcony and got a can of charcoal lighter from under the Webber. He grabbed a fire extinguisher, set it down next to Mark's door, squirted lighter fluid under the door, and tossed on a match.

"Fire!" he yelled. Noreen ran out first, stark naked, followed by Mark, who was fully erect. Nick and Leo, who had drifted into the common room in their boxers, applauded Noreen's nudity while George extinguished the small blaze.

"Mark, move the headboard away from our wall. Noreen, stop screaming." George held back a grin.

"You just did that to see Noreen naked," joked Sue when George returned to bed.

"Why would I do that? You have a much better body than she does." George was right. Noreen had voluptuous breasts, but she was a little flabby. Sue was a hard body. She had run cross-country and track and played basketball in college, and had kept fit in the gym since graduation.

Sue and George resumed their embrace. After a while Sue started putting the moves on George. She wanted to go again. They were kissing deeply when the phone rang. Sue protested, but George managed to wriggle from her grasp and answer it. It was Vijay Varghese, head of European trading at City Trust, calling from London to talk about Russia. George quickly flicked on the trading screens on his desk to check the news stories and prices. The hard-line communist mutineers had been crushed so completely that a consensus was forming that they had had their last hurrah. All of the European markets were up. Vnesh was 30 bid. Vijay asked George how he thought the American hedge funds would react in the morning. George told him that the higher prices would eliminate the forced selling to meet margin calls. The hedgies would be buyers. When George finally got off the phone, Sue had dressed and left. She must be really pissed off this time, thought George. At least prices were up. George guessed that Ecuador would be back in the mid-40s. He was back on track to earn a big bonus this year. And he'd won 5 grand on the Jays.

He relished out-trading Steinie, but he had to share that victory with Enrique. He had outwitted Vegas on the ball game by himself, which was more satisfying. He recalled a table stakes game of seven-card stud with some rich preppies at Princeton. After five rounds of maximum raises, the nonscholarship portion of his next semester's tuition was on the table. He savored the memory of the acute tension he had felt during the final stage of betting. Sweat had trickled down his spine into the crack in his ass and he had nearly puked. When he laid down his king high full house against Skip's jack high full house and Tyler's flush, the rush was incredible. It was better than sex.

He lay back and tried to sleep for a couple of hours before his 6:00 A.M. alarm, but after an hour he gave up. He showered, shaved, dressed, and headed into the office to trade with London for a couple of hours while waiting for New York to open up.

3

George quaffed black coffee to stay awake in the morning research meeting. Most days, the conference call consisted of a series of reports from City Trust's emerging market branches on political or economic events that could affect the markets for sovereign debt. São Paulo, Buenos Aires, Mexico City, and Caracas reported daily. Lima, Quito, and the smaller branches or agencies reported on an ad-hoc basis. Since the London office made the trading decisions on Eastern European and African debt, those branches only reported in to the New York research meeting when major events required global coordination to manage the trading book. Today was such an exception. Sasha, Pablo's deputy in London who headed EM research for Europe, Africa, and the Middle East, and Yuri, the head of the Moscow branch, dominated the call. Their view was that, having weathered the storm, the Yeltsin government was stronger than ever. Prices of Russian debt would continue to recover.

After the call, Enrique pulled George and Pablo into Pablo's office. The walls were covered with diplomas from prestigious South and North American universities and certificates of recognition from the World Bank, IMF, and Inter-American Development Bank. A photograph of Pablo shaking hands with Treasury Secretary Brady hung in the center of the back wall.

"Well, not only have you guys bet your own bonuses on the Ecuadorian Brady deal, but after doubling down yesterday you've bet a good chunk of mine as well. Maybe even a sliver of Gold's." Enrique had succeeded in getting Pablo and George's attention. "Gold wants a sanity check ASAP. Pablo, he wants you to go to Quito. George, you and I are going to D.C. to meet with Treasury and the IMF. Let's shoot for next week. Meanwhile, I'm going to talk to my friends on the bank steering committee to make sure everything is cool."

"Steering committee members are subject to a strict confidentiality agreement," stated Pablo matter-of-factly.

"Yeah, right. You worry about your end, and I'll worry about mine."

"OK, I'll call Jorge this morning to coordinate setting up the meetings," replied Pablo, with a hint of disdain. Jorge ran City Trust's Quito branch.

"The best part of Jorge ran down his mother's leg," snapped Enrique.

"Must you be so vulgar?" Pablo replied disgustedly. "Jorge may not be brilliant, but he'll get me an audience with the president and the head of the opposition party. What you don't understand is that, in Ecuador, who you know is more important than what you know."

"What about the finance minister?" Enrique ignored the lecture.

"Cesar Robelino is an old friend of mine. I don't need Jorge's help there."

José stuck his head in the door. "Sorry to interrupt, but I thought you'd want to know that Ralph at Panther Capital cut us off. He found Paribas, the seller of the $10 million Sudan block that I sold him, and he's pissed about the 2-point markup." George rubbed his temples with both hands. Enrique steamed, and Pablo looked puzzled.

"What's wrong with a 2-point markup on a totally illiquid loan?" asked Pablo.

José grinned. "That's exactly what I said, but Ralph doesn't see it that way. He sees it as a 100 percent markup." Pablo looked even more puzzled.

George picked up his head. "We bought them from Paribas at 2 and sold them to Ralph at 4."

"Four cents on the dollar? I see," nodded Pablo.

Enrique threw his arms in the air and began pacing the room. "You guys are fucking amateurs."

"You approved the trade," countered George.

"You're supposed to know your market and your clients well enough to know when you're going to get caught speeding." Now Enrique was yelling. "And you get caught by the biggest trader on the buy side. Now I have to go over to his office and do the Bugsy again."

"The Bugsy?" George asked.

"You didn't see the movie? I crawl around the carpet barking like a dog and oinking like a goddamned pig while Ralph yells at me." Enrique stormed out of Pablo's office, ending the meeting.

At the Treasury desk, Sam sat hunched over with his phone in his ear.

"Yes, this is Samuel Thorn at City Trust."

"Mr. Thorn, this is Dr. Galena from the New York City Health Department. I have some very serious information for you. We have diagnosed a young lady with syphilis. She has reported you as one of her recent sexual contacts. Mr. Thorn, it is virtually certain that you have contracted syphilis. We believe that it is a strain from Southeast Asia that has proven to be resistant to antibiotics, making it extremely dangerous. Mr. Thorn, we need information to contact each of your sexual contacts for the last five weeks. You also need to come in for an examination."

"What's the young lady's name?"

"Amber Dickerson. That's confidential, but you obviously need to know to be convinced of your condition."

Sam gulped. "I can't really talk right now, Dr. Galena. Give me your number and I'll call you back." Sam copied down the number and hung up. He stared at his screens in stunned silence.

During a lull in trading, Mark pulled George away from his desk. They leaned against a pillar, sipping coffee.

"George, take a look at Sam." Mark was laughing.

"Jesus, he looks terrible. Totally ashen. He must have lied about one quick drink last night. What happened, he buy your coke and try to snort it all?"

Mark was laughing harder. "He got a call from the City Health Department telling him that he has syphilis. That Amber has it and reported him as a contact."

"Jesus, that's terrible. If Amber has it, it's going to be an epidemic. And he's supposed to pick up Joy from Hong Kong tonight."

"Exactly. Except it wasn't the Health Department. It was Tim Mayer." Mark's laughter had him tearing.

"You're a sick bastard, and so is Mayer."

"Anybody tells him it's a prank gets the death penalty."

"All he has to do is call someone else who planked Amber. Compare notes. Or call Amber."

"Well he hasn't yet. He's been comatose for over an hour."

George observed the Treasury desk. Periodically, guys would peer over the screens at Sam, then sit back down and snicker to themselves or with their buddies.

"How many guys know about this?" asked George.

"Most of the Treasury desk. Half the mortgage desk. Other guys around the floor who know Sam. Remember, death penalty if you tell."

George returned to his desk. He traded Vnesh at 31, Peru at 36, and Ecuador at 45. Forty-five on Ecuador meant George had earned a profit of $7 million on the $50 million that he had bought the previous day. He made the appointments at the Treasury and IMF. For the third time he called Sue at her office and for the third time she refused his call. He saw Sam walking like a zombie toward the elevator, carrying his briefcase and jacket. He waited for someone to intercept him and set him straight, but nobody appeared. How could they let him go while he was still duped? When Sam left the trading floor, George sprinted after him but failed to catch him before he disappeared into an elevator. George grabbed the next elevator, got off on the top floor of the parking garage, and ran to the exit just as the gate was lifting for Sam's BMW. He stood in front of the car, but Sam kept driving, forcing George to sprawl on the hood.

"Stop! It's a joke!" George banged on the windshield. The BMW skidded to a stop at the top of the ramp. Sam jumped out of the car.

"What the fuck?"

"You don't have VD. The call from the Health Department was a prank."

Sam's pallor instantly flushed red. Trembling, fists clenched, he chased George around the car. "You fucking asshole, you sick, prick fuck . . ."

"It wasn't me. I'm your pal—I'm the one who's telling you before you hook up with Joy."

"Who fucking did this?"

"I'll only tell you if you promise to get back in the car and drive to JFK. You start a fistfight on the trading floor, you're fucked. It'll impair your career, regardless of the circumstances. You've got too much going for you to blow it in a rage."

"Who fucking did this?"

"You're going to the airport, right?"

"I promise. Now who?"

"I know that Tim Mayer impersonated the doctor. That's all I know. And you didn't hear it from me."

"Got it. Thanks, George. I owe you." Sam quickly turned away as he got in the car so George wouldn't see him fighting back tears. Girding himself against the abuse he would take on the floor, George headed back to the elevator. He wondered if there were any other professional cultures that inspired pranks as crude and ruthless as those played by traders.

4

The sand-colored concrete walls of the IMF building encased the windows like a giant waffle holding syrup. It looked more like a big-city airport hotel than a government building. Enrique and George proceeded through security to the stuffy, cluttered office of Alfredo Gomez, one of the senior officials in charge of the IMF's economic aid program for Latin America. The walls were decorated with photographs of Gomez with South and Central American presidents and finance ministers, including a shot with former Brazilian President Fernando Collor de Mello. George thought it was odd that Gomez kept that one up after the Brazilian Congress had impeached Collor last winter for stealing billions in government funds.

Trudy Waite, Gomez's associate, joined them in the office just before they sat down. Alfredo was middle-aged, bespectacled, balding, and soft-bellied under his plaid brown suit. Trudy was in her late twenties, with a plump but pleasant face. She wore her blonde hair in a bun and her wire-rim glasses halfway down her nose. Having worked with Alfredo and Trudy at the IMF, George made the introductions and everyone shook hands.

"It's a pleasure to see you again, Mr. Wilhelm," said Alfredo, smiling genuinely. "What can we do for you and Mr. Guerrero?"

"The pleasure is ours, Mr. Gomez," replied George respectfully. "We came down because City Trust is now one of Ecuador's largest creditors."

"Really? I was not aware of that."

"We've been building a loan position in the secondary market. We were hoping you would update us on your negotiations regarding Ecuador's adoption of structural reforms that would be acceptable to the Fund."

"I see." Gomez tamped tobacco into his pipe and then launched a twenty-minute discourse on Ecuador's fiscal, monetary, and trade policies. He felt the IMF was close to a standby agreement, which would be a necessary precursor to a Brady deal. When Trudy made a point or provided statistical support for one of Gomez's points, he lit and puffed his pipe. He was optimistic about the country's ability to generate the foreign exchange necessary to service its debt again should a Brady exchange be agreed to.

"How do you see the negotiations with the Bank Advisory Committee playing out?" asked Enrique.

"The banks will not forgive more than 65 percent of principal because that would jeopardize the Brazilian debt reduction agreement. I think that the government understands this, and will agree to something in the vicinity of 65 percent."

"What about past due interest?" asked George.

"PDI? That's a fascinating question, since Ecuador's payment history differs on each tranche that came out of the multiple restructurings. Since 1987, Ecuador has paid interest periodically on the MYRA, ERA, and New Money loans, about 40 percent of interest due in aggregate, and no interest on the MYRA-to-be and Consolidation loans. Obviously, it would be unfair to grant the unpaid lenders the same past due interest claim as the lenders that received periodic interest payments. Therefore, PDI forgiveness will have to be greater on the partially paid loans. I estimate PDI forgiveness of 50 to 65 percent on the MYRA, ERA, and New Money loans, and 30 to 50 percent on the MYRA-to-be and Consolidation."

"What about timing?" asked Enrique.

"I think they'll agree to heads of terms early next year. What do you think?"

Enrique and George agreed. Trudy nodded as well. They talked shop about the other Latins for another few minutes before Enrique and George took their leave. In the corridor, Enrique excused himself to visit a friend on the Brazil desk. George doubled back toward Trudy's office. She emerged from the ladies' room with her blonde hair flowing over her shoulders, and no glasses.

"Where are we going for lunch, Mr. Wall Street money bags?"

"That's up to you."

"How 'bout your hotel?" Trudy raised her eyebrows mischievously. George knew Trudy had a crush on him, but apart from a brief necking session at his going-away party with the IMF crowd, they had done little more than flirt. At the time George had been dating a brilliant classmate from grad school. Trudy didn't know about Sue, so George was not entirely surprised that she had now abandoned all subtlety.

"No hotel. It's a day trip." When Trudy just smiled, he added, "I have to meet Enrique for another meeting at 2:30."

Trudy pouted, "Then we'll have to go to François's."

They sat at an elegant table for two, decorated with pink orchids. The clientele was older, mostly men in business suits. Lobbyists entertaining government officials, figured George. At a few tables distinguished men dined with attractive young women. More likely mischief than father-daughter bonding, he thought. George and Trudy chatted briefly about mutual friends and acquaintances. Then Trudy's manner became serious. "So how can an IMF desk officer with a Ph.D. in developmental economics get a high-paying job on Wall Street?"

"You mean you?"

"Of course I mean me, silly."

"Well, what I did was, I went to all of the big commercial and investment banks with a business plan. Pre-Brady arbitrage. City Trust bought it."

"What's pre-Brady arbitrage?"

"First you identify a country that's likely to enter into a Brady debt exchange. Then you estimate the likely terms and the price where the Brady bonds will trade after the exchange. If the pre-Brady loans are available at a significant discount to the level where the reconstituted debt will trade in Brady-bond format, you buy the loans."

"That's what you do? You buy defaulted loans and pray for an exchange under the Brady plan?"

"Pretty much. I also trade the loans. I'm the most aggressive trader on Wall Street in loans to Ecuador, Peru, and the Dominican Republic."

"What about Brazil?"

"Much more competitive. Enrique trades it. The Brazilian Brady bonds trade on a 'when issued' basis. I just trade the illiquid stuff."

"So you're just a speculator?"

"No, I'm providing a critical economic function by facilitating the redistribution of defaulted debt from the global banks to high-risk-oriented investors. This frees up dead capital for the banks, enabling then to make new loans which create global economic growth, adding to the wealth of nations, eradicating poverty—"

"You're so full of it." Butter from Trudy's escargot trickled down her chin as she laughed. "So what do they pay you for saving the global economy?"

"Well, my salary is about the same as at the Fund."

"Bullshit."

"Honest. My bonus will make up most of my compensation."

"How much is that?"

"I don't know. It will be a percentage of my trading profits."

"How much is that?"

"Just between you and me, over $20 million, year to date."

Trudy's eyes got big. "Wow. What percentage do they pay you?"

"I've never gotten a straight answer to that question."

"How'd you make the $20 million?"

"When I first joined City Trust last year, I convinced them to buy $50 million face of Peruvian debt in the high teens. Those prices have more than doubled. Then we started buying Ecuador, which has rallied substantially as well."

"So you'll get a huge bonus?"

"Well, the issue is that the chips are still on the table."

"Meaning?"

"Meaning that we employ mark-to-market accounting. The loans have appreciated by more than $20 million, but we still own them."

"So if the Brady deals collapse and the loans go down?"

"I get no bonus. If it's a hard landing, I probably get fired."

"That's intense. Can't you sell? Put the money in the bank?"

"With the size of my positions, and City Trust's prominence in these trades, I'd obliterate the markets if I tried to sell. And the whole premise of the trade is to exchange the loans and sell the Brady bonds."

"I see." Trudy dug into her lamb chops. "So I know as much about the Brady process as you do."

"More."

"So can I get a job in New York?"

"You sure you want the pressure? Wake up in the middle of the night with nightmares about a coup in Quito? Tanks rolling through the streets of Lima?"

"Sure. I'm game. Will my econometrics help me?"

"I still model foreign exchange flows, but I'm the only trader on Wall Street who does. The most profitable trader I know lives in Caracas. He says trading Venezuela is easy—you just short it every autumn."

"What?"

"When the students go back to school, they start rioting. I called him one day to ask him why Venie was getting hammered. He was ecstatic—he'd just made a ton shorting. Said he'd started smacking bids as soon as he smelled the tear gas from the campus."

"Screw Caracas, I want to work in New York."

"Of course. I'll send you a copy of the business plan that I used to get hired last year. We'll take it from there."

"You'd do that for me?"

"Sure."

In the cab back to the IMF George initially resisted Trudy's advances, thinking of Sue. But Sue hadn't taken his call since the night of Noreen, more than a week ago, so he figured, what the hell. They only made out. It was broad daylight.

The international economist at Treasury was just as positive on Ecuador's Brady prospects as were Gomez and Trudy. George was all fired up. Enrique seemed merely relieved. On the plane back to LaGuardia, George started badgering Enrique about his prospects for a seven-figure bonus.

"Look, George, 10 percent of your profits is only a rule of thumb. There are a lot of variables. Most importantly, you're only a rookie."

"So I'm going to get screwed because I'm a rookie? That would be really stupid. I've gotten calls from Citibank, Chase, and Goldman. They don't talk about me being a rookie. They talk about me being the *man* in the pre-Brady market."

"You're not going to get screwed. I just don't want you carving the 10 percent in stone."

"But it will be close to that?"

"Unless the bank has an earnings disaster in the fourth quarter, yes."

"And I won't be disadvantaged because most of my profits are unrealized?"

"You'll be required to mark your positions conservatively due to illiquidity. But I've never seen the bank differentiate between realized and unrealized trading income."

George could barely contain his glee. His trading profits of $20 million were likely to grow before year end, if the bureaucrats he had just met with were right. A $2 million bonus. Unbelievable. He was rich. At LaGuardia he split up with Enrique and called Pablo at his hotel in Quito.

Pablo sounded like he was in good spirits. "I had an excellent meeting with Robelino today. Even though the structural reforms demanded by the IMF are politically unpopular, he is determined not to back down. He claims to have the president's full support in that regard."

"What about the negotiations with the banks?" asked George.

"He desperately wants the country to return to the international capital markets, and he knows full well that the Brady exchange is the only practical route to that goal. He's demanding 75 percent forgiveness of principal and substantial forgiveness of past due interest, but I think he's posturing. In the end he'll do what's necessary to complete the exchange."

"So how do you handicap a signed Brady deal this spring? Eighty percent? Ninety?"

"You and your percentages. Let's just say it's looking good." George started to ask another question, but Pablo cut him off. "George, I have to go now or I'll be late to my dinner with the chairman of the Monetary Board. I'll call you tomorrow."

George decided that he would plug an 85 percent probability weighting into his Ecuador return formula. He viewed all trading as probability analysis. He had modeled the prospective Brady exchanges by assigning probabilities to the potential levels of debt forgiveness and other terms. His econometric models, which predicted each country's ability to service its Brady debt, were stressed based on computer-driven Monte Carlo simulations of oil and other commodity prices. In draw poker, George always calculated the exact probabilities of winning hands based on the number of players and their draws. In stud poker, he adjusted the calculation for every up card that landed. The challenge was always the human element—gauging the other players' proclivities to bluff, etc. In EM trading, politics was the unquantifiable element. George thanked God that Pablo was on a first-name basis with every significant finance minister in Latin America. He picked up the pay phone again and called Brooklyn.

"Hello."

"York for TD."

"Phillies are 9, York."

"Give me the Jays plus the 8 . . ." George hesitated. With a $2 million bonus coming on February 1st, why should he bet like a piker? When he was paying off student loans at the IMF in D.C. his limit had been $100, and that was only on big games where he thought Vegas was way off the mark. Even after he got to City Trust, he kept himself to $100 on regular-season NBA games. He had still been pretty green at City Trust when he was introduced to TD and started betting $500 on the NCAA tournament. Now as a millionaire-to-be he could afford to bet exponentially more. A thousand dollars was nickel ante stuff, thought George. The old stakes were suddenly boring. He *had* to bet more now to get the same charge.

TD was impatient. George was small time for him. There was bigger action holding on the other lines. "How many times, York?"

"Four thousand times."

TD sniffed. The kid was stepping up. Must be bonus time or something. "You're betting 20 large on the Jays plus the 8."

"Yes." George would lose $20,000 or win $32,000.

"OK. Good luck, York."

George jumped into a cab and rode to McNabb's to watch Game 5 of the World Series. Autographed jerseys and photographs of New York sports heroes hung on the walls, and large TVs hung from every corner of the room. The dark, heavy wooden furniture needed refinishing. George grabbed the only available stool at the bar, next to a half-drunk old-timer wearing a Phillies cap, and ordered a beer and burger.

"You a Phillies fan?" asked the drunk.

"You bet."

"From Philly?"

"Bethlehem. Born and raised." George clicked glasses with the old man and turned his attention to the game. Dykstra led off the bottom of the first with a walk, stole second, and took third when Borders's throw went into center field. George cursed.

"Hey," said the drunk. "I thought you were a Phillies fan."

"I am, but I bet the Jays tonight."

"Too bad. Phillies are gonna cream 'em tonight."

"I figure it's a toss-up. Guzman and Schilling are both hot, but Guzy outpitched Curt last Saturday in Toronto and has a good chance to do it again. And the Jays' bats are hotter. On the other hand, they are playing at the Vet, which evens it out."

"So why'd you bet the Jays?"

"I'm getting 8 to 5."

"You bet against your own team in the World Series? You're pulling for a team that's not even American because you like the odds?"

"Eight to 5 for a game that should be even is a huge overlay in my book. I can't pass it up."

"You're fucked up, boy." George shrugged. Dykstra scored on John Kruk's grounder. In the second, Daulton doubled and scored on Stocker's double to give the Phillies a 2–0 lead. Apart from that, Schilling and Guzman pitched brilliantly. The Jays didn't even put a man in scoring position until the eighth, when Borders singled and the pinch runner Canate took third on Butler's single. Then Canate got caught between third and home when Schilling knocked down Henderson's grounder. Some pinch runner. White fanned, Alomar bounced to second, and that was that. Schilling pitched a complete-game, five-hit shutout for the victory.

George walked back to his apartment feeling light-headed after six beers. He enjoyed walking the streets of New York with a buzz on. He loved the prewar architecture. He always looked up to study the gargoyles holding up the eaves of the older buildings. George wondered how he was supposed to feel about the loss. In thinking about his bonus he had completely lost his bearings. George knew how badly he had felt about a $100 loss against his $60,000 IMF salary, but what did $20,000 mean against a $2 million income? All those zeroes dulled the pain of losing, and he felt curiously unhinged. In any case, it had been the right bet—the game was virtually even. The Phillies just got the breaks. Guzy had only given up five hits, just like Schilling, and only one of the runs was earned. When he got back to Club 16B Mark was taking a hit off a bong with a girl George had never seen before. They were both wasted.

"Hey, George, this is . . . uhhhh, Jill. Want a hit?"

George mumbled a no-thank-you and went to bed, reassuring himself that at 8–5 the odds had been in his favor. If he got the chance, he'd make the same bet again—in a second.

5

Virtually every available foot of space in Philip Gold's office was decorated with tombstones. Mounted on plaques or encased in Lucite blocks, they were the trophies of a distinguished career, each one memorializing a City Trust bond deal. Gold was forty, six one, with an average build and close-cropped black hair. He was all business. Enrique and George sat on a couch, backs to the huge window on the trading floor, facing Gold's desk. Gold scanned his screens as Pablo, clearly audible on the speakerphone, concluded his remarks.

"Sounds like you guys have done your homework on this Ecuador trade. I'm OK. Thanks. Bye, Pablo. Safe trip back from Quito." Gold hung up the phone.

"Before we go, I wanted to post you on the arbitration with KQB Bank this afternoon," said Enrique.

"I thought you were going to settle that," replied Gold.

"We tried, but the other side was unreasonable."

"That's the trade from midsummer, right?"

"Right. Go ahead, George," instructed Enrique.

"We bought $20 million Ecuador from KQB at 32. I very clearly specified MYRA-to-be. KQB is trying to deliver MYRA."

"Multi-Year Restructuring Agreement," said Gold. "The MYRA-to-be loans were never contributed to the program."

"Exactly right," said George.

"What's the difference in price?" asked Gold.

"The market is illiquid, so it's hard to say exactly. If they contributed every loan they made to the MYRA program and have to go into the market to buy the MYRA-to-be loans, it will probably cost them 5 points or so."

"Five points on $20 million. That's a million bucks. No wonder they want to arbitrate," said Gold. "Sounds like you picked them off."

George was about to get defensive, but Enrique anticipated him and jumped in.

"George was very precise. We have it on tape. KQB are big boys—they're supposed to know what they're doing."

"Was there a market on the screen at the time, George?"

"Thirty-two bid, 34 offered. The quoted market presumes MYRA."

"But the bid was sure as hell not good for $20 million. KQB might have figured that MYRA-to-be was worth a couple points more, but sold at the MYRA price because they were trying to move a big block that would have depressed the market by a couple of points if they'd decorated the screens with it," Enrique interjected.

"Any screen quotes on the other stuff, the non-MRYA?"

George shook his head. "Only if I put them up. Pretty arcane stuff."

"I don't know, Enrique. Sounds like KQB may have made an honest mistake. We don't stick guys for honest mistakes. The guy probably didn't hear George say 'MYRA-to-be,' or didn't appreciate its significance."

"He sure as hell heard him. As to its significance, no one knows how the accrued interest differential will be treated in the Brady exchange. It's a matter of speculation. Maybe KQB changed their valuation analysis after the trade. That's not our problem." Enrique paused, then added, "If it were a client, I might reconsider, but in this sector KQB is a competitor. They wouldn't give us quarter if the situation were reversed."

Hank Price, the head of the bond syndicate desk, stuck his head in the door. "The World Bank wants to issue a billion ten-year notes. They want a firm price in fifteen minutes. Want to join us, boss?"

"Of course." Gold grabbed a spiral notebook and a calculator. At the door he turned to Enrique. "What's our downside?"

"No downside. If we lose, we take MYRA. We already have it marked as MYRA, as a reserve."

"Got it." Gold headed to the syndicate desk.

"I don't know." George was squirming. "I don't feel real good about this. I picked them off, cut and dried."

"Goddammit," hissed Enrique. "This is Wall Street, not Sesame Street. You snooze, you lose! C'mon, let's go."

Twelve dark suits filed into the somber, mahogany-paneled conference room at the Park Avenue law firm of Weiss and Gottrack. Enrique, George, and two of City Trust's in-house litigators sat on one side of the table. The head of all bond trading, the head EM trader, the sovereign loan trader, and two litigators from KQB sat on the other side. The arbitrators—a desiccated, professorial lawyer in his sixties, a matronly woman with a bad wig, and an overweight forty-something man who was already sweating profusely—sat at the head of the table. KQB's lawyers contended that the market for MYRA was 32 bid, offered at 34, and they had executed the trade on MYRA in the context of that market. If they had indeed intended to sell something more valuable than MYRA at 32, they would have been doing so outside the context of the market, nullifying the trade. They argued that they had been picked off. The City Trust litigators contended that it was ludicrous to assume that a bid in the screen for $2 million represented a level where $20 million would trade in such an illiquid market.

The KQB trader must have been trying to break the trade because he subsequently changed his valuation of MYRA-to-be. The arbitrators asked the traders a few technical questions, then played the tape recording of the trade. For several minutes the group could hear the voices of George and Andres, the KQB trader, negotiating the terms. Then came the following exchange:

"So I'm buying $20 million principal amount of Ecuador, MYRA-to-be, at 32."

"Right. I sell you 20 at 32. Done." Then came a click, but the tape kept playing. Four or five voices, including George's and Enrique's, cheered wildly, and in the background was the sound of flesh slapping flesh. Then came Enrique's best imitation of a Caribbean pirate: "AAAARRRGGGHH! HURTCHYA!" The tape ended. George slid down in his chair, staring at his hands. Stone-faced, Enrique fixed his eyes on the KQB traders. After a long moment, both pairs of lawyers began whispering to each other. KQB's head bond trader was sputtering, spittle running down his chin. Andres, the loan trader, screamed at Enrique, "You cocksucker, you fuck, you slimy piece of shit—"

The head arbitrator slammed the table with authority. "That's enough! Counselors, do you have anything further before we conclude?" The lawyers shook their heads. "Fine. I will inform you of our decision next week." When George looked up, Enrique was already halfway out the door. When the elevator came, Enrique, George, and the City Trust litigators got in. Andres, who had resumed cursing, was being physically restrained by his boss. The KQB lawyers stood with their backs to the City Trust team, blocking the KQB traders' entry. The last thing they needed was a fistfight in the elevator. The arbitrators looked on in amazement.

When the elevator door closed, Enrique started laughing raucously. Unsure how to react, the litigators pretended to laugh along. George was silent.

After walking a couple of blocks toward City Trust, Enrique peeled off from the lawyers and pulled George into one of the boutique hotels that had sprung up in midtown Manhattan. At the bar, they touched glasses and drank scotch.

"George, I have a confession to make. You've just witnessed my worst nightmare. I've been trading fifteen years, and I have it two or three times a month."

"You dream that you pick somebody off and have a nasty arbitration?"

Enrique laughed aloud. "No, goofball. I dream that I do a big trade and when I hang up the traders on the other end of the phone are laughing and high-fiving. That's my fuckin' nightmare." He drank off his scotch and ordered another round.

6

On Saturday morning George jogged three laps around the Central Park reservoir—about five and a half miles. He liked the uptown section because he could look south over the water and view the skyline of midtown Manhattan at Central Park South. Back at Club 16B, he showered and hoovered a bowl of Cheerios while watching ESPN. For the next two hours he pored over the *Sporting News*, the sports pages of the local papers, various college football magazines, and two newsletters for gamblers. Then he placed a call to Brooklyn.

"Hello, York for TD."

"Yeah, York."

"Game 6?"

"We'll have the World Series at six o'clock."

"OK, how 'bout college football?"

"OK." Cigars, who worked the phones every Saturday, read off the point spreads on all the Division I games, and George jotted them down on the weekly betting sheet that TD mailed to his clients.

"OK, give me Pitt plus the 20, a thousand times, USC plus the 17, five thousand times, Wisconsin minus the 9, two thousand times . . ." George bet twelve games for a total of $110,000. Home teams, visitors, favorites, underdogs, Big Ten, Pac Ten—there was no pattern or bias to his selections. He analyzed each game using won-lost records, including opponents' strength, offensive and defensive statistics, and "insider" information on injuries, suspensions, etc. If the point spread was too small, he bet on the favorite. Too large, he bet on the underdog. The more the spread was off, the bigger the bet. If it was about right, he never bet. He thought that made him a disciplined gambler. There were forty games on the board and he had bet fewer than a third of them.

The early TV broadcast was USC at Notre Dame. The Irish quarterback, Kevin McDougal, was injured and Paul Failla was starting his first game. Coach Robinson would stack eight in the box against the powerful Notre Dame running game, forcing Failla to pass. USC quarterback Rob Johnson would hook up with Johnnie Morton for at least one TD. George conceded that Notre Dame would win, but probably not by more than two touchdowns. Seventeen points was the biggest overlay on the board.

When George got up to clear the newspapers and magazines off the coffee table, an emaciated girl with eight gold rings piercing her ears and eyebrows wandered out of Mark's room and passed out on the couch in front of the TV. She wore nothing but one of Mark's dress shirts. George squeezed in between her feet and the arm of the couch and watched Lee Becton weave his way through the Trojan secondary for a 70-yard touchdown run on Notre Dame's first possession. Ouch. Then Marc Edwards bulled into the end zone from the two, making it 14–0 in the first quarter. None of the other games were going well either. Gopher Jeff Rosga intercepted a Darrell Bevell pass and returned it 55 yards for a touchdown to put Minnesota up 21–0 over Wisconsin. West Virginia scored on four of their first five possessions against Pitt. When Jeff Burris's 4-yard touchdown run put the Irish up 21–0 just before halftime, George buried his head in his hands.

"Here," said Mark, who had shuffled out of his bedroom in his boxers, "maybe this will cheer you up." He pulled the tails of his starched white shirt up above the punk girl's shaved pubis, revealing a tattoo of a fire-breathing dragon and a ninth gold ring. George started to laugh, then stopped abruptly when he saw a highlight of Illinois linebacker Simeon Rice stripping the ball from Michigan back Ricky Powers. The Wolverines had been clinging to a four-point lead, trying to run out the clock in the fourth quarter. Illinois scored off the turnover to upset Michigan 24–21. George had Michigan minus 4, a thousand times. Leaving the punk girl uncovered, Mark whistled his way into the kitchenette and began frying eggs.

Late in the fourth quarter Johnson hit McWilliams for a touchdown, making the score 31–13. The extra point would make the game a push, but Coach Robinson decided to go for two. Transfixed on the try, George did not hear his suitemate Nick and his girlfriend Missy enter the room and drop their shopping bags. Johnson's pass fell incomplete, costing George $25,000.

"Why, Ah nevah!" cried Missy in a tone of indignation that could only be mustered by a female bred south of the Mason-Dixon Line.

"I know," groaned George, as if he'd been kicked in the gut. "Down eighteen in garbage time and Robinson goes for two."

Missy covered the punk girl with her wool blazer and whacked George with her purse. "George Wilhelm, you are a degenerate. Ah cain't imagine how a nice girl like Sue puts up with you. Ah'm moving Nick out of this . . . this den of iniquity."

Mark stood in the kitchen laughing uncontrollably. Tears were running down his cheeks. Nick backed away, straining to hide his laughter from Missy.

"I'm just watching the game," protested George. He liked Missy and was genuinely sorry that she was upset with him. What else could go wrong today, he thought. In the late games, Kansas State kicked a late field goal to tie Colorado 16–16. George had the Buffs minus 1, a thousand times. Oklahoma quarterback Cale Gundy was tackled for a safety late in the Sooners' 38–23 victory over Kansas.

George had Oklahoma minus 16, two thousand times. George lost nine bets totaling $95,000 and won three bets totaling $15,000. Subtracting $9,500, TD's 10 percent vigorish on George's losses, netted to a loss of $89,500 for the afternoon. George wondered if he'd feel worse if he got run over by the Second Avenue bus. He stuck his football sheet in his pocket, kneaded his temples until they hurt, then dug into his magazines for yet another look at the Game 6 pitching matchup. It was southpaw Terry Mulholland for the Phillies versus righty Dave Stewart for the Jays.

George couldn't figure out why the Jays were so heavily favored. Mulholland's regular season ERA was 3.25 versus Stewart's 4.44. Mulholland had out-pitched Stewart decisively in Game 2 in Toronto, so why did they think he wouldn't do it again tonight? The Jays were only 22–25 against lefties during the regular season. The DH would be in effect in the American League park, but Molitor wasn't *that* big an advantage over Duncan at DH. The bullpens were equally rested. Vegas was *way* overweighting the home field. George placed a call to Brooklyn.

"York for TD."

"Jays are 7½, York."

"Give me the Phillies plus the 6½, ten thousand times."

"You want the Phils plus the 6½, ten thousand times? Fifty large on the Phillies?"

"Correct."

"Good luck, York."

George was not in the mood for the usual Saturday night circus in Club 16B so he walked over to McNabb's. It was a Phillies crowd—a mixture of rabid fans from eastern Pennsylvania and Yankees fans who just hated the Blue Jays. The bar stool next to the old drunk in the Phillies cap was empty again.

"So, if it isn't the yuppie from Bethlehem that sells out his home team in the Series."

"Relax, old-timer." George slapped him on the back of his Mike Schmidt shirt. "I'm with you tonight."

"Learned your lesson, huh?"

"You bet." George ordered a shot of house bourbon for the old souse and a beer and burger for himself. The Blue Jays scored three runs in the first inning, casting a pall over McNabb's. George's stomach knotted up. He waved off his half-eaten burger and drank his beer somberly. The other patrons were equally glum as they watched the Phillies struggle against Stewart. Trailing 5–1 in the seventh, Dykstra tagged Stewart for a three-run homer. The McNabb's crowd let out a roar. When Thompson hit a sac fly to put the Phillies ahead, George found himself dancing a jig with the old drunk. Everyone was boisterous until Mitch Williams jogged out of the bullpen to pitch the bottom of the ninth. George winced, and the other Phillies fans let out a collective groan. Wild Thing, who had already blown game 4, promptly walked lead-off hitter Ricky Henderson. White flew out and Molitor singled, bringing Joe Carter to the plate with one out. George felt a play of needles up his spine. With the count 2–2, Daulton called for a slider, low and away. Carter drove it over the left-field fence to win the World Series for the Blue Jays. Rounding second, Carter leaped high in the air with the stadium erupting around him. McNabb's fell silent.

When the old drunk put his arm around him, George turned and suddenly puked on his shirt. Reflexively, the old drunk shoved hard, toppling George off his stool to the floor. He stood over George, dripping beer and burger vomit, and started to stomp him. George popped up and reeled backward into a table full of despondent Philly fans, knocking over several beer glasses and a full pitcher. A bearded, heavily tattooed three-hundred-pounder in a John Kruk uniform caught the pitcher's contents in his lap. The man grabbed George by the lapels of his brown leather jacket. George puked again, soiling the Kruk jersey. Enraged, the fat man hoisted George by the throat and the belt buckle and, with a running start, hurled him through McNabb's plate-glass window and onto First Avenue. Sparks from the broken neon Budweiser sign showered George as he struggled to get off the sidewalk. The old drunk came out and started dodging the sparks. Everyone else was inside watching the showdown as the bartenders squared off against the fat man and his friends.

"You're fucked up, boy," offered the old drunk as he wiped himself with a bar towel. George nodded slowly. Hearing approaching sirens, he hurried north on First. He felt blood on the back of his neck. It was a good thing he was facing away from the window when he crashed through, he thought. He pulled three shards of glass out of the back of his head and dropped them in the gutter as he walked. At the door to Club 16B he heard the party inside. He tried to slip into the bathroom unseen, but there was a knock on the door.

"George, it's Sue. Let me in."

"Hi, Sue."

"What happened?"

"Minor accident."

"Where's the blood coming from?"

"Back of my head. I think I got all the glass out."

"Turn around." Sue parted his hair and examined his head. "There's no glass. I don't think you need stitches. Get in the shower and scrub those wounds. Do you have any antibiotic?"

"It would be in the cabinet above the sink. What do you know about first aid?"

"Nothing. I'm winging it." When George got out of the shower, Sue was sitting on the toilet, scrubbing the blood off his jacket.

"This is all I could find." She held up a bottle of Qwell lotion for body lice. "Do you have crabs?"

"Not me. It's a four-man suite."

"I'll be right back." Sue returned in ten minutes with a bottle of hydrogen peroxide and a tube of bacitracin.

"What are you doing here?" George asked while she dressed his cuts.

"I came to see you, stupid. I almost left when Missy told me about your couch toy with the vulva jewelry, but I wanted to see you."

"Hey, she was with Mark, not me."

"Do you think I would be here if I didn't already know that?"

"It's good to see you, Sue. I'm sorry I'm not better company tonight."

"I know. Let's get a drink." When they entered the living room, George wearing his red flannel robe, everyone was filing out to hit the dance clubs.

"You should go, Sue. Have a good time." George was so devastated by the day's losses that he feared he wouldn't be able to concentrate on sex. He'd never failed to perform before (the time he drank the bottle of tequila didn't count), and he didn't want there to be a first time.

Sue frowned. "I came here to see you."

"I'm really glad you did. I'm sorry about last week, and I want to make it up to you. But right now I feel weak—probably from the loss of blood. I need to sleep." Sue grabbed his hands, pouting. "Now go," he said, raising his voice authoritatively, "or you'll miss a fun night."

"I understand." Sue kissed him on the lips and rushed out to catch the gang at the elevators.

George gathered up the sports sections and football magazines. He had to bring his debt to TD down to a manageable level, and there was a full NFL slate tomorrow. He wondered if TD would shut him down. Pinky and Dog worked the phones on Sunday, never Cigars. Would TD reconcile accounts between Carter's homer and the 1:00 P.M. kickoffs? Did they have a counterparty risk management system, like City Trust? Doubtful. George dug in. The Bills were favored by 7 over the Jets. . . .

On Sunday morning George ran around the reservoir to clear his head. Then he called Brooklyn.

"Hello." It was Dog.

"York for TD."

"Yeah, York. Bills 7, Browns 2½."

George bet seven teams at an average of $25,000 each and settled in to watch the games. It was a repeat of Saturday's college debacle—George couldn't catch a break. He lost 20 large on the Steelers when Eric Metcalf ran a punt back 75 yards for a touchdown with two minutes left. Browns 28, Steelers 25. When the Lions' Jason Hanson kicked a field goal with four seconds left to beat and cover over George's Rams, costing him 30 large, George puked on the sports section of the *New York Times.* Mark and Nick goofed on him as he carried the mess to the garbage can in the kitchenette.

"Last time a man puked in Club 16B it was Mark," laughed Nick. "Except he threw up a black, lacey thong."

George retreated to his bedroom to tally the damage. He'd lost $65,000 on the World Series, including the $50,000 on Game 6; $89,500 on college football; and $115,000 on pro football—a grand total of $269,500. The Bears were 6 over the Vikings on Monday night, a ridiculous overlay, but TD probably wouldn't let him bet. He'd have to work a deal with TD first where he could pay him when he got his bonus in February, if he was still down. George wondered how TD would react to that.

The next afternoon, after slogging through a day of unfocused trading, George called Brooklyn. "Hello, York for TD."

"Yeah, York. Hold on, TD wants to talk to you."

TD picked up. "York, I got you minus $269,500 for the week, right?"

"Yes."

"Meet me tomorrah at 6:00."

"Uh, OK . . . but I won't have it all."

"How much will ya have?"

"Fifteen or so."

"When will ya have the rest?"

"February 1st."

"You're pullin' my leg, right?"

"No. That's when I get my bonus."

"We gotta problem, York."

"Don't worry, TD. You'll get paid."

"I know I will. Six o'clock. Bring as much as ya can."

"Can I bet the Bears game?"

"Don't be a jerk. Be there tomorrah."

"I'll be there."

George arrived early at the coffee shop on 96th Street so he could take the table farthest in the back. He knew people in the neighborhood and didn't know how he'd explain or, God forbid, introduce TD to one of his colleagues. TD labored to plunk one foot in front of the other as he made his way to the table. He was sweating and wheezing heavily as he squeezed his legs under the table. George figured he had to weigh at least 350 pounds—maybe more.

"How are you, TD?" They shook hands. George felt like he'd opened the refrigerator and shoved his hand into a juicy roast beef. He wiped his hand on his napkin under the table.

"Not too good. High blood pressure's killin' me. That and the diabetes." TD tossed his leather-sleeved Yankees jacket and his Yankees cap on an empty chair and coughed up a hunk of phlegm. He spat it into a napkin and then looked at George. "So, whaddaya got for me?"

"Nineteen-five." George handed him an envelope full of hundreds. "Makes the balance an even two-fifty."

"When do I see the rest of it? And don't tell me February."

"That's when I get my bonus. Until then, all I have is my salary, which barely covers the rent."

"I'm a reasonable man, Georgie, but don't lie to me. It really pisses me off."

"I'm not lying. Why do you say that?"

"Georgie, I been doin' this for twenty-t'ree years, and for whatever reason, I've had a lotta clients work on Wall Street. Senior executives, send their secretaries to make payments; back-office guys, every type o' job on the Street. You think I'm stupid? I checked you out. Hotshot trader at City Trust. I've had dozens of hotshot traders. I've had hotshot traders didn't wanna pay me, but they all did. I never had a hotshot trader *couldn't* pay me. I know what traders at big banks earn. Now when do I get my two-fifty?"

"What you have to understand is that this is my first full year on Wall Street. Most of last year I was working in Washington in a government-type job, struggling to pay off student loans. I have no savings, only student loan debt. I stayed up nights playing dollar ante poker to put myself through college and grad school. February will be my first real payday. That's when I'll pay you. With interest, of course."

"I don't gotta unnerstand nothin', Georgie. Here's what you gotta unnerstand. You don't pay the principal, the vig is 10 percent per week. Got it?"

"Twenty-five grand per week?"

"You got it."

"That's loan shark stuff, what loan sharks charge junkies, street people."

"You're wrong, Georgie boy. Shylocks charge 20 percent a week. I think you're a good kid, got over your head, so I'm givin' ya a break. Ten percent a week. You're into me two-fifty means I'm into my guy two-fifty. He charges me 10 percent a week. I'm a nice guy, I pass it t'rough. You pay any less, I'm losin'. I like ya, Georgie boy, but I lose money for nobody."

"I can't raise 25 a week until February," George hissed, struggling to keep his voice from rising. He glanced around the room. "I'll pay the vig, but I've got to do it in a lump sum when I get my bonus. You have to work with me on this, TD." A frazzled, nasty looking waitress in a T-shirt and jeans finally took their coffee orders.

"They got the best apple pie here, but my doctor would kill me.

Diabetes. You should have some. Listen, you don't like the terms, get the money from a bank. You work at one. This bonus is in the bag, get an advance on it."

"I have no collateral to borrow against, and advances on bonuses are against bank policy."

"Family?"

"My dad is a retired steelworker, Bethlehem Steel. He's got Alzheimer's. I'm helping my kid sister with her tuition at Penn State."

"You work on Wall Street, have rich friends."

"Rich *new* friends. My old friends are in Bethlehem. Blue collar. I don't mean this to sound like a sob story, but I have no place to go for that kind of money before February. You have to work with me on the repayment terms."

"I'm workin' witchya, Georgie boy. You don't gotta pay the principal 'til February. But you gotta pay the vig every week. You don't pay the vig, it's outta my hands."

"Out of your hands?"

"You don't pay your credit card, company turns it over to a collection agency. You don't pay my vig, I gotta turn it over to the collection guys. I got no choice."

"What collection guys? What kind of guys?"

"You went to Princeton, right?"

"Yes."

"Kevin went to Princeton too. He got a Ph.D. in advanced collectin'."

"You're goofin' on me," choked George. He was perspiring heavily.

"No shit, Georgie." TD rolled his eyes and shifted his weight. "These guys collect overdue gambling debts for a livin'. What kinda guys you think they are?"

"So I get behind with the vig, you're going to get tough with me? That's what you're saying?"

"I work inna organization. It ain't City Trust, but we got rules.

Client doesn't pay his vig, the collection guys take care o' it. That's the way it is, Georgie boy. I gotta make a couple more stops." TD rocked the table as he pushed himself to his feet. "See you here next Tuesday. Twenty-five minimum. You're a smart kid. You'll find a way."

7

On Wednesday morning Enrique strutted up to the trading desk and announced that they had won the arbitration with KQB Bank. There were cheers and high fives all around.

"George, you can mark up the $20 million position at the end of the day. Nice going." The 4-point markup would add $800,000 to George's P&L—his profit and loss ledger.

"Thanks, Enrique. Say, do you have a minute?"

"Sure. What's up?"

"Off the desk?"

"No problem, we'll use Pablo's office." They darted behind the glass door. "I hope you're not going to tell me your conscience is bothering you about hosing KQB."

"It's not about that." George's dress shirt was chafing his neck. His drycleaner had used too much starch. "I was wondering if I could get an advance on my bonus."

"It's against bank policy. I've never heard of an exception. Why, you buying a car? A co-op? What?"

"None of that. It's just that when you hired me from the IMF I had no savings, and living on the East Side is tough on just my salary. Rent, social obligations . . . plus, I pay my kid sister's tuition. . . . What are you doing?"

Enrique was writing a personal check. “Here. Pay me back in February.” The check was for $5,000.

“Uh . . . wow . . . I mean, thanks Enrique, but I couldn’t.”

“Don’t worry, it’s my pleasure. Hey, you’re my top money maker this year.”

“Hey, I really appreciate it, but I wasn’t really thinking of 5 grand, I mean . . . relative to my bonus . . .”

“How much do you need, George?” Enrique’s stare suddenly focused, alert, like a big cat tracking its prey.

George was taken aback. “Uh, I don’t know. . . . I mean . . . uh . . .”

“You can trust me, George. What’s the problem?”

“No problem. I mean, I just figured why should I be living like a pauper when I’ve got this big check coming on February 1st?”

Enrique studied him closely. He spoke in a tone more serious than George had ever heard from him. “George, if you’ve got a problem, I’ll work with you. If you and I decide to take it to human resources, the bank will work with you, if it’s a family health issue or something with your sister’s college, whatever. But you have to level with me.”

“No problem, boss. Nothing like that.”

“Take this.” Enrique stuck the folded check in George’s shirt pocket. “This will keep American Express off your back until February. If you need more, for whatever reason, you come to me. Understand?”

“Understood. Thanks a lot, Enrique.”

At lunchtime George pulled his friend and mentor Sam Thorn away from the Treasury desk. They stood with their backs to a pillar where they wouldn’t be overheard.

“Thanks again for intercepting me on the way to JFK last week. I still have no idea what I would have told Joy,” said Sam.

“No problem. Say, I have a question. You know my trading ledger is up over $21 million.”

"Congratulations."

"Thanks. I'm not trying to brag. So I asked Enrique for an advance on my bonus and he got really weird on me. All of a sudden it was the Spanish Inquisition. What's up with that?"

"Enrique's a pro. That's all."

"Yeah, I know he's a pro. But why'd he take out the rubber hose?"

"You're really naive, aren't you? There's nothing more dangerous on a trading floor than a trader with a money problem. It's Enrique's job to know if you have one."

"Dangerous?"

"Yeah, you know, potential fraud. Couple of years ago we had a mortgage trader who cornered the market for some obscure security. Did off-market trades with a buddy and took kickbacks. Went on for months. They only caught him because the derivatives trader was trying to price a trade off of the guy's trading marks, which were way off because he was pricing the securities off market to match his overtrades. The auditors dug in and the guy was cooked."

"What happened to him?"

"Six months at Danbury, then probation."

"What drove him to commit fraud?"

"I don't know if it was drugs, gambling, or just plain greed, but I'm surprised you never heard the story. Management likes to tell it to scare people. You EM guys are in your own world."

"What does the bank do if a trader has a drug or gambling problem?"

"If it's drugs, they offer to take him through rehab. That's what they're doing with your roommate."

"Mark?"

"Yep. He missed a big FNMA auction on Monday. Just didn't show up for work. Heard he was holed up on Avenue B with an ounce of coke, a hooker, and a bottle of Wild Turkey."

George realized he hadn't seen Mark since the Notre Dame–USC game. He wondered what else he'd missed since the weekend. "I hope that's not true."

"I don't give a damn. That asshole had me shitting razor blades for a whole day about that syphilis thing. Even his daddy won't be able to save his job if he doesn't lighten up on the nose candy." Sam was usually pretty coolheaded, and George could tell he was pissed. Sam continued. "Anyway, I think Enrique knows about Mark. He's probably thinking that because you're his roommate you might also have a coke problem. Guilt by association."

"You know I don't touch the stuff."

"Yeah, but Enrique doesn't."

"What about gambling? Bank finds out a trader has a gambling problem."

"I think gambling is actually tougher than drugs. You can't give a gambler a urinalysis to see if he's cured. Last year there was a guy at Silverstein Brothers who shorted a long shot in an NCAA tournament pool and lost a few hundred thousand dollars. He couldn't pay. He got fired and he'll never work on Wall Street again."

"Why can't he work on the Street again if he pays the money back?"

"Judgment. Guy's judgment is so poor that he loses more than he can pay, he's too dangerous to sit in a trading seat. You don't have a gambling problem, do you, George?"

"Of course not. Don't be silly. I'm just a little stretched right now. Living at Club 16B isn't cheap."

"I'd be happy to lend you a few hundred bucks until bonus time if that helps get you over the hump."

"Thanks, I appreciate it, but that's not why I grabbed you. I just wanted to know why Enrique wigged out on me. Thanks for the explanation. I'll let you get back to work." George turned quickly and walked away. He was shaking a bit, and his stomach had turned sour. Sam gave him a funny look and went off to get a cup of coffee.

George told Enrique he had a lunch date with a government economist and went to his bank to cash in the $50,000 CD that he had bought with last year's bonus. There was a significant interest penalty for early redemption, but George didn't hesitate. He also applied for a personal loan. Over the next few days he visited half a dozen banks. The questions were all the same. Did he have any collateral? No. Did he have a credit history? No. Based on his pay stubs from City Trust, he managed to open four checking accounts with $1,000 overdrafts, a Visa card with $20,000, a MasterCard with $20,000, and a Diners Club card with $10,000. This was in addition to his City Trust–sponsored American Express card with $7,800 available and his personal American Express card, which was virtually tapped out. Including Enrique's check he had about $117,000 of cash and credit. He could pay next week's vig and pay off $92,000 in principal, or he could pay the $25,000 vig for the next four weeks and come up 8 grand short of the fifth payment. The former got him lower payments, but he'd be up against it after a week. The latter got him a month to negotiate. The choice was clear.

George paid TD the $25,000 vig on the next two Tuesdays. At each meeting he pleaded for extended terms, which only infuriated TD. On the third Tuesday George was standing under his umbrella on 96th Street when TD pulled up in a green Pontiac. George leaned in the passenger's window and handed TD an envelope.

"How much?"

"Twenty-five."

"I was hopin' you'd make a dent in the principal."

"How? I tapped every conceivable source of credit and I've only got enough for this and next week's payment."

"Get in the car." George obeyed. He hit a wall of stench—a combination of TD's body odor and flatulence.

"Whaddaya tellin' me? Are ya tellin' me that after next week you ain't payin' me?"

"I'm telling you that I've exhausted every way I know to get the money and after next week I will be broke with no prospects for further credit."

TD started to turn red and tremble with anger. He scowled and spat. "Don't fuck with me, Georgie boy."

"I'm not fucking with you. I'm just telling you the facts. I don't have the money and I can't get it until February. You have to let me pay you then, with interest."

TD leaned in George's face, hitting him with another foul odor. "I only gotta do one t'ing, and one t'ing only, and that's to turn this over to the collection boys"—TD started coughing up phlegm but then continued—"which is gonna cost me which is why I'm so pissed off. My doc tol' me I can't get pissed off like this, so get outta my sight. Next week you meet Kevin and Frank. Same time and place. Now get lost."

George got out of the car. He was hoping TD's doctor was right—that he'd have a heart attack. George wondered if he could trick TD into running after him. Maybe he could induce cardiac arrest. George's probability analysis told him he shouldn't try and provoke the guy. The heart attack was too much of a long shot, he decided.

TD rolled down the passenger window and leaned over to yell one last piece of advice to George. "And if you don't make the meetin', they'll find you even if they have to go to City Trust! So don't get no ideas!" As TD pulled away into traffic, George tried to envision two thugs trying to get past the bank's security to the trading floor. One thing was for sure: no matter what happened, Enrique would demand an explanation. Adios bonus. Adios Wall Street. How would he ever pay TD then? He *had* to keep this mess away from the bank.

George walked back to Club 16B in a freezing drizzle. He changed into his sweats, stuck his apartment key in his sock, and pulled on a pair of gloves. Grabbing two rolls of nickels, he took the elevator to the lobby and jogged across the East Side to Central Park. His Uncle Mike in Bethlehem had recommended the nickels for self-defense when George had told him that he often ran in Central Park at night.

The dirt track around the reservoir was covered with puddles. George had to dance to avoid a big puddle and an oncoming jogger, which ticked him off. It was one of his pet peeves about New Yorkers. George always ran the reservoir counterclockwise, as did the vast majority of runners. In Bethlehem and Princeton, all joggers ran the right way, and every track meet he had ever seen, live or on TV, was run counterclockwise. He figured it dated from the ancient Greeks. George could never understand why some people insisted on running the reservoir clockwise. In the summer it was always the young guys, shirtless or in tank tops. He assumed they did it because they could show off to more women, or men if they were gay. But on a moonless, rainy November night?

On the northeast side of the reservoir, puddles covered the entire track save a narrow strip on the inside next to the cement berm that anchored the chain-link fence. On his second lap, George was running on the inside strip when he saw an oncoming jogger. He was a big Caucasian guy, slightly taller and probably twenty pounds heavier than George.

Screw this guy, I've got the right-of-way, thought George. It was like Robin Hood and Little John. When the big guy didn't yield, George dipped his shoulder and caught him in the sternum. George's lower body position offset the big guy's extra weight and they both bounced backward. The guy threw a roundhouse left which glanced off the top of George's head as he ducked. George countered with a right cross, flush on the jaw. He put everything he had into the punch, and could feel it from his fist to the ball of his right foot. He also felt the sickening crunch of the guy's jaw shattering. The roll of nickels he clenched had transformed his fist into a club. The big guy slumped to the track. George rolled him over so he wouldn't drown in a puddle. His face was bloody and misshapen. George looked around for witnesses and, seeing none, hurled the rolls of nickels into the reservoir. He ran down the forested slope, across the bridle path, and out of the park onto Fifth Avenue. At the first phone booth he called 911 and reported the injured jogger. He flexed his right hand to see if it was broken as he ran back across town to Club 16B.

George was disgusted with himself. The gambling debt had been looming all month, but only then did he realize what the pressure was actually doing to him. There was a message on his machine from Sue. He filled a baggie with ice and held it against his sore right hand. He dialed with his left hand and cradled the phone on his shoulder.

"Hi, Sue. How are you?"

"Great. What have you been up to?"

"Ran the reservoir. Just got back."

"In this weather?"

"I needed the exercise."

"So, what are you doing for Thanksgiving?"

"Going to my folks'. I told you that."

"That's right, you did."

"You're going to your mom's, right?"

"I was. She called today to tell me that she's going to Aruba with her boyfriend."

"What about your dad?"

"I can't handle Thanksgiving with him. Not right now."

"So you're going to stay in the city?"

"I guess so," sighed Sue. There was silence on the line for a good ten seconds.

"Do you . . . uh . . . do you want to come home with me for the holiday?" asked George cautiously.

"You don't have to do that. I'll be fine. My roommate Cheryl is staying in the city also."

"No, I mean it. My parents would be thrilled to meet you. They won't believe I have such a terrific girlfriend."

Sue covered the receiver for a moment and smiled. If George was taking the step of bringing her home, what they had must be more than lust. Not that Sue had a problem with lust. Sex had dominated her previous relationships, but none had lasted more than six months. The boys had always been willing to continue, but she'd always looked for new men, new conquests.

"Yeah, right. Are you sure this isn't an act of mercy?" She repressed her delight.

"Not at all. What time do you get off tomorrow?"

"Day before Thanksgiving the office empties out around noon."

"I can't get off that early. Would you mind renting a car? I'll pay for it, of course."

"Sure."

No, George was different from the rest. He could be a stubborn bastard, but he wasn't afraid of sparring with her. When she challenged the others, they either pushed back to protect their eggshell egos, or they rolled over so quickly that they lost her respect. Bullying George was like charging a judo master—she always wound up on the mat with him grinning at her. Not that she ever stayed on the bottom for long.

"Since you'll have the car, why don't you pick me up at three o'clock? I'll be waiting outside my building so you won't have to park."

"How long will we be staying?"

"We'll drive back Saturday or Sunday, if that's OK."

"Fine. See you at three. Bye," said Sue enthusiastically.

George was more apprehensive. His Uncle Mike had taught him that courtship was all about selecting good breeding stock. He was sure Uncle Mike would take one look at Sue and give his hearty approval—if not a wolf whistle. But how was this upper-crust girl going to react to the Wilhelms?

8

At five past three Sue pulled up to the curb on York Avenue in a white Taurus from Hertz. George shoved a green canvas duffle, a cardboard box containing five bottles of wine, and a wet umbrella into the backseat. When he approached the driver's door, Sue waved him off.

"You're not insured. You can navigate," she ordered. George shrugged and got in the passenger's side. He leaned over and kissed her on the lips. She held the back of his head to make it last.

"Good wine?" she asked.

"Passable. Can't buy wine with a cork in it in my neighborhood back home."

Sue zipped through Central Park on 79th Street. The rain, the gray sky, and the bare, wind-whipped trees made the park look bleak. Holiday traffic jammed the Lincoln Tunnel. They made out behind the wheel as the traffic crept toward the tunnel. During an especially long kiss, Sue let a gap develop in front of her and a taxi cut in. She paid no attention to the angry honking behind her. On the New Jersey Turnpike she wove from lane to lane, passing every vehicle at seventy to eighty miles an hour. George moved over and fastened his seat belt. They sped west on Route 78 past the stately bedroom suburbs of northeast New Jersey and the gentlemen horse farms of north-central Jersey.

"So, is your mom serious about this Aruba guy?" asked George tentatively.

"Oh, please. I'm sure he's just some airhead, boy-toy stud. The only thing my mom is serious about is suing my dad for more money to support her lifestyle."

"Doesn't sound like it was an amicable divorce."

"It was a shit show. Still is. I'm just glad that I was in boarding school in Switzerland. I came home for the summer after ninth grade and I had to stay with the neighbors for a day. My mom wasn't around and she had changed the locks. So what are your parents serious about?"

"Family mostly. The church. They could never afford a lot of distractions."

"I see." Sue paused momentarily. "So what are the sleeping arrangements chez-Wilhelm?"

"What would they be at your mom's?" countered George.

"We could sleep together. If she was sober enough to notice, she wouldn't care."

"And at your dad's?"

"Purely theoretical, but he wouldn't care either."

"Well, that's not the case at my folks'. You'll probably sleep in my old room and I'll sleep on the couch."

"What time are we expected?"

"Sometime in the evening. I told Mom not to hold dinner, that we'd eat on the way."

"Well, you might have to exaggerate about how bad the holiday traffic was. Big accident in the tunnel." Smiling, she exited the highway and parked in front of a Motel 6. The Hilton was more to Sue's taste, but she was a practical woman. Two hours later they were back on the road.

The city was hidden in pitch darkness as they drove along and across the Lehigh River. Lights dimly illuminated the great Bethlehem Steel Works, but they could smell it better than they could see it. George directed Sue to a neighborhood of compact wooden houses built in the 1930s and separated only by hedges and an occasional driveway. Some had outdoor stairways which led to private entrances for second-floor residents. In the darkness, the homes appeared well maintained. This was unfamiliar territory for Sue. It reminded her of Archie Bunker's Queens neighborhood from *All in the Family,* but with front yards.

They pulled into a narrow driveway beside a white, two-story house. The front yard was small and covered by bare bushes that bowed to the late autumn weather. A single lantern-style lamp illuminated the front steps—there was no porch. A sturdy woman in her early sixties opened the door as Sue and George approached. She wore her gray hair in a bun, with glasses and a smile that dimpled her plump, rosy cheeks. She gave George a hug and a loud kiss on the cheek.

"Mom, this is Sue Collier. Sue, my mom, Greta."

"How do you do, Greta?"

"So wonderful to meet you, Sue. So nice of you to come all the way out here. George has told us so much about you." George rolled his eyes. He had told his mom very little about Sue. He guessed that was just something you said. Sue was wearing a Burberry raincoat belted over tight corduroys and a white ribbed turtleneck sweater. Her face radiated the glow of a woman coming off multiple orgasms. George thought his mom would guess that they had stopped to make love. In high school she had always figured out exactly when he had become intimate with his girlfriends. "You and Jane better be careful," she'd say, immediately after they'd gone all the way. At first he thought it was a sixth sense that all moms had, but none of his friends' moms, including his girlfriends' moms, seemed to have a clue.

Inside, to the left, there was a cozy parlor where rust-colored wing-backed chairs flanked a modest fireplace. The walls were decorated with Currier and Ives prints. On the right was what appeared to be a dining room, because of the antique maple sideboard, but it was dominated by a low, shiny steel hospital bed. One wall was decorated with framed black-and-white photographs of Bethlehem, including the river, the bluffs, and the steelworks. On another wall hung the family photos: a soldier, a bride and groom, babies, and a family of four at various ages. A half dozen military medals, pinned to navy blue velvet, hung above a photo of a squad of young soldiers hugging each other playfully on a beach.

George walked straight back to the kitchen where his dad sat in his wheelchair. He was tall and gaunt with short, wispy white hair and parchmentlike skin. His head tilted slightly, and spit dribbled from the lower corner of his mouth. When George hugged him, he could feel every rib under his father's red flannel shirt. As he stepped back, his dad made eye contact with him, much to George's delight.

"Dad, this is Sue Collier. Sue, this is my dad, Kurt."

"How do you do, Kurt?" Sue grabbed Kurt's hand and squeezed it gently. She thought she felt him squeeze back. George saw his dad's eyes register an obscure approval.

"What can I get you kids to eat and drink? Please, sit down. I've got homemade apple strudel, or I could make ham sandwiches." Smiling broadly, Greta clasped her hands in front of her chest.

"A beer would be great," said George.

"For me too, please," said Sue. Greta set four Rolling Rock bottles on the table next to four old-fashioned pewter mugs. She pushed Kurt's wheelchair up to the small steel-and-linoleum kitchen table and poured a beer with each hand. Grabbing a plastic turkey baster from a kitchen drawer, she dipped it into Kurt's beer and carefully squirted some into his mouth. Without asking, she washed and sliced a few radishes and placed them on a saucer in the center of the table next to the saltshaker. Finally, she placed a wooden bowl of walnuts and a brass nutcracker on the table.

"Where's Heidi?" asked George.

"Your sister's out with friends. She won't be home 'til late. Tell me, how was your trip?" Sue and George told her all about the big accident at the Lincoln Tunnel, the terrible weather, and dinner at Wendy's outside Easton. Greta talked about the glorious day of cooking ahead of her.

"We have to start by boiling the giblets for the dressing. What kind of dressing does your mom make, Sue?"

"Umm . . . to tell you the truth, Greta, what my mom makes on Thanksgiving is, uh, reservations," replied Sue uncomfortably.

"Well. . . ." Greta hesitated. "Perhaps you'd like to learn how to make Pennsylvania-style giblet dressing?"

Sue smiled sincerely. "I'd love that. I've never cooked poultry before."

"Wonderful!" Greta clasped her hands again and smiled. By the time Kurt and Greta finished their beers, George and Sue had each finished two. Greta stood up and announced, "It's way past Papa's bedtime. He stayed up late to visit with you two." George stepped between Greta and Kurt.

"No, Mom, I'll help Dad tonight."

"Don't be silly. You and Sue should visit. Sit together on the couch."

George raised his eyebrows to Sue, who nodded. "No, Mom, I want to. Get acquainted with Sue. Really."

"All right. Papa doesn't usually have beer at bedtime. Make sure . . ."

"I know, Mom."

Greta grabbed another beer for Sue and led her into the parlor. George wheeled his dad into the bathroom that had been added on to the back of the house ten years prior, when Kurt could no longer climb the stairs. It was cramped, but Greta and Kurt's cousin, who was a plumber, had laid it out carefully to accommodate an invalid. George brushed his dad's teeth, then took his trousers down and slid him on top of the toilet. He seemed lighter than ever. Shockingly light. George wheeled him into the dining room and drew the curtains that his mom had sewn by hand. He slid his dad onto the hospital bed, undressed him, checked him for bedsores, and put his pajamas on. His dry, wrinkled skin hung loosely on his fragile body. It felt like Naugahyde. George hugged his dad, told him he loved him, and turned out the lights.

Sue and Greta were watching the 11:00 news on TV. Greta kissed George good night and went upstairs to bed.

"Is your mom always this nice?" Sue asked. George looked at her inquisitively. "I mean, she's like a character from a children's book."

"Mother Goose?"

"You know what I mean. I mean, does she ever get, you know, bitchy?"

"She had a little trouble with menopause, maybe."

"Thank God. I mean . . . you know what I mean."

"I know," replied George softly. Sue kissed him, and they began necking fervently on the couch. When she started getting carried away, he pushed her back. "Avast, ye wench," he snarled, imitating Enrique's Caribbean pirate routine. "To bed with ye." He carried her bag upstairs to the bedroom he had grown up in. She was taken aback by its smallness. George read her mind.

"My sister and I shared a room until puberty. Then my dad built this partition." He knocked on the inner wall, which sounded paper-thin. He kissed her again, softly, and headed downstairs. She looked at the ribbons, medals, and trophies that cluttered the room. Football, wrestling, and baseball. Sue had better trophies. She wondered if it was because she was a better athlete, or because she competed in leagues that could afford better trophies. George went downstairs to watch *SportsCenter.* When he remembered that his parents didn't have cable, he vowed to buy it for them when he got his bonus.

Awaking at dawn, George quietly slipped on jeans and a sweatshirt and headed out into a chilly mist. He found a small wheelbarrow, a spade, and a pair of work gloves in the garage. He pushed the wheelbarrow to a large pile of dead leaves at the corner of the rusty chain-link fence that separated the Wilhelm's backyard from the neighbor's, swept the current year's leaves off the top of the pile, and filled the wheelbarrow with the decayed leaves from prior years. Then he pushed the wheelbarrow into the front yard and shoveled the mulch onto each of Greta's dozen rosebushes. Squatting next to each one, he patted the mulch with his gloved hands to compact it against the lower canes. George saw his dad looking at him from the dining-room window. Greta had wheeled him in front of the window because she knew it would please him to see his son tending the roses. George waved to his dad and smiled.

A wiry old black man and a teenager with a scraggly blond beard, both wearing green hospital scrubs, stood in the kitchen. They had just finished bathing and dressing Kurt. Greta was sliding fried eggs onto thick slices of dark bread.

"Sorry we can't stay for breakfast, Miz Wilhelm," said the black man.

"Nonsense, Jim," replied Greta, handing each man an egg sandwich wrapped in wax paper. "You finish with your other patients so you can spend the rest of the holiday with your families." George walked in and greeted Jim, who introduced him to young Stan.

"Good meet you," said Stan in a heavy Slavic accent.

"Likewise," said George. "Tough duty working Thanksgiving. Hold on a minute." George grabbed two of the wine bottles he had brought from New York and handed one to each man. "Happy Thanksgiving." They thanked George and Greta profusely and left. George called to Sue from the bottom of the stairs, and a minute later she came down in her stocking feet wearing designer jeans and a maroon T-shirt. Greta served eggs scrambled with big chunks of boiled potatoes to Sue and George. Then she pureed a smaller portion in a blender and fed it to Kurt with a teaspoon while she ate.

After clearing the table, Greta handed Sue a flowery muslin apron that matched her own. Sue put it on and fastened her hair in a ponytail with a rubber band. Greta chattered gleefully about cooking as she scooped the giblets from the twenty-pound turkey. She was like an avid fisherman baiting a young child's first hook.

When George returned from more yard work, Greta was instructing Sue and Heidi on the art of spicing the giblet dressing. Heidi gave George a long, warm hug. She was prettier than ever. She wore a navy Penn State sweatshirt and faded jeans.

"Hey, big brother," she said, beaming.

"Hey, shrimp." George smiled. "How's college? Straight As?"

"Like you? No, all Bs. But I love it."

"Still dating the linebacker from Cleveland?"

"I dumped him. He kept passing out drunk everywhere."

"Replace him yet?"

Heidi shook her head. "I'm not in any hurry. I see you're doing all right." She tossed a glance at Sue and grinned. Sue blushed, ever so slightly.

Greta was in a zone. George wondered if a cooking zone was like a pitching zone. When the dressing tasted perfect, did Greta feel like she had just wobbled a batter's knees by starting a curve at his chin and snapping it over the inside corner for strike three? Did she feel like Enrique when he out-traded Goldman Sachs? George showered, put on clean jeans and a denim shirt, and borrowed the Taurus keys from Sue. When he returned with a cold case of Rolling Rock, his cousin Harry was carrying an identical case into the house.

George introduced Sue to his Uncle Mike and his cousins Harry and Marlene. Mike was ten years younger than his brother Kurt and a hundred pounds heavier. He had shaved cleanly for the occasion and dressed up in a white shirt and a threadbare suit that was a size too small. Mike's son Harry was George's age. He was built like an offensive lineman and wore his blond beard long and unkempt. His disheveled hair fell over the collar of his plaid flannel shirt. Marlene was two years younger than her brother, with long, straight, mahogany-colored hair and pale, fleshy cheeks.

She carried a sleeping infant in a frilly pink basket and wore a powder blue maternity dress with a white, embroidered collar. Her figure had not yet recovered from childbirth. Mike and his kids had been joining Kurt and Greta for Thanksgiving ever since Mike's wife had divorced him and moved to Allentown with the owner of the local Chevy dealership.

Marlene moved to the kitchen and watched the other women fuss over her baby daughter. The men stayed in the living room. They twisted the caps off their Rolling Rocks and settled in to watch the NFL pregame show. Mike stayed busy with the turkey baster, helping his brother to sips of beer. George grabbed fresh bottles for Mike, Harry, and himself, located the carving knife and whetstone, and sat down to hone the blade. Watching Barry Sanders run was the best part of Thanksgiving, decided George. No back in history cut as sharply as Sanders. When he spread his knees in the hole to shake and bake, he squatted so low he nearly dragged his butt on the turf. Late in the second quarter, Lions quarterback Rodney Peete fumbled on his own 42-yard line.

"They'll never win with a spook quarterback," declared Harry.

"Do me a favor, will you, cuz?" asked George irritably. "Can you hold the racist comments when Sue's around?"

"Don't want her to find out your family is a bunch of rednecks?" Harry snickered.

"Exactly," snapped George. Harry smiled and turned his attention back to the game. At halftime he helped George move Kurt's bed to the cellar and replace it with the old, maple dining-room table. They screwed the legs on the table, flipped it upright, and inserted the leaves to maximize the length. The smell of the roasting turkey made their mouths water as they worked. George asked Harry if he knew if the city was cutting trees down anywhere. Harry called his friend Stash, who worked for the parks department and was happy to tell George where he could find some free firewood.

In the third quarter, Sanders grabbed his knee and writhed on the turf. Harry said it was a shame that the greatest back since Jim

Brown had to play on artificial turf. For the Lions no less. They all speculated as to whether or not he would need surgery. With Sanders out, the Bears defense dominated, winning 10–6. The men had finished three six-packs, and the women had finished the fourth and broken out the second case. George opened a bottle of Chardonnay, but everyone except Greta and Marlene stuck with the Rolling Rock.

As soon as the gun sounded, Mike wheeled Kurt to the head of the dining room table. Greta had timed the meal to be ready at the end of the fourth quarter, so the dressing, cranberry sauce, peas, sweet potatoes, and sourdough rolls were already laid out. George carried the turkey in from the kitchen and set it on his place to his dad's right. After everyone was seated, George surprised Sue by leading the family in prayer. When she realized that everyone had their heads bowed she did the same, but she whiffed on the collective "Amen."

"So how's Gus?" George asked Marlene as he cut into the turkey. She smiled longingly at the mention of her husband.

"He called from Kuwait this morning. He's fine, except he pulled a hamstring playing flag football in the sand. We didn't talk long. He said most of his platoon was lined up behind him waiting on the phone." Everyone said they were glad that Gus was well.

"What kind of work do you do, Sue?" asked Mike. Greta returned from the kitchen with Kurt's pureed turkey and listened attentively.

"I work for an advertising agency on Madison Avenue."

"Really? Sounds exiting," Mike replied.

"Do you write commercials?" asked Marlene.

"I'm not creative enough for that. I'm a media buyer."

"What's a media buyer?" asked Marlene.

"We buy time from television and radio stations, or space from newspapers, magazines, billboards, et cetera."

"Do you put commercials on the football games?" asked Harry.

"That's mostly trucks and beer. I work on the Procter & Gamble account. We do a lot on the daytime series."

"Selling soap. That's why they call them soap operas," offered Marlene.

"Precisely," replied Sue.

"The Procter & Gamble account. How wonderful," said Greta.

"And you're still brokering the Latin stocks, George?"

"Latin loans, Uncle Mike. Yes."

"Can you believe this NAFTA vote? At least the House Democrats voted against shipping our jobs to Mexico. The damn Republicans and that goddamn Clinton. . . . You know I voted for every Democratic candidate since Adlai Stevenson—every one endorsed by the United Steel Workers. I should have voted for Ross Perot."

"Protectionism isn't going to solve the problems of American industry. Tariffs just make us less competitive," said Sue. Mike glared at her icily.

"Hey, what do you get when you cross a Mexican and an octopus?" interjected Harry. He paused expectantly, then continued. "I don't know either, but the sombitch sure can pick tomatoes." Harry laughed aloud in an unsuccessful attempt to ease the tension.

"You see that picture, young lady?" Mike pointed to a framed newspaper photo on the wall. It showed several dozen workers wearing boots and overalls in what appeared to be a picket line. "That's 1941. The man in the center with the fedora is John Waldony, who organized the USW in Bethlehem. The skinny kid on his right is Kurt. Sixteen years old. Fifteen minutes after this picture was taken, Robert Wilkens's goons started bustin' heads. Kurt was unconscious for three days. Waldony finally won out in '42, but Kurt wasn't here to celebrate. He was fightin' Japs at Guadalcanal. He fought in the Solomons right through '43, took Saipan in '44, and was damn near killed at Iwo Jima in '45." Mike stared at Sue. "Do you think that Kurt made these sacrifices so we could give American jobs to Mexicans and the goddamn Japs?" Sue didn't reply.

Mike chugged half of his eighth beer and continued. "During World War II, thirty thousand USW members made steel here for the war effort. Now there are a few hundred, and this time next year they'll be making the works into a museum."

Greta jumped in. "Did you know that James Carville and Mary Matalin are getting married in New Orleans tonight?" She beamed at Sue and Marlene. "What a wonderful example of political opponents getting along. The Olympia Brass Band is playing at their party in the French Quarter. I'm sure it will be on the news tonight."

"I've had it with Clinton and Carville too," growled Mike. "Next week Clinton's going to sign the 'Don't ask, don't tell' bill. Queers in the military. How 'bout that, Kurt? How would you like to have shared your foxhole on Iwo Jima with a pansy?" Mike cracked another beer. "I was in the Marines too, in Korea. It was thirty below zero at the Chosin Reservoir. Our whole platoon slept squished together, hugging each other to keep from freezing to death. Imagine if we'd had to worry about queers too?"

"Big, good-looking hunk like you?" Sue smirked. "I'm sure that at least one marine in that pile lusted after you in his heart. That cute one that was hugging you from behind, kind of rubbing . . ." Horrified, Mike glowered silently. Marlene and Heidi started giggling. Harry guffawed. Shaking his head, Mike gradually broke into a smile and chuckled.

"Homosexuality is a hard issue these days," offered Greta. "No one ever had to talk about it before. Now there's all this clamoring, but after four years the Lutheran Church still hasn't come out one way or the other. Bishop Chilstrom finally had to fire Reverend Bloomquist as head of the national panel. What church do you belong to, Sue?"

"I'm, uh . . . unaffiliated."

"Unaffiliated. Sounds like, you know, a runner at a track meet," quipped Heidi.

"I race in 5Ks and 10Ks," Sue replied. "Unaffiliated."

After apple strudel and pumpkin pie, everyone complimented Greta on the wonderful meal. The men adjourned to watch the Dolphins play the Cowboys while the women cleaned up. Dallas lost in the final seconds on a brain fart by Leon Lett, but Harry obediently laid off the racial slurs. When the second case of Rolling Rock was gone, Mike drove his family home.

Kurt, George, Heidi, Greta, and Sue drank Chardonnay and watched Texas A&M beat Texas 18–9. George put Kurt to bed, and everyone else retired. After a half hour, Sue tiptoed downstairs wearing nothing but one of George's old T-shirts. She slid into the fold-out couch beside him and wetly licked his neck. Soon she was straddling him and rocking leisurely. As she gradually increased her intensity, the old bedsprings creaked ever more loudly. Looking past Sue's naked, bouncing torso, George could see Heidi scrambling down the stairs with her index finger to her lips.

"You guys are going to wake up Mom and Dad for sure," she whispered. Sue turned to see Heidi retreat back up the stairs. Without hesitation, she grabbed George by the wrist and led him down to the unfinished cellar. She spread her legs apart and bent over the dryer, her sweaty breasts flattening against the white steel. Privacy insured, George took his time concluding their first Thanksgiving together. He hoped it would be the first of many.

It rained heavily all night and cleared just before dawn. Sue drove George north toward the city center as the low autumn sunlight was beginning to dry the streets.

"Your uncle seems to idolize your dad," remarked Sue.

"He sure does. My dad was a local hero for standing shoulder-to-shoulder with Waldony during the riots of '41. Then he came home from Iwo Jima with two Purple Hearts and a Bronze Star. He was badly wounded, and to top it all off he contracted malaria. He didn't get out of the hospital until 1947, and he never fully recovered. The union carried him for years, even though he couldn't do much around the plant. In the '60s he finally went on full disability. The USW really took care of us."

"How did he court your mom if he was, you know . . ."

"She was a teenager—a candy striper at the VA hospital. She's been a saint her whole life, I guess."

"Is your dad's disability the reason you weren't born until '65?"

"Oh no. He was 100 percent in that way. My mom had nine miscarriages. She was almost forty before she found the right doctor."

"Oh my god. She is a saint," exclaimed Sue. She drove over the South New Street Bridge and parked. George pointed back toward the Lehigh River and Canal Park.

"There's the running trail. You can run west, all the way to Allentown, or east, all the way to Phillipsburg."

"The steelworks are east, right?"

"Right."

"See you in a couple of hours. I love you."

"I love you, Sue." It was the second time they had exchanged those words. The first time had been nine hours earlier, when they were draped over the old Westinghouse dryer.

Sue grabbed her plastic water bottle and ran toward the river. After two miles she could see the blast furnaces—massive, decaying behemoths that towered above acres of motley brick buildings along the river. The tall stacks belched smoke, clouding the humble row houses that clung to the bluffs. Looking across the river into the morning sunlight, the only person she could see in the dreary shadows was the engineer in the window of a locomotive that was unloading several dozen coal cars. Suddenly, Sue was overcome by a haunting feeling brought on by the towering presence of something once so proud and great that was clearly fading into history. The uneasy emotion ebbed as she ran on through the outskirts of eastern Bethlehem and settled into a familiar rhythm.

After another few miles, she imagined that she was a senior at Wellesley again, racing for the Seven Sisters cross-country championship. She had run on the heels of the defending champion from Smith until the last forty yards, when her final burst carried her to first place by a step. Smiling, she recalled the exhilaration of victory as she was mobbed by her coaches, teammates, and friends. Then she remembered searching the crowd for her parents and realizing that neither was in attendance. Her smile faded then, but she didn't slacken her pace.

George drove to Harry's house and swapped the Taurus for an old pickup truck. The address that Stash had given him was on frat row, near Lehigh University. The trunk of a pin oak lay on the lawn, sawed neatly into eighteen-inch sections. George loaded the tree into the truck, dropped half of it in his parents' driveway, and returned the truck to Harry with the other half onboard. Returning in the Taurus, he brought out the eight-pound sledge hammer and three antique steel wedges. Greta wheeled Kurt down the wooden ramp that Mike had built in back and parked him in a sunny spot in the yard to watch his son work. George quickly tapped a wedge into a crack in the center of the largest trunk section. Standing back, legs apart, he swung the sledge high over his head and drove the wedge through to the ground, neatly splitting the trunk in half. He loved the feel of the hickory sledge handle in his hands, dispatching his power to the task. It was like the bliss he felt hitting a line drive off the sweet spot of a Louisville Slugger. He pitied today's kids, who would only feel the ping of aluminum unless they turned pro. Talking to himself, he mimicked Woody Harrelson in *White Men Can't Jump.* "I'm in a fuckin' zone, maaann." By noon he had split and stacked enough firewood for the winter. He carried an armful into the house to dry by the fireplace and returned to the yard with a large old wicker basket which he filled with bark and splinters for kindling. Then he wheeled his dad back in front of the TV and made a fire in the fireplace. He found his mom alone in the kitchen making lunch.

"You know, Mom, things are going pretty well for me at the bank. I mean, if you get to the point where it's tough for you to, you know, to take care of Dad, we can afford a first-class retirement home. No problem."

"Don't be silly. I'm still as strong as an ox. Jim and Stan do all the lifting anyway, and Medicare pays for it. You save your money. You're doing more than enough helping Heidi with her tuition."

"Well, it's there if you need it."

"You're so sweet." Greta gave her son a big hug. "I can't tell you how proud I am." George wondered how proud she'd be if she knew about his problem with TD.

Minutes later, Sue appeared looking totally exhausted. Greta was astonished that she had run eighteen miles. Sue and George drank two pitchers of ice water between them, then retreated to the showers. When they returned to the kitchen, Kurt and Heidi were already at the table. Greta served them leftover hot turkey with dressing, gravy, and sweet potatoes, and the five of them drank the last bottle of Chardonnay. George took his dad to the bathroom, wheeled him back to the parlor, and stoked the fire. He lay on the couch with Sue and watched college football. While she slept with her head on his shoulder, George dozed only fitfully, despite his exhaustion. The games reminded him of the disastrous afternoon of Game 6, and he knew he'd have to meet with TD on Tuesday.

9

On Saturday, George woke up at 7:00 A.M. when Jim and Stan came in to bathe Kurt. He dressed quickly and puttered around the yard. The weather was cold and dry, and it smelled like football. George added more mulch to the rosebushes where it had settled too low after the rain and split some logs into kindling. When he reentered the house his dad was back in the dining room so he showered and shaved in the downstairs bathroom. When he emerged, Greta was serving Kurt, Jim, and Stan eggs, potatoes, and fried leftover turkey instead of bacon. George joined them, and Sue soon came down the stairs with her bag. Jim talked about his other patients. Most were considerably older than Kurt, but they all suffered from the same bedsores, constipation, and other ailments. Sue helped Greta clear the table but was not permitted to help with the dishes. George hugged and kissed his mom and dad good-bye. When Sue hugged and kissed Greta and Kurt, George could tell it made his mom happy.

Before Sue had driven a block, she asked, "Are you glad you brought your godless, liberal, spoiled WASP, Boston slut home for Thanksgiving, George?" From her tone, it sounded as if she had rehearsed the question.

"My mom really likes you. She told me," George half lied.

"How could she?"

"My mom's a special person. She looks through the background, the politics, the religion, et cetera. She looks through to a person's heart. She knows you have a good heart."

"I'm not sure she's right, but it's nice to hear."

"Nonsense."

"And your dad?"

"He likes you too. I can see it in his eyes. He also thinks you're hot." Sue chuckled. George had loosened her up.

"You can see that in his eyes also?"

"Absolutely. Plus he drools ten times as much." Sue was smiling now. After a few blocks she cleared her throat.

"You know, it's really touching to see the way you and your mom take care of your dad."

"My sister helps."

"Right. And your sister."

"That's the point of marriage, right? Finding someone you want to grow old with," said George earnestly. Sue drove a few more blocks. She was losing her smile.

"I obviously can't see one of my mom's boyfriends sliding her off the wheelchair onto the toilet when she's disabled."

"Your folks are rich. They can afford a first-class retirement home. They'll get good care. Make friends with the other residents."

"You know it's not the same thing." Sue paused. "I hope I'm not too much like my mom."

"I'm sure she's a good person."

"Yeah, right. When I was in the eighth grade she seduced my dad's best friend. I mean, this guy was the best man at their wedding. They got really drunk at a party at the club and she jumped him on the golf course. It was like she wanted to get caught, and she did. The ninth hole became known as Sarah Collier's hole. The guy's wife divorced him."

"Is there a Sue Collier hole at the club?"

"None of your damn business." Sue gave him a little sideways smile. "I do know one thing that I inherited from my mom. My sex drive."

"That's the part that I like best about you," George said with a grin.

"A doctor told my mom that she's a nymphomaniac."

"Your mom told you that?"

"She was really drunk one night. I was thirteen. Pretty weird, huh?"

"I don't know," mused George. "So your mom started the infidelity?"

"Strangely enough, I don't think so. I'm pretty sure it was my dad."

"If she was all over him, why did he, you know, stray?"

"Good question. Plus, she was really hot. I've seen pictures of her as a newlywed, in her bikini. Smokin'."

"What does she look like now?"

"The drinking hasn't helped her face, but she's still got a great body."

George smiled. His uncle had taught him that when evaluating breeding stock, one should always look at the mom, because that's what the daughter will look like.

Sue continued. "So tell me why the bastard cheated on my mom."

"Do you want the scientific answer?"

"What are you talking about?"

"All animal behavior has evolved to maximize reproductive success. Over hundreds of generations, behaviors that do not maximize reproductive success are selected out of the gene pool. With humans, males have evolved to be more promiscuous than females."

"This sounds more like an excuse than science, but I'm listening."

"Well, a human male has to invest five minutes in a sex act."

"Premature. What a loser."

"The female has to invest the time and physical strain of pregnancy as well as the effort to raise the offspring to maturity. Nine months plus eighteen years for humans. So the female has to be a lot more careful who she mates with. The promiscuous male can mate with twenty females in a week, and he's got a chance of reproductive success with all twenty. A woman can only get pregnant once a year, so what's her upside in promiscuity? She'd only be genetically disposed to promiscuity if her mate couldn't fertilize her."

"Was Lorena Bobbitt genetically programmed to chop off her hubby's dick?" Sue swiped at George's lap. He shuddered. Laughing, she continued. "So males are genetically disposed to sow wild oats, and females are not because historically it was a bad deal for them if they did."

"A bad deal for their gene pool. You hit the nail on the head." Sue considered this as she turned off Route 412 onto 78 East.

"You make it all sound like a math problem. So how did love evolve?" she asked.

"Romantic love evolved to strengthen the bond between a man and a woman so they will pool their energy to raise their offspring."

"That's your idea of romantic? What about lust? What does your science book say about that?" asked Sue.

"Animals that are lustier mate more often, increasing their chance for reproductive success. Deer rut only in the fall, when the females are fertile. Otherwise it's a waste of energy. But where females are fertile year-round, like dogs and humans, males lust constantly because they can't miss an opportunity for reproductive success. Have you noticed that you're horniest around your fifteenth day?"

"I have. But what I'd like to know, Mr. Science Nerd, is why I'm horny every other day of the month?"

"You're genetically programmed to use sex to attract a mate

and keep him from straying, even on days when he can't get you pregnant."

"Well then," she said with an impish grin. "I guess I'm going to surrender to my genetic programming." She pulled off onto the shoulder, stopped, and ordered George to drive. When they were back on the highway she unbuckled his belt. George pushed his seat all the way back. He set the cruise control on sixty and tried to concentrate on keeping the car in the middle of the right-hand lane.

10

Frank woke up around noon. His square face was covered with acne, and his small head seemed to connect to his body-builder's shoulders just below the ears. The apparent absence of a neck made him look like a caveman. Sitting on the side of his bed, he rubbed his eyes, farted, and tried to reconstruct the events of the prior evening. He knew that Kevin had said something about a job today, but he couldn't remember the specifics. He pissed, brushed his teeth, and pulled on jeans, sneakers, and his green Jets jacket. He grabbed his half-gallon thermos and gym bag and walked the two blocks to a small, greasy diner on Flatbush Avenue. As soon as he sat down at the counter, the fry cook threw his eggs and sausage on the griddle.

A homely, middle-aged waitress sloshed coffee into his mug. She hadn't spoken to Frank since September, when she'd suggested he needed a bath and he'd threatened to shove the ketchup bottle up her snatch and break it. She grabbed his thermos and filled it with coffee, sugar, and ice while Frank stuffed the food in his mouth. A minute later, she slammed the thermos down in front of him, making the glasses on the counter shake as she stomped away. Frank threw her a big toothy smile with his mouth full of eggs and walked out. On the subway platform and the subway he lifted the thermos above his head and alternated between loud gulps and even louder belches. He ignored the disgusted looks of the other passengers. By the time he got to the gym, the thermos was empty and the caffeine had his heart racing.

The piney smell of disinfectant pierced, but did not mask, the smell of stale sweat in the small, deserted locker room. Frank changed into green gym shorts (the Jets logo had long since worn off) and a black spandex tank top. He took a vial from the pocket of his Jets jacket, sprinkled the powdered meth on the back of his hand, covered it with his right nostril, and snorted. He repeated the process with the left nostril, roared like a tiger, locked his locker, and swaggered into the gym. Treadmills, steppers, and Nautilus machines occupied one half of the gym. Racks of free weights, benches, and canvas mats covered the other half. A heavy bag and two speed bags hung in the back. The wall opposite the locker room was mirrored, floor to ceiling. A young man with gold rings piercing his ears and eyebrows admired his own bare torso in the mirror as he curled twenty-five-pound dumbbells. Two middle-aged tough guys, with paunches and tattoos, panted on the treadmills. A professional bodybuilder, cleanly shaven from head to toe, pulled the high pulley bar behind his neck—thirty slow, smooth reps.

Frank bench-pressed one hundred pounds twenty times rapidly to get the blood flowing through his deltoids and pectorals. After consulting a chart in his pocket, he slid a total of 405 pounds onto the bar. Frank was surprisingly organized when it came to his workout. He took three deep breaths and accompanied each of his first seven repetitions with a loud, fierce grunt. On his eighth and final rep the grunt became a violent roar as he strained mightily to straighten his arms. He squatted 455 pounds, military pressed 275, curled 185, pulled 280 on the high pulley, and rowed 255 on the low pulley. Each set was seven grunting reps with a roaring rep number eight.

Frank was on the eighth rep of his second set of squats when his heart began to flutter. He sat down to compose himself, wondering if he'd snorted too much methamphetamine. A tall man in his thirties wearing a brown leather coat appeared at the entrance to the gym just then and nodded to him. They met in the locker room, where the man looked around like a nervous squirrel and bent low to check for feet in the toilet stall. He handed Frank a syringe.

"Delatestryl, twenty milligrams. Breakfast of champions," he whispered. Frank stepped into the stall, removed the plastic safety cover, plunged the needle into the top of his butt, and injected the anabolic steroid. He recapped the needle and handed it back to the man along with a fifty-dollar bill.

"Solid. See you next week," said Squirrelly. They touched fists, like boxers before a fight.

"Yeah. Next week." Frank returned to the gym. He had finished three cycles and was punishing the heavy bag when Kevin walked up behind him with his leather jacket slung over his shoulder.

"Time to go," said Kevin.

"Where?"

"Lower East Side. I told you last night, remember?" Kevin was checking himself out in the wall mirror.

"Kinda. Better tell me again."

"I'll tell you on the way."

"Do I need anyt'ing?"

"Your Browning. And we have to bust a door down."

"Steel or wood?"

"Wood. Heavy wood."

"Runnin' start?"

"Yeah. End o' the hall. It's perfect." Kevin grinned.

In the shower room, Frank approached one of the tough guys from the treadmills. "Nice tattoos, man. I really like da dragons," offered Frank.

"I got 'em in Saigon in '69. I was with the Air Cav—" Feeling something warm on his thigh, the guy looked down to see Frank pissing on him. He recoiled two steps and clinched his fists. Frank just laughed. After studying Frank's imposing build for a moment, the veteran quickly washed his leg, then retreated to the locker room muttering something about Frank's sick sense of humor. The vet was gone when Frank came in to dress.

Kevin waited on a bench, curling thirty-five-pound dumbbells in his street clothes. Frank removed six forty-five-pound plates from the bar he had been bench-pressing, leaving 135 pounds. He handed Kevin his thermos and gym bag and carried the bar out the door.

"A, whey you gwan wi' dat?" yelled the fat Jamaican front-desk attendant.

"Don' worry, honey, jus' borrowin' it. I'll bring it back." Ignoring her further protests, Frank carried it to the back of Kevin's Impala.

"Not that way, you'll bend it. I won't be able to close the lid."

Frank removed the plates from one end of the bar and stuck the weighted end in the trunk with the bare end sticking out. He stacked the loose plates flat in the trunk and returned to the gym. The attendant yelled at him again as he removed two more forty-five-pound iron plates and strolled out the door. While Kevin tied the trunk down with the sweat-soaked drawstring from Frank's gym shorts, Frank went to the deli next door and bought two six-packs of Colt 45 and a big bag of onion-flavored potato chips. He handed the chips and a beer to Kevin's seventeen-year-old brother, Brian, who was in the backseat. As Kevin drove down Flatbush Avenue, Frank popped Pantera's "Vulgar Display of Power" into the tape player, lit a joint, and cracked beers for Kevin and himself.

"So, what's up?" asked Frank.

"Don't you remember last night?"

"I remember that you were fuckin' around wit' Ritchie's wife."

"Yeah, I fucked her behind the Dumpster while Ritchie was losin' his paycheck at cards. Almost froze my ass off."

"I can't believe you fucked your boss's wife. Mortal sin, ya know."

"Look, Ritchie is a rebar guy with the Builders Union. He was crew boss on a couple of masonry jobs I did. Doesn't make him my boss."

"Like Saint Peter's gonna give a shit, crew boss or boss?"

"I can't believe this shit. Listen, we're hittin' a couple o' Jamaican dealers on Avenue A."

"Yeah?"

"Jimmy the Rat was late again, so I told him I'd cut his dick off if he didn't give me somethin'. He was late because his guy didn't show up with the Ecstasy that he was supposed to sell these guys. I kicked him a few times and he gave me the address."

"How much?"

"Enough to buy five thousand tabs of ex. Who knows what else."

"They got guns?"

"Jimmy said he didn't know."

"Bullshit," said Frank.

"Couple o' Rasta dealers." Kevin shrugged. "Whaddaya think?"

"What if he's settin' us up t' get us offa his back?"

"Nah, Jimmy's chickenshit. We know where he lives. Tha Rastas probably don't."

"Why can't we wait 'til dark?"

"'Cause they're expectin' Jimmy this afternoon. Who knows if they're around with the cash tonight?"

Frank took a deep hit off the joint and chugged the beer to cool his throat. "Why we gotta bust da door? Why not bring Jimmy, make 'im get us in?"

"'Cause Jimmy would shit himself and the Rastas would smell it." Kevin hit off the joint. "Besides, if they're carryin' they'll be holding their pieces when Jimmy knocks. They obviously have reason to be suspicious of the little scumbag, right? Better we surprise 'em."

Kevin parked in an alley between the back of a gas station and a tall wooden fence. Brian jumped out and quickly replaced the license plates with plates he had lifted from a Trans Am an hour earlier.

"Why ya always gotta change da plates?" asked Frank.

"'Cause it's my car," snapped Kevin.

"Pain in da ass."

"What if a Rasta sees us drive away, traces the license?"

"How's a Rasta gonna trace a license?"

"Same way we do. Friend on the force."

"Dere's Rastas in da NYPD?"

"Or we hafta shoot 'em. John Q. Citizen hears the shots, gives the license to the cops."

Frank considered this as he held the smoke in his lungs. Exhaling, he answered, "John Q. Fuckin' Citizen don't live on Avenue A."

Kevin drove over the Manhattan Bridge from Brooklyn to Alphabet City, named for Avenues A through D. The neighborhood was overrun by pushers, pimps, and prostitutes. They passed a squalid park with a colorful mural that had been marred by graffiti. Kevin parked in front of a five-story tenement made of crumbling red bricks.

"You hear shots, wait three minutes. No more. Then leave," Kevin instructed his little brother, who jumped into the driver's seat. Frank was crouching in the gutter, sliding the plates back on the bar. "Relax, the apartment's in the back. Window's on the alley."

"How d'ya know?"

"I checked it out this morning." Kevin jimmied the entrance lock with a screwdriver, and Frank followed him to the second-floor landing, carrying the barbell. Frank examined the nearest apartment door, tapping lightly to gauge its thickness. He hurried back to the car and returned with the two forty-five-pound plates. As he was sliding them on the bar, a young Hispanic woman walked up with a bag of groceries.

"You hombres going to lift in the hall?" she asked cheerfully.

Frank leered menacingly and flicked his tongue at her. She scurried into her apartment and slammed the door. Kevin put on a black ski mask and handed one to Frank. Frank pulled out his Browning 9-millimeter automatic, flicked off the safety, and shoved it back in his jacket pocket. He lifted the 225-pound barbell and cradled it under his right armpit like a jousting lance. He took three deep breaths and charged down the hallway. Kevin followed right behind him with his .38 caliber Smith and Wesson revolver held high.

Frank splintered the door and barreled over a table, smashing the couch behind it and knocking two startled Jamaicans over the back of the couch onto their heads. When one of them rolled over and reached for his handgun, Kevin hammered him with his revolver, knocking him out and opening a deep gash in the back of his scalp. Frank shoved his Browning into the other man's face so hard that he broke and split his nose.

"Give me da money or you're dead," growled Frank. Holding his mangled nose, the man pointed to the unconscious man's pockets. Kevin removed a wad of hundreds, then searched the conscious man's pockets, removing only a few bills. "Now da drugs!" ordered Frank." Still holding his nose, the man led Frank to the kitchen and opened a drawer containing a baggie full of crack cocaine and a hundred vials. Frank pocketed the crack, then hit the man on the temple with his Browning, cracking his skull.

"Let's go," ordered Kevin calmly.

In the hall they saw heads duck inside several doors, like gophers into their holes, and heard the locks being bolted. They removed their masks as they stepped onto the sidewalk. They got into the Impala coolly, but Brian sped away before they had even closed the doors.

"Easy does it, little bro'," instructed Kevin. "Take a left up here. There's an alley, we can change the plates back."

"Fuckin' plates," grunted Frank as he pulled a fresh joint from the glove compartment. "How much we get?"

"Relax. I'm countin'," replied Kevin. He marked his place in the money roll with a rubber band so he could hit the joint and drink his beer. "We got $5,350. Two large for you and me and $1,350 for Brian."

"Hey, we coulda got shot," protested Frank. "I say $2,250 for us and $850 for da kid, plus he can have da Rasta's Glock. It's a nice gun. Cop gun."

"How 'bout he sells the crack and we split it in thirds?" offered Kevin.

"Deal," agreed Frank. Brian finished changing the plates and hopped in the backseat. Frank dropped his empty can out the window. "Finally. Let's go t' Daisy's."

"I'd rather go when the night shift comes on. Day-shift strippers are too skanky," said Kevin.

"I want skanky."

"Vice catches Brian in the club, it's a big problem for Anthony. He'll kill us."

"I got a fake ID," interjected Brian.

"Kid'll be fine," assured Frank, as he passed the teenager the joint. "Crystal'll blow him in da office. He don't need to hang out in da bar."

Brian passed two Colt 45s to Kevin and Frank and cracked a fresh one for himself.

"Hey, Kevin." Frank burped in a deep staccato. "Ya got another joint?"

11

The Tuesday after Thanksgiving, a red Impala pulled up in front of the coffee shop on 96th.

"Get in, George. I'm Frank." He nodded toward the driver. "Dis here's Kevin." The car smelled of marijuana. Kevin and Frank were drinking Colt 45 and listening to loud heavy metal. Pantera's "Cowboys from Hell." All three men were in their midtwenties. They drummed on the car seats to the music, saying nothing, until the car was crossing the Manhattan Bridge and Frank offered George a joint.

"No thank you." George waived it off.

"You wanna beer?"

"Sure." George accepted gratefully. It would take more than a couple of Colt 45s to slacken his nerves, which were strung tauter than he could ever remember.

George had been to a party in Brooklyn Heights once, but he'd never been to the heart of Brooklyn, and he immediately lost his bearings. They drove past dollar stores and dilapidated restaurants. He saw signs for fast-food chains he'd never heard of, like Kennedy Fried Chicken and Golden Krust. They pulled over in front of a yellow brick tavern with a green neon shamrock in the window. Frank chugged the rest of his third beer, handed the joint to Kevin, and marched into the bar.

"Get in front with me," ordered Kevin. George silently complied. Seconds later a medium-sized man with a scraggly brown ponytail and a shaggy mustache emerged from the bar with Frank behind him holding the collar of his suede jacket. Frank shoved the man in the backseat and pulled his gun out of his Jets jacket as he followed him in. Frank slammed the door, and Kevin pulled away from the curb.

"Put your hands in fronta ya, wrists togetha," snarled Frank. Petrified, the man didn't move. Frank smashed him with the automatic, splitting his nose open. The man stuck his hands out and Frank slapped on a pair of plastic handcuffs and drew them tight.

"Dammit, Frank," scolded Kevin. "You get blood on the seat again, you clean it up." Kevin noticed that George was staring at Frank's gun. "Nice piece, huh? I prefer a revolver myself. Totally reliable, can't jam. Frank wants fourteen in the clip. Thinks he's gonna fight the OK Corral."

"Valentine's Day massacre." Frank grinned his crooked grin. "Fifteen in da clip and one in da chamber." They drove through a run-down residential neighborhood to a light industrial area of machine shops and warehouses. Kevin handed George a black ski mask.

"Put this on backwards and pull it over your eyes until I tell you to take it off," he ordered. Sweating under the mask, George thought that Frank reminded him of Moose Raczak, who had briefly lived next door in Bethlehem. One night in the spring of his senior year of high school, George had heard horrific female screams. He rushed over in his boxers and burst in to find Moose beating his wife bloody with a fireplace poker. The man had gone completely berserk, but George stood his ground in the hallway. George had just taken third place in the Pennsylvania state wrestling tournament. He instinctively ducked the poker, took Moose down with a fireman's carry, and held him in a guillotine until the police arrived. Moose was threatening him the entire time. Even with the restraining order, George had looked over his shoulder constantly until he moved to Princeton that September.

After ten minutes Kevin pulled the mask off George's head. They were parked in front of a large garage with a wooden sign that read "Body Shop." Smithereens of broken glass littered the far side of the parking lot. The four men got out of the car.

"This is the Spa," Kevin told George.

"The Spa?"

"Yeah, the Spa. Where you take the treatment."

Kevin knocked on the metal door and an ancient, gnarled dwarf answered. Kevin handed him a pint bottle in a brown paper bag and the dwarf disappeared around the corner. Frank shoved the ponytailed man through the door and motioned to George to follow. Inside were half a dozen late-model cars in various states of disassembly. Frank gagged Ponytail with a red ball with leather straps, *Pulp Fiction*–style. Then he lowered a ceiling hoist, hooked it around the man's handcuffs, and hoisted him two feet off the floor. Ponytail cried out through the gag as the cuffs cut into his wrists. While Ponytail dangled, Frank switched on a boom box on top of a tool chest and calmly swayed his hips to the music. Kevin motioned for George to sit with him on a ragged, mildewed couch against the wall.

"The thing is, guys owe money have to do tough things to get money to pay it back. Take this drug dealer. Probably have to rip off another dealer to get the money. Dangerous stuff. My job, I make sure that he's more afraid of the Spa treatment than he is of the thing he's gotta do to get the money. I do that, the money always appears."

Frank squirted lighter fluid on the coals in a small hibachi and lit them. Then he sat on the hood of a car, chugged half a can of beer, and started rolling another joint.

"Now Frank, he really enjoys his job. My job, I gotta keep Frank from goin' too far."

"What's too far?"

"Frank cripples a guy where he can't work, how's he gonna pay us back? Guy dies o' shock, how's he gonna pay?"

"Does he always get so wasted?"

"Only time he's not wasted is when he's liftin' weights. If you had the spiders and snakes crawlin' in your brain like Frank, you'd stay wasted too. He's certified."

"Certified?"

"Put it this way, last time he got busted they sent him to a loony bin instead of the joint."

"Why'd they let him out?"

"They didn't," deadpanned Kevin.

"You're telling me he escaped from a hospital for the criminally insane?"

Kevin just looked at George.

"You're messing with me. Trying to scare me."

Kevin nodded toward the hoist. "Judge for yourself."

Frank pulled Ponytail's pants and boxers down to his ankles. He took a long hit off the joint, then started flogging the dealer with his weight-lifting belt. It was four inches wide, and the heavy leather raised angry welts. Every time Frank whipped around Ponytail's hips and snapped his genitals, he stretched the belt out and pretended to play it like a guitar while he danced. The ball gag muffled the screams.

"*Reservoir Dogs* came out on video last year. Frank watched it a hundred times." Kevin smiled for the first time. "Keeps asking me can he cut a guy's ear off so he can talk to it like Mr. Blonde." Kevin drank his Colt 45. "The FBI asked Willie Sutton why he always robbed banks. You know what he tol' 'em? He said, 'Cause that's where the money is.' Lotta guys need money to stop the treatment, they get it from their work. You work in a bank. Where the money is."

Frank pulled a long, red-hot screwdriver out of the hibachi, laid it on the inside of Ponytail's thigh, and whooped. "YEEAAHH!" The dealer screamed and writhed. "'Ey, be still. You kick me, I'll shove this up your piss hole," Frank yelled at him.

When George caught the smell of searing flesh, he threw up on the floor. "Clean that up," ordered Kevin. "Can't leave my buddy's place a mess. There's a mop in the bathroom."

George went into the bathroom and threw up in the toilet. He filled a bucket with water and started mopping. Frank burned Ponytail's thigh again, inching closer to his genitals.

"Look at this." Kevin showed George a Polaroid of Sue. George froze. "We can't find you for your Spa treatment, we bring her. I'll have to put a leash on Frank, though. He gets a woman on that hoist, somethin' snaps." George finished his beer. "Hey, look at this." George's parents' address in Bethlehem was written on the back of the photo. "We can't find you or Sue, we find your parents. Wouldn't bring 'em here, though—might get stopped by a Pennsylvania trooper or somethin'. Probably gag 'em good, give 'em the treatment right in their house."

George collapsed on the couch and buried his face in his hands. He looked up at Kevin and mouthed, "How?"

"I got this private dick, Henry, who owes me. You want, I can have him check on Sue—make sure she's not fuckin' around on you."

Frank was dancing, whooping and burning Ponytail. When the dealer passed out, Frank grabbed the bucket of puke water and threw it on his face, waking him up.

"I think that's enough, Frank. Guy dies we don't get paid." Kevin leaned over to George and whispered, "I don't stop Frank, he'll kill 'im."

Frank pulled the screwdriver out of the coals and pressed it on the tip of the dealer's penis, uttering another enthusiastic "YEEAAHH!" Ponytail passed out again. Kevin got up and lowered the unconscious body to the floor. Frank sighed with satisfaction and flopped on the couch.

"Fill this up, will you, George?" Kevin gestured toward the mop bucket, and George obeyed. Frank got up and threw the water on the dealer's face. He looked a little upset that he couldn't continue.

"Wake up, Crispy." Frank grinned. "Pull your pants up. I ain't takin' ya in da car wit' your charred dick flakin' off onna seat."

The dealer curled up in the fetal position. Frank kicked him a few times, then gave up. Kevin and Frank pulled the man's pants up and dragged him out to the car. George sat on the couch in a stupor. Kevin returned to the shop and casually slapped George's cheek.

"C'mon, Georgie. We're outta here."

The dealer was curled up in the backseat, sobbing. Frank smoked dope, drank beer, and joked about what he had just done. "You see Crispy's eyes bug out when I burned 'im? Looked like some kinda deep-water fish on Jacques Cousteau." He slapped Kevin's shoulder, seeking his approval. Kevin handed George the ski mask, and he pulled it back down over his eyes. When he was told to take it off, they had stopped in a residential neighborhood on a dark stretch in front of an empty lot. They shoved the dealer out onto the curb.

"Hi, Crispy. Bye, Crispy." Frank mimicked Chef's "Hi, Tiger. Bye, Tiger" from *Apocalypse Now.* He kept laughing his sinister laugh and slapping Kevin on the shoulder. George wondered if he'd picked the laugh up in the loony bin.

"Hope you don't mind takin' the subway back to Manhattan." Kevin pulled over at the subway station at Flatbush and Atlantic. "See you Tuesday at six on 96th."

"I don't see TD on Tuesday?"

"No, you're ours now, Georgie. Pay the vig and we're best friends. Don't pay and we visit the Spa, 'cept you'll be the guy on the hoist."

George went into a liquor store and bought a pint of Johnnie Walker Black for the subway ride. He had never been in a store where both the cashier and the inventory were behind bulletproof glass. As he walked out with his pint in a brown paper bag, he pictured the old dwarf limping away from the Spa with a similar package. He swigged the scotch on the subway. His pulse slowed and he felt the tension ease in his throat. He stared hard at his reflection in the window across the train as the lights of the tunnel flashed by. He knew what he had to do.

12

The following evening George rang the buzzer of the high-rise on Lexington.

"Who is it?" The voice was guarded.

"Hey, Morgan. It's George. Mark from City Trust's roommate. We met about a month ago."

"What's up, George?"

"I need to talk to you. Do you have a minute?"

"Anyone with you?"

"No, I'm alone." The lobby door buzzed open. At the apartment door Morgan raked George with narrow, suspicious eyes. The apartment was furnished just as George remembered it, but it seemed sleeker this time. Furniture, drapes, rugs, kitchen appliances, electronics—everything was either glass, steel, black, or white. The only color emanated from a couple of Salvador Dali prints that hung on opposite walls. A haggard-looking girl sat on a leather sofa behind a bong. A mirror, a razor blade, and a rolled-up twenty lay on the clear glass coffee table.

"Trish, this is George. George, meet Trish." The girl gave a burned-out smile. "Can I get you anything?" asked Morgan. "No? Have a seat. What's up?"

George stood where he was. "Uh, actually uh, I need to speak to you privately."

"It's OK. Trish knows my business."

"Uh, actually, it's about my business. Maybe I should come back," said George haltingly. He had spent the last twenty-four hours girding himself to cross the line. Now, the drugs and Morgan's junkie girlfriend were giving him cold feet. Then he thought of the Spa treatment and quickly decided to proceed.

Morgan's curiosity had been piqued. He flipped Trish a vial of coke. "Can you wait for me in the bedroom, Sweetie?" Trish rose, steadied herself, picked up the bong, grabbed a Heineken from the refrigerator, and swayed into the bedroom without a word.

"Thanks. Sorry to be rude."

"No problemo. So, what's up, George?"

"This is just between you and me. Two EM traders. Nobody else in the world can know about this conversation. Nobody. OK?"

"Sure. I'm the most discreet guy in the world."

"Swear it?"

"Sure. I swear. What's up?"

"I need to come up with 258 grand in thirteen days or I'm dead."

"What's that got to do with me?" asked Morgan coolly.

"Well, I've got an idea how to make the money, with your help. Obviously there's a ton of money in it for you also."

"I'm listening."

"Well, I've gained a lot of credibility at City Trust with some big winning trades on the Dominican Republic, Peru, and Ecuador. So when I recommend a proprietary purchase, they pretty much let me do it. The cleanest way to do this would be for you to source a block of low-dollar-priced loans that never trade. Something with zero price visibility. Say you source $25 million face at 8. City Trust buys them at 10. Two points on $25 million is $500,000. We split the profit. I solve my problem and you walk away with a clean quarter million."

"I understand why price discovery is an issue. Why does it have to be such a low dollar price?"

"I can get City Trust to buy $25 million at 10 cents, invest 2½ million dollars, without a ton of scrutiny. To get them to buy $25 million at 40, invest $10 million, I have to jump through more hoops. I don't have time for that. Also, if it's a higher price it's likely to be a more established trading name, like Ecuador or Panama. They'll wonder why I'm sourcing it from some mysterious account."

"Low dollar price. Hmmmm. Can you do sub-Saharan Africa?"

"London makes proprietary decisions for Africa and the Middle East. It has to be Western Hemisphere."

"OK. That's how we did it at Commerce Trust. But why me?"

"Because you've done it before. Know the ropes setting up offshore accounts, et cetera."

"But I got caught. What makes you think I'd be stupid enough to do it again?"

"I've done a little research." George leaned forward with his elbows on his knees. "Every one of these types of situations where the trader got caught, including your own, it was because of a pattern of dealing. Someone—another trader, an auditor, a back-office guy, whoever, got wind of a suspicious pattern. Now this deal, we do one block trade and that's it. Finished. You're barely even breaking the law. You're sourcing paper in an unregulated market and selling it to a bank. The only violation is when you split it with me, and I'm never going to tell. After the trade we close the account. If you want, we never speak again."

Morgan cocked his head and studied George with a gleam in his eye. "One shot, take the money, and close the account. Wham, bam, thank you ma'am." He walked over to the window and looked at the skyline. "Still, I have to think about it a little more."

"I appreciate that it's not a decision you would take lightly, but I need to know if I'm doing this with you. I've only got thirteen days. If you're not onboard I need to move in a different direction right away."

"You know, I meant to tell you, this can't happen in thirteen days. You know that the convention for executing loan documents is three weeks."

"I can force an accelerated close from my end. I'll tell the back office and the lawyers it has to close early and they'll do it. I'll tell them that, given the unconventional counterparty, I need to close quickly to ensure that the trade doesn't bust."

"And the seller?"

"You'll have to make sure that he's incentivised to close early also."

"I assume you want cash currency. Hundred-dollar bills?"

"That's right."

"How do you plan to turn a Fed wire to a bank account into currency?"

"I haven't the foggiest. I figured that's your department. I'll get City Trust to wire the money. You turn it into currency. You know how to do that, don't you?"

"Sure." Morgan smiled. "I've got a banker friend in Nassau. He'll require a commission. You'd better work that into your calculations. We also have to get it into the country. I'm not taking my half through an airport. We'll take a boat to Florida. I can arrange that also."

"The commission is off the top, right?"

"Sure. We'll take all expenses off the top. Banker's cut will be 5 percent or so. I'll do the best I can. I'll make some calls tomorrow and see what I can source. How do I reach you?"

George reached for a business card, then thought better of it. He scribbled his home number and his unrecorded office number on a scrap of paper and swapped Morgan for his number. "Call me at work tomorrow, but only from a pay phone. I'll only call you from pay phones also. We don't want our numbers on each other's phone records."

"Very good. I like your thinking, partner. I'll call you tomorrow from a pay phone. Want to seal it with a line?"

"No thanks." George stood up and shook hands with Morgan. "Do it with Trish."

George walked back to Club 16B, put on his sweats, and grabbed a roll of nickels in each hand. He was on his third lap around the reservoir before his head stopped buzzing.

On the trading desk next day almost everyone was off the phone, staring at Enrique. The head EM trader was pacing frantically with a phone in his ear. He alternately barked profanity and listened with gritted teeth. A few traders wandered over from nearby desks to see what was up. George intercepted Sam and they stood by the pillar.

"He's on with Kenneth Dart. Getting interesting."

"Who's Kenneth Dart?" asked Sam.

"He's the point man for the Dart Family on the Brazilian Brady restructuring."

"I read something about that. One of the richest families in America, right?"

"Yep. They own a billion and a half dollars of the forty-four billion of the Brazilian bank debt that's eligible for the Brady exchange. They bought a ton of it from Enrique. They're refusing to participate in the exchange that's supposed to close in February. We lose a bundle if they crater the deal."

"A family can crater a sovereign debt exchange?" asked Sam incredulously.

"Well, the Darts won't accept the terms that the banks agreed to, the Brazilians refuse to close with the Darts out there suing for repayment in full, and the banks refuse to allow the Darts to receive a special deal. Some guys think they're just trying to force the banks to buy them out at a premium, but they're too big for that to happen." There was a loud crash. George and Sam flinched as pieces of Enrique's phone went flying across the floor. Enrique was moaning in pain and bleeding profusely from his forearm. When he shattered the receiver he had driven a thumb-sized shard of plastic deep under his skin. George wrapped Enrique's arm in paper napkins and rode the elevator with him to the bank's dispensary.

When George returned to the trading floor the crowd had dispersed from the EM desk, but there was a new commotion in the corporate bond sales area. A few traders were attempting to high-five an attractive blonde woman whose face was fire-engine red. She was having none of it. George knew Gwen Friestadt because she covered Ralph for corporate bonds and relayed his EM trading inquiries when José was off the desk. Sam stopped to speak to George on his way back from his reconnaissance mission on the corporate desk.

"It seems that Gwen and Sheldon, the utility bond trader, were having this heated exchange via the internal email system. She types 'Eat me in Macy's window.'" Sam smiled. "Except she hits the wrong button and it goes to the whole department as a flashing, red alert." Sam's smile broadened into a roguish grin. "America is a great country." He narrowed his eyes at George, who was not laughing. "You all right?"

"I'm fine," George replied distractedly. The EM trading assistant shouted across the floor at George and he returned to his desk to take a call. He noted that the call came in on his unrecorded line.

"It's Morgan."

"Are you on a pay phone?"

"Yes. Listen, we're in luck. I've got a guy that'll sell $25 million Nicaragua at 13."

"Nici? How am I going to convince the bank to invest in that basket case?"

"Hey, it's the only Latin country that fits the bill. Cuba's illegal for U.S. banks to buy. None of the other distressed Caribbean or Central American paper comes out in size. Low dollar price, no visible two-way market, and the paper's available. Nici's perfect."

"Is 13 a reasonable price? I haven't heard a quote in a couple of months."

"Guy says the last trade was $5 million at 12, about two months ago. I can get the counterparties if you want to check. Since then we had those kidnappings in Managua and San Ramón, which are perceived to have damaged the credibility of the Chamorro government."

"That's the first time I've heard Chamorro and credibility used in the same sentence," George interjected.

"On the other hand, as you know, the whole market for exotics is up at least 20 percent in the last couple of months, so 13 seems fair."

"I hear you. Can the seller do an accelerated close?"

"He thinks he can. Yes."

"Thanks for moving so fast, Morgan. This may save my ass. Now I've got to convince the bank that Nicaragua is about to rally. Any ideas?"

"No clue."

George immediately began researching Nicaragua. He called friends at Treasury, the Inter-American Development Bank, and the State Department. He spoke to a pal from Fletcher who staffed for the Senate Foreign Relations Committee. Over the next day and a half he constructed an argument for investing in defaulted Nicaraguan loans. George decided to try it out on Pablo before going to Enrique. In deference to the economist's formal comportment, he knocked on his office door. Pablo waved him in and motioned toward a chair as he spoke on the telephone in Portuguese. After a few minutes he hung up and turned his attention to George.

"Sorry to interrupt, Pablo."

"Not at all. I was happy to get off the phone. Brazilian Finance Ministry. If Enrique had his way, I'd be spending all of my time on Brazil. What can I do for you?"

"Well, I'm thinking that Nicaragua is the next Peru. What do you think about Nicaragua as an intermediate-term candidate for a Brady exchange?"

"Are you serious?"

"Dead serious." He pictured Ponytail lying on the curb in Brooklyn. George wondered if the guy was still alive.

"A discussion of structural economic reform in Nicaragua is premature. The country's been at war for over a decade. Some sort of political reconciliation must take place before they can move forward economically. For more that three years Chamorro's government has had opportunities to make progress, but they have proved dysfunctional. Recent events, the kidnappings, General Ortega's refusal to step down next year as army chief, these things have only deepened the quagmire. What do you see that will solve the political problems?"

"Basically, the Clinton administration. My sources on Capital Hill tell me that Jesse Helms is on the verge of losing his battle to make further U.S. aid contingent on the removal of Sandinistas from the government. Congress will authorize an increase in aid and Clinton will make sure it is directed toward the repair of the economic base, not the pockets of the ex-Contras. Clinton doesn't want Nicaragua and El Salvador to continue to stagnate. It will undermine his ability to leverage the Contra scandal against the Republicans going into the midterms and the '96 elections."

"If it is the case that Washington will drive Nicaragua's political and economic recovery, then you are better positioned to make a judgment than I. My best relationships are in Mexico City, São Paulo, and Buenos Aires, not D.C." Pablo smiled in a way that suggested he was ready to turn his attention back to the important countries. On his way back to his desk, George could barely contain his glee. Pablo had ducked. He wouldn't interfere unless Enrique prevailed upon him to engage. George pulled his boss away from the desk to speak to him privately.

"Enrique, I think I've found the next Peru." Debt prices were up 150 percent in Peru, and the desk was up $10 million on the position that George had talked Enrique into buying late last year. He got Enrique's attention. "Nicaragua."

"You're kidding. Nici is a piece of shit."

"I'm not kidding."

"Hey, I know you're a baseball fan, but just because Dennis Martinez is running for president doesn't mean it's time to invest."

"Dennis Martinez the pitcher? What?"

"The pitcher. He's a national hero. The Third Democratic Way party is collecting the signatures to get him on the '96 ballot. C'mon amigo, you need to read the Latino papers—figure out what's going on." Enrique was grinning.

"Piece of shit. Those are the exact words you used in describing Peru last November."

"OK, amigo. I'm listening."

"All the pre-Bradys are trading in the 30s or 40s. Peru, Ecuador, Panama, Poland. Away from Africa, Nici is the only paper available in the teens in any kind of size. From a trading perspective, it's perfect. When Peru and Ecuador sign their Brady deals next year, most of the juice will be out of those trades and everyone will be looking for the next trade. We'll roll the aggressive hedge funds out of those countries on signing and into Nici, probably into the high 20s or low 30s. We can probably double our money on the momentum trade alone, even if there's no tangible improvement in the country's credit profile."

"These hedge fund guys aren't stupid," countered Enrique. "Peru and Ecuador were moving in the right direction when you talked them into investing. The war in Nicaragua has theoretically been over for three years since Chamorro has been in power, and the country is still in the shitter. Where's the hope?"

"The Clinton administration . . ." George made the political case that he had made for Pablo.

"What's Pablo think?"

"He agrees that the country is being driven by Washington. It has been for a dozen years. He thinks I have better contacts in Washington to determine this than he does."

"Sounds like he punted."

"He says you want him to focus on Brazil."

"How much do you want to buy?"

"I'm in touch with $25 million face in the midteens. I recommend that we buy the block to get a toehold, then continue to research the situation, including in-country due diligence, and potentially build the position going into next year."

"In country? Good luck getting Pablo to Managua."

"I'll go to Managua if the opportunity to build the position warrants a visit."

"We build a controlling position, we could hire Ollie North to negotiate the exchange for us. I hear he's looking for work." Enrique grinned again. George was glad he was in a good mood.

"Tell you what," Enrique continued. "I'm in D.C. on Monday for some meetings on Brazil, this damn Dart problem. Angie's got my schedule. Why don't you set up meetings for us on Capital Hill, State Department, whatever?" George panicked. He had made up the part about Jesse Helms losing his battle to hold aid hostage to a purge of the Sandinistas from the government—that could be an ongoing stalemate. He'd really stretched on the Clinton administration's agenda also. He knew no one in D.C. who would back him on that.

"We're talking about an initial investment of less than $4 million here." George strained to keep his voice from cracking. "Are you sure it's worth your time?"

"When Gold sees Nicaragua hit our ledger, he'll want an explanation. Want to know that we've done our homework."

"OK, but my friend who staffs for the Senate Foreign Relations Committee was really speaking off the record on the Helms thing. Same with my guy at State." George fought against a shortness of breath. "They wouldn't be interested in a formal meeting with City Trust." Needles pricked George's spine.

"Do the best you can, amigo." Enrique returned to his desk and jumped on the phone. George headed for the men's room. He felt nauseated.

Returning to his desk, George worked on loan trades for an hour. He managed to buy $5 million Ecuador MYRA from the Miami branch of a Spanish bank at 49½. Then he placed a call to the U.S. Treasury.

"Mr. Johnston's office."

"Hi, Rose. This is George Wilhelm."

"Hi, George. How are you?"

"Very well, and you?"

"Fine. How can I help you, George?"

"I was wondering if Tom would be available for a meeting on Monday."

"He's very busy on Monday. . . ." George knew that everyone at Treasury had staff meetings on Mondays. "But . . ."

"Sorry, hold on one second, I have to confirm a trade." George put the line on hold and counted to twenty before reengaging. "Sorry, Rose. If Tom is busy Monday, I'll catch him another time. I've got to go."

"Don't let New York give you an ulcer, George. Bye."

"Bye, Rose." George sighed in relief. He had covered himself as to why there would be no meeting with Treasury on Monday. Enrique wouldn't be seeing Tom Johnston on Brazil, but if he spoke to him George could say that Rose said that Tom was busy. Next George hit a direct line to one of his interdealer brokers.

"Yo, George," answered Dennis in thick Brooklynese. It was Dennis who had introduced George to TD.

"I called to ask a favor." George knew it would be granted. When George wanted to show a bid or offer to the market, he could push any of five direct lines and the result would be the same. Since the brokers struggled to differentiate their commodity service, they entertained heavily, hoping that the trader for whom they had bought $500 worth of lap dances the previous night would hit their wire. George was uncomfortable accepting the more lavish gratuities—limousine services, Las Vegas or Super Bowl junkets, etc., but he hit the brokers up occasionally.

"Anyt'ing ya want, hittah."

"Rangers-Islanders?"

"How many ya need?"

"Is four too many?"

"If our box behind da Rangah bench is taken, I'll get 'em low between da blues. You'll have 'em dis aftahnoon, hittah."

"Thanks, Dennis. While I have you, bid 49½ for five Ecie."

"You got it, hittah."

George took a deep breath and called the IMF.

"Trudy Waite."

"Hi, Trudy. George Wilhelm."

"Hi, George." Her tone shifted from formal to playful. "Did you call to explain why you haven't sent your business plan like you promised?"

"Exactly. I called to say that I want to deliver it personally."

"When?"

"Monday."

"And what brings you?"

"I want to talk about Nicaragua."

"Why would you want to talk about Nicaragua?"

"I'm thinking of investing there."

"You're kidding, right?"

"Dead serious."

"Why?"

"Number one, it's the lowest dollar price Latin pre-Brady that's available in size. Number two, I think that the Clinton administration will help move the country in the right direction."

"Clinton certainly won't do worse than Bush and Reagan," replied Trudy. George exhaled heavily. That was the most positive statement he had heard on Nicaragua from anyone in Washington.

"Can you meet with Enrique and me on Monday morning?"

"Will you take me to lunch?"

"I won't have time. But if you're not busy Sunday night, I'll take you to dinner."

"That would be nice. Where are you staying?"

"Haven't booked yet."

"Why don't you stay with me in Georgetown?"

George took a deep breath. "OK. Make dinner reservations in Georgetown then." George took down Trudy's home phone number and address.

"In the meantime I'll bone up on Nicaragua." She said "bone up" mischievously.

When George got off the phone he accepted an AAA Brokers envelope from a messenger. He called Dennis to thank him and to pull his bids and offers from the screen so he could leave the desk. He took the elevator to the operations floor and weaved his way through endless rows of gray, soundproof cubicles to the work area of the loan closers—the clerks who handle the documentation associated with transferring sovereign loans. The head closer, Dominic Palermo, was a paralegal and extremely competent.

"Hey, Dom."

"Hey, George. Slummin' today? What's the problem?"

George tossed the four Ranger tickets on Dom's desk. "No problem. Just came down to thank you for the great job you and your crew have been doing."

"Jesus, Section 53 for the Islanders. Awesome. Thanks, George. Are you comin'?"

"No, I have to go to D.C. Take whomever you want."

"Thanks a lot, George. How's everything on the floor?"

"Couldn't be better. Peru and Eci keep moving up. No clouds on the horizon. By the way, we may be trading some Nicaragua soon."

"You kiddin' me?"

"Dead serious. Can you check with the lawyers and see if there are any wrinkles, please?"

"Sure, but I don't think we've ever traded it at City Trust before. Probably need outside counsel. Anyone you want to use?"

"Good question. I'll find a firm that has experience documenting Nici trades and get back to you." George left the building and walked five blocks uptown to a pay phone.

"Hello, Morgan?"

"Yeah. You on a pay phone?"

"Yeah. Listen, I'm almost there on the Nici trade, but my boss wants to do a little due diligence in D.C. on Monday."

"What if he doesn't like what he learns?"

"I'm working on that. Listen, we'll probably use outside counsel. Do you have a view?"

"I'll call my buddy at Friedman, Cohen."

"Are you crazy? You can't get anywhere near anyone on the buy side of this trade. Why don't you find out who the seller will use and get their recommendation. If they've dealt with another firm in Nici before, it will streamline things."

"OK."

"How is it going with the bank?"

"I confirmed that my banker friend will be in Nassau next week. I'll fly down as soon as we print the trade."

"We'll print it on Monday. You should fly down this weekend. Every trade I do has to be executed on the recorded line. Bank policy. Since City Trust's counterparty is going to be a Bahamian bank, you'll have to call from there. We'll need to pretend to negotiate, et cetera, in case the tape is reviewed. And think of an alias to use."

"I like the way you think. Are you sure you'll print the trade on Monday?"

"If I don't, I'm cooked."

"I'll be at the British Colonial Hilton. Talk to you Monday."

When George returned to the trading desk there was a message to call Sue. Oh Christ, he thought, of all the things that could have been waiting for him. He felt that they had something special over Thanksgiving, and he didn't want to blow it. It had been long enough that Sue would probably jump him as soon as he walked through the door. He wondered if he'd even be able to get hard now after what he'd witnessed at the Spa. George shuddered. And now he was definitely going to have to sleep with Trudy on Sunday night. Necking with Trudy in the taxi had been easy when Sue was being a bitch, but this didn't feel right at all. He picked up the phone.

"Hi, George. It's good to hear your voice."

"It's good to hear yours too." There was an uneasy silence.

"So, George, can I take you to dinner tonight?"

"Didn't I tell you? I'm going to D.C. this weekend."

"Great! Can we go to the Smithsonian?"

"It's a bunch of guys. We're going to see the Terps on Saturday and the Skins on Sunday."

"What are Terps?"

"Maryland Terrapins. The football team. I'm headed down tonight to be there for a tailgate party in the morning." George wished that his money problem would end soon so he could quit lying to people.

"You're seeing someone else in D.C., aren't you?"

"No, of course not. You think I'm lying about the pregame?"

"George, we haven't made love since Saturday and you're the horniest guy around. If it's not another girl, what is it?"

"I'm going to D.C. to meet my buddies. That's all."

"The October or November George would be trying to talk me into a quickie before the flight, or taking an early-morning flight and spending the night with me. What's up with the December George?"

"Let's go to dinner tonight. I'll change my flight. I'll pick you up at seven thirty. And no more talk about some other girl." George reflected on Sue's sudden jealousy. Maybe she had really fallen for him as well. She had told him that she loved him. Three times.

George and Sue had dinner at La Cantina. He asked her to tell him more about her job at Grey Global.

"It's great. I deal with statistics, from Nielsen, Arbitron, focus groups, et cetera. I've become an expert on P&G's advertising budget. A lot of the stuff is financial, but I'm glad I'm on Madison Avenue and not Wall Street."

"Why is that?"

"Female professionals are accepted here. My Wharton classmates on the Street say it's like, 'Who do I have to blow around here to get one of the important jobs?'"

"It's not that bad."

"Bullshit, George. Have you ever seen the statistics on the percentage of female managing directors at the bulge bracket firms?"

"I know, but City Trust is working on that. All of the managing directors are required to take six hours of sensitivity training. There's a big campaign to ensure that it's not a hostile environment for women and minorities." George drew air quotes with his fingers around "hostile environment."

"Sure, it may not be hostile, but no amount of sensitivity training would get them to hire someone like me for a management position."

"Hey, don't look at me." George gave her a wink. "I'd hire you in an instant." He took a bite of his enchiladas and started talking about his research on Nicaragua. Sue had been to El Salvador in college and was well informed on Central American economies.

"At the time, I was actually convinced that I wanted to go down there to help alleviate the suffering," she said. "Now I wonder if I was just trying to get my parents' attention."

"I take it they were against it?"

"I'm sure they would have been. I couldn't see Peace Corps stickers next to the Wellesley stickers on their Mercedes. My plan was to call them from the airport."

"What changed your mind?"

"The Peace Corps wouldn't let me pick my station. They train you and assign you. I need to control my situation."

"I've noticed. Like always being on top."

"Not always."

"You're right. There was that time on the dryer."

"So what? Now you want to make it in the laundry room at your building?" Sue had had three margaritas, George four. They went back to Club 16B and made love until two in the morning—in George's bed. No problems until the nightmare jerked George awake at dawn. He had dreamt that Frank had Sue up on the hoist, naked. He put on a dry T-shirt and went back to sleep.

On Sunday night Trudy took George to a four-star French restaurant in Georgetown. They were the youngest couple in a room where everyone else was older and dressed to kill. Though she didn't have diamonds or pearls like the other women, Trudy had done up her hair and wore a gold necklace. This was one of the best restaurants in D.C., and she had had to call in a favor to get the reservation. She was convinced that George was rich and wouldn't mind the expense. Her friends at the IMF would be jealous. She opened his business-plan outline at the table and grilled him on it while they drank wine, waiting for their appetizers. When the food came, she put the business plan away and George asked her about Nicaragua.

"George, you're not pulling my leg, are you?"

"Dead serious."

"That's what you said before and I believed you, so I did a little research. George, it's a wasteland. Sixteen years of civil war, which isn't quite over, by the way, have taken a terrible toll on the people and the economy. Chamorro hasn't found a solution to the country's poverty and economic stagnation."

George ran through his argument about Clinton and Jesse

Helms again. With practice, the speech had gotten better, but Trudy's facts overwhelmed him.

As they walked out of the restaurant, George kept his hands in his pockets. "Trudy, I would really, really appreciate it if you could be more constructive when we meet with Enrique tomorrow."

"Why are you so desperate to make an investment you can't support, George? Something weird is going on here." George was taken aback. It hit him that if Trudy could smell a rat, Enrique must have the whole caper nailed. He was trying to sort reason from paranoia when Trudy planted her mouth on his and pushed her tongue in deeply. She must have sensed the evening going in the wrong direction, but this mood swing was peculiar and abrupt. He had never experienced anything like it.

George tried to rationalize what was about to happen. He needed Trudy's support for the Nicaragua trade, because without the trade he wouldn't be able pay the vig. Sue could be threatened or even tortured. He did his utmost to convince himself that what he was doing was for Sue's safety.

Back in Trudy's apartment he had to drag her into the bedroom or she would have had him on the piano bench. George wondered how long it had been for her. He thought about the sex guides he had read as a teenager which insisted that women liked foreplay and taking it slow. The surveys had definitely missed Trudy Waite. She jumped on top of George and rode him in a frenzy. It seemed more the mating instinct of some nocturnal feline than the passion of a woman. George was more than a little spooked. Squeezing Trudy's thighs, he contrasted the softness of her muscles with the hardness of Sue's. The difference between thousands of hours in the library and thousands of hours in the gym, he thought. The lack of muscle tone did not inhibit her ability to hump, however. After three of these sessions, each one bizarre in a different way, George lay exhausted with Trudy's head on his shoulder. All he could think about was how to adjust her attitude on Nici. Could he level with her? Offer to share the money? Threaten her with the Spa treatment? He blinked himself back to reality. If Enrique nixed it, he didn't have time to hatch another plan. And even if he did, would Morgan be game after flying back from Nassau, ticked off by the false alarm? George felt the familiar tightness returning to his throat and gut.

"Trudy, you've got to help me with this Nici trade. It's really important to me. You can't be so negative with Enrique in the morning." Trudy bolted upright and stood naked beside the bed, her hands on her hips.

"I am an officer of the International Monetary Fund. If you think you can wine, dine, and screw me into conspiring with some trading scheme, you are badly mistaken, big guy. I would resign before I would compromise the IMF with one of the world's largest banks." George was stunned by her self-righteous rage.

"Relax, Trudy." He stood to face her, and she stiffened as he grabbed her shoulders. "I'm not asking you to lie. I'm just asking you to try to say that the glass is half full, not half empty." Trudy didn't relax. She folded her arms under her droopy breasts and debated George hotly, standing face-to-face beside the bed. After several minutes she conceded only that she would provide Enrique a balanced view. Then she put on her cotton pajamas, got back into bed, and went to sleep. George wondered why, out of the dozens of public officials he knew who were involved with the Latin debt crisis, he had decided to bet his life on a head case.

George met Enrique in the lobby of the IMF at 9:30 A.M.

"Angie said that this is the only meeting we have?" asked Enrique.

"Like I said, my contacts on Capital Hill and State want to keep their comments off the record. I tried to get Tom Johnston at Treasury, but he was booked."

"So we're only meeting with Alfredo?"

"Trudy. It's off Alfredo's radar screen." Enrique shrugged and followed George to the elevator.

Trudy's cramped office was decorated with her diplomas and academic citations. Her leather-bound doctoral dissertation, "Structural Economic Reform: The Precursors to Mexico's Return to the International Capital Markets," was prominently displayed on her bookshelf. With her bun, wire-rimmed glasses, and shapeless black suit, Trudy looked like a stripper trying to be the uptight schoolteacher—before the music started. As greetings were exchanged, her manner was formal, almost cold. She launched into her spiel with minimal ceremony.

"Nicaragua has the highest debt per capita in Latin America because of chronic fiscal and current account deficits during the 1980s. Approximately $4 billion is owed to the former Soviet Union and approximately $6 billion is owed to Western banks and multilateral lending institutions. . . ." George tried to will himself to stop perspiring, lest Enrique notice. Trudy droned on until Enrique interrupted.

"Can it get any worse, Trudy?"

She pondered the question before answering. "Coffee and banana prices are near record lows. Our agricultural economists are predicting a cyclical recovery in both commodities, as well as in cotton, so those economic drivers are unlikely to get worse and will probably improve. It could certainly get worse if the level of violence, which is currently sporadic, escalates materially."

"What are the chances of that happening?" asked Enrique.

"Perhaps the CIA could help you with that. I'm an economist."

Enrique nodded. "What about the Clinton administration? Are they helping?" George held his breath. Trudy had totally disparaged his political argument the night before.

"The administration has not informed the IMF of any change in aid policy." Her reply could not have been more dispassionate.

Enrique nodded thoughtfully. "So what are you hearing on Ecuador?"

Trudy provided an upbeat assessment of the upcoming IMF mission to Ecuador. George and Enrique shook hands with her. When her eyes met George's they were icy.

"You have contacts at the CIA, don't you?" asked Enrique in the corridor.

"You bet. I'll meet with them ASAP. Do you want to join the meeting?"

"Only if I'm down here anyway." In the elevator they stared at the floor numbers. By the time they reached the sidewalk George could no longer contain himself.

"I'm not sure when I'll see the CIA. I'd hate to lose the offering in the meantime. The paper hardly ever trades."

"What offering?"

"Twenty-five million Nici at 15ish." George could hardly breathe.

"Less than 4 million bucks, right?"

"Right."

"Go ahead." Enrique waved for a cab. "How 'bout that Trudy. Couldn't pull a needle out of her ass with a twenty-mule team. She really needs to get laid."

"She needs a lot more than that." George smiled for the first time in a long time. He grabbed a separate cab to National Airport. He stopped at a convenience store on the way, got $10 worth of quarters from the cashier, and placed a call to the British Colonial Hilton.

"It's on."

"Great. There are some complications on my end, though."

"Complications?"

"My seller is at 14 now."

"And?"

"The banker needs a 10 percent commission on the cash conversion."

George assumed that Morgan was padding his end of it, but he knew he'd never know for sure. He certainly wasn't going to try to meet the Bahamian banker in order to dig into it. A quick calculation told him he'd have to pay 16½ to cover expenses and net him $275,000. That would be $4,125,000 gross.

"I have to stay under $4 million total purchase price. I'm not authorized above that."

"The deal is that we each net a quarter million after expenses. You need to pay 16⅜," said Morgan.

"I need $275,000 now with an extra week's vig, but I'm authorized to pay less than $4 million, not more. You want to risk the bank investigating this trade, make me pay more than I'm authorized."

"Get authorized higher."

"I got authorized by the skin of my teeth. If I go back, I risk losing it altogether. You've got to do better on your end." A recording gave George a thirty-second warning. He was out of quarters. "I'll be back at my desk by two o'clock. Call my trading line from the bank. Remember it's recorded."

"OK. The seller is using Boykin and Glatfelter. They documented an Eci trade with Friedman, Cohen quite recently. And I'll be Anastasio."

"As in Anastasio Somoza? Clever."

"I'm a clever guy."

George picked up his trading line at 2:00.

"Hello, George, this is Anastasio from Bank Mori. I'm calling because I've been able to firm up the offering on the restructured Nicaraguan bank debt."

"Same block that we discussed last week? Same credit agreement?"

"Yes. The only difference from what we discussed is that my seller wants to close within a week."

"That would be very difficult."

"My client's counsel, Boykin and Glatfelter, are very familiar with the documentation and stand ready to execute. They say it can be done. I don't have the authority to proceed on any other basis."

"OK. What's the price?"

"16⅜."

"Too high," countered George. There was silence on the line for a minute.

"My seller says that Salomon Brothers will pay him 16, maybe more."

"I know for a fact that Solly is not involved in Nici. 15¾ bid."

"At 16."

"15.875 bid. That's my best."

"Done. Twenty-five million Nici at 15.875." They exchanged details on their respective operational and legal contacts and rang off. George was delighted. He had stayed under $4 million and it was a real negotiation—he didn't even have to act. The tape would sound perfect. George wrote a trade ticket, time stamped it, and tossed it in the bin. Then he went down to operations to see Dom.

"Yo, George. Thanks for the tickets. Great game. Messier is the balls."

"No problem. We bought the $25 million Nicaragua. The seller is Bank Mori Geneva through their Nassau branch, acting as agent for a private client. We'll be using Friedman, Cohen."

"Bank Mori? Jesus. Wonder how many countries their client is wanted in."

"Why do you say that?"

"There's a smell around that bank, ya know. Probably some Contra general war criminal. Or maybe Ollie North did a guns-for-debt swap, stuck the debt in Switzerland and wants to sell it, raise money for legal expenses." Dom appeared pleased with himself.

"What's with all the Ollie North jokes?"

"Marine colonel cries on TV, he's a joke."

"Bank Mori is not taking ownership, so we'll need the lawyers to set up an escrow account there. We'll wire the funds into escrow, and the lawyers will release them when the documents are executed."

"We've done that before. No problem."

"One more thing. The trade settles next Monday."

"You're kiddin' me."

"Dead serious. The seller is requiring it."

"Told you he's a desperado. Don't worry. I'll push them back to something more reasonable."

"The trade settles Monday," George commanded.

"Why?"

"Number one, because I agreed to it. Number two, it's a good price and there's no other paper available. I don't want the seller to find a better price and weasel out of the trade because we didn't close as agreed." George almost cringed. He hated lying to people he respected.

"You don't trust Bank Mori either."

"Look, tell Friedman their future business with us depends on this, whatever. You want me to whip and drive them, I will. But this has to close on Monday." On the way back to his desk George wondered if he'd pushed too hard. If he behaved strangely he would arouse suspicion, and Dom's antenna was already up because of Bank Mori.

George left work right at 5:00 and ran four laps around the reservoir. He hoped that the sweat would cleanse him somehow. It didn't, but it made the beer at McNabb's hit him like a punch. They didn't blame him for the broken window. He had watched Monday Night Football before without having money on it, but only when Las Vegas had the spread right on the mark, denying him an advantage. Here, the Cowboys should be two touchdown favorites at home, but the spread was only 9. It pained him to watch Emmitt Smith slicing up the Eagles' defense. He had to find a new bookie. With Dallas up 16–3 at halftime, he took a cab to Sue's apartment.

13

On Tuesday George constantly fought the urge to badger Dom and the lawyers at Friedman, Cohen. He would have camped on the operations floor to monitor the closing except that it would look crazy. Enrique was so busy trading Brazil that he didn't even ask about Nici. George bummed hockey tickets from a different broker and headed down to see Dom at 5:00.

"Hey, thanks again, George. I hope you don't have to cough up too many chips to the brokers to get these."

"No, all in due course. How's Nici?"

"I've never seen lawyers move so fast. They've already telexed the agent bank and the borrower requesting consent to transfer. The agent bank is Chase, so that's no problem. The Central Bank of Nicaragua is the wild card."

"Wild card?"

"Yeah. Who knows when they'll consent. Could be today, could be January."

George took a deep breath against the panic. "Does anybody know the people at the Central Bank? Any way to expedite it?"

"I asked all those questions and nobody has any ideas. Latin bureaucratic morass."

"Can we close without the consent? Get the seller to warrant that they'll obtain the consent postclosing?"

"Are you nuts?" asked Dom. George just stared at him, and Dom resumed. "We could consider it if Bank of America were selling as principal, but you understand that until the borrower formally recognizes the obligation we have nothin'. Mori's Contra general war criminal client could disappear with our 4 million and we'd have bupkis."

Back at his desk, George called the senior partner at Friedman, Cohen and got nowhere. He pulled out his Rolodex and called around to try to get an angle on the Nicaraguan Central Bank until it was time to head uptown. When he got to 96th Street, Frank was standing in front of the coffee shop in his Jets jacket. No Kevin, no red Impala. "TD tol' me to try da apple pie here." George tried to lead Frank to the back, but he took a table near the windows. George handed him a fat manila envelope.

"How much?"

"Twenty-five."

"Dat's da minimum. When's da rest comin'?"

"Next week, I hope."

"I don' care whatchya hope."

"I might have to take a trip to get the money. But I should have it all sometime next week."

"Trip where?"

"Why do you need to know that?"

Frank flexed his bodybuilder muscles and leaned across the table. He smelled strongly of marijuana and stale beer. "Ya gotta un'erstan' somet'in'. Until ya pay me back, I *own* ya. Ya wanna take a shit, ya ask my permission. I let ya leave town, I get your flight numbah, hotel, everyt'in'. Ya leave town widout my say-so, or you ain't where ya supposta be, I assume ya skipped and I go aftah Sue. Take 'er t' da Spa." Frank looked over George's shoulder. George turned around to see Nick's girlfriend Missy and another girl standing right behind him. They were decked out in their preppie finest, cashmere sweaters and all. George wondered how long they had been standing there.

"Hey, George. How're y'all. This is mah friend from Carolina, Melanie Parker. Mel, this is George Wilhelm, one of Nick's suite-mates." Missy smiled primly. George was paralyzed. After a moment of awkward silence, Missy finally asked, "Aren't you going to introduce us to your friend?"

"Uh . . . this is Frank."

"Missy Lee. How do you do?"

"How ya doin'?"

Another awkward silence passed before Missy declared, "Ah don't seem to see any open tables in heah."

"We were trying to talk some business," said George.

"Yo, have a seat, girls," offered Frank.

"I'm glad one of you Yankees has some manners," scolded Missy. Frank leered at them as they took off their pea coats. Tasty bodies. Nobody said anything for a minute. Frank stared at Melanie's ample breasts.

"Ah didn't mean to eavesdrop, but ah did hear y'all mention taking Sue for a spa treatment. Ah just love to spoil mahself that way. What spa are y'all going to?"

Frank laughed the asylum laugh, and the girls exchanged troubled glances. "Brooklyn Body Spa," snickered Frank.

"Ah haven't heard of it. Brooklyn Heights?"

"Just Brooklyn. Da four o' us should go out dere. Have a party."

"It's a little early in the week for a party," said Melanie uneasily. Frank was still staring at her breasts.

"Yo, I got some killah Thai sticks. Getta couple bottles o' good wine on da way out. Great party." The girls went rigid in their chairs. Melanie suddenly looked down and slapped Frank's hand off her lap.

"What is the matter with you?" shrieked Melanie. Frank started flicking his tongue at her like a snake. George saw Missy raise her purse to whack Frank, and he leapt between them. He guided Missy out to the sidewalk, and Melanie followed. Frank just laughed.

"What is that man's problem?" shrieked Missy.

"He's criminally insane. Now you know why I was rude and didn't invite you to sit down."

"You are judged by the company you keep, George Wilhelm, which makes you a degenerate. Ah'm moving Nick out of Club 16B tonight!"

"I'm sorry, Missy. And Melanie, sorry I didn't meet you under better circumstances." In fact, George hoped never to see Missy again. First the living-room labia display. Now this. Do I go in there and admonish an escaped criminal lunatic for his behavior, he asked himself. No way.

"Nice girls." Ice cream dripped from Frank's lopsided mug. George wondered if he practiced the grin in the mirror, like De Niro in *Taxi Driver.* "So where ya thinkin' o' goin'?"

"Bahamas, to pick up the money."

"Like I was sayin', you wanna leave town, you lemme know." Frank wrote a phone number on a paper napkin and tossed it over. "Whateveh ya wanna do next week it's 25 large, minimum, on Tuesday, or else. Got it?"

George nodded, then walked deliberately out of the coffee shop. He got a pocketful of quarters from a deli down the street and placed a pay-phone call to the British Colonial Hotel in Nassau. Morgan said he had no idea how to prod the Nicaraguan Central Bank.

"Why don't you go down to Managua with a fistful of dollars and grease the skids?" suggested George.

"I'm a self-employed felon. How long do you think it would take me to get a visa?"

"Fly to Costa Rica and cross through the jungle."

"You're losing your mind. But City Trust could probably sponsor you for a visa on an accelerated basis."

"People are already suspicious because I've jammed this thing. They're suspicious of Bank Mori also. If I fly down to help close the trade, I'll set off alarms. Look, can you at least make some calls and try to find someone who knows someone at the Central Bank?"

"I thought we didn't want me nosing around."

George pondered that for a moment. "You're right. Just try to locate a contact and then we'll discuss how we might approach him for help."

"Got it. Everything is arranged at Mori."

"Great. I'll keep you posted."

George spent the rest of the week trading well enough to keep Enrique happy while scrambling to expedite the consent he needed from Nicaragua. By midday Friday he still had no idea when he would get word from Managua. He had $17,000 of cash and credit against the $25,000 he owed for vig on Tuesday. He decided to start hitting friends up for personal loans of a few hundred or thousand dollars which he would agree to pay back in a week. Sam lent him $500, but he wrote a check, which would not clear and become cash in time for Tuesday's payment. George couldn't figure out how to explain to Sam, or anyone else for that matter, that he needed them to go to their bank and make a cash withdrawal. Mark, who understood quite a bit about cash commerce, agreed to lend him $8,000 in cash on Monday. Without asking, he figured that George had a problem with his bookie. Shocked and delighted, George hugged Mark on the trading floor.

The level of revelry at Club 16B was unusually low that weekend because Mark and Leo were not around. George played flag football in Central Park with some of the guys from the desk on Saturday and ran four laps around the reservoir on Sunday. He took Sue to dinner and a party and slept at her apartment on Saturday night. Before leaving for work on Monday morning, he looked for Mark to touch base with him on the loan, but he had not returned. When he asked about Mark's whereabouts on the mortgage desk later that morning, everyone shrugged.

"You're his roommate, aren't you?" asked Lucas Roth, the head of mortgage trading. "Don't *you* know where he is?" When George shook his head, Roth let out an ominous sigh.

It was midafternoon when George watched Roth trudge across the trading floor to John Peters's office. Philip Gold and Ann Lansky, the head of human resources for all the capital markets businesses, followed him in. George pulled Sam off the Treasury desk. They stood at the pillar watching Peters's door.

"Is this what I think it is?" whispered George.

"I told you they gave him a warning. Offered counseling, et cetera. There was another FNMA auction this morning."

"Any possibility they'll give him another chance if he agrees to rehab, whatever?"

"Not if what I'm hearing is true."

"What?"

"It's gone beyond coke and hookers. This time a client of the bank was involved."

"Jesus."

"It's really a shame. He may be an asshole, but I've heard he's one of the best traders on the floor, when he doesn't have the shakes," concluded Sam.

A short while later a uniformed City Trust security guard escorted Mark to John Peters's office. Even across the floor George could see that Mark's face was pasty and damp with perspiration. He looked totally strung out. Twenty minutes later Mark emerged with the guard and was escorted to the elevators. He appeared to be crying.

George fought the urge to race after him. Enrique probably knew why Mark was getting canned, and the last thing George wanted to do was to show intimacy with a junkie. Not this week. But with Mark now unemployed, would he be willing to front George the cash? Maybe he should offer Mark double his money back in February when he got his bonus. His heart started racing. He had to meet Frank in less than thirty hours and he was 8 grand short.

Under Enrique's eye, George focused on trading for the rest of the afternoon and dutifully attended the 5:00 research meeting. When he left Pablo's office, Pam, one of the mortgage trading assistants, was removing Mark's personal effects from his desk and placing them in a cardboard box. Standing next to her, Roth caught George's eye and motioned him over to a pillar.

"Can you get this stuff to Mark?"

"Sure."

"You should get your boy some help before he kills himself. Betty Ford clinic or something. City Trust's insurance will pay for it. He won't listen to us."

"He's not my boy," said George sternly.

"You know what I mean."

George accepted the box from Pam and took a cab straight back to Club 16B. Nick and Missy were sitting on the couch drinking wine. A tall, powerfully built man in his late fifties stood in front of Mark's bedroom door with his arms folded. He wore an immaculately tailored three-piece pin-striped suit. George had seen the man plenty of times on the cover of *Institutional Investor* and the *Wall Street Journal*, but he had never met him in the flesh. Mark Frost Sr. usually looked statesmanlike and paternal. Now he was scowling.

"Good evening, Mr. Frost. I'm George Wilhelm." Mr. Frost shook hands reluctantly. His huge palm was cold and wet. "Is Mark in his room?" Mr. Frost nodded. "I've got a package for him."

"I'll give it to him." Mr. Frost blocked the door.

George held on to the box. "If you'll excuse me, I need to speak to him."

"Mark is going away from this place. From now on he will be having no contact with his junkie friends who have destroyed his career. None." George had never been spoken to in a more authoritative and intimidating tone.

"Ah beg your pardon, Mr. Frost, but your son's problems do not give you the right to insult us," declared Missy indignantly. Nick squeezed her hand and hissed at her to shut up. It never worked.

Mr. Frost glared at her for a moment, and then spoke deliberately. "You're right, young lady. I apologize if you thought I was calling you a junkie." He shifted his glare to George. "But there will be no more contact. My secretary will be in touch with you to clear up loose ends as to rent, furniture, et cetera. Give me your business card." Nick, who handled the rent, popped up and handed him a business card. George handed him the box and sat down on the couch next to Nick. After a few minutes Mark skulked out of his room carrying two suitcases. Avoiding eye contact, he followed his father out of the apartment. He looked like hell. Nick, Missy, and George all wished him luck, but he did not respond.

"Ah cain't believe that you big strong men just sat there and let that man insult us. Where's your sense of honor?" Missy folded her arms indignantly.

"William Frost Sr. is probably the most powerful man on Wall Street, Missy," replied Nick.

"Ah don't care if he's the president of the United States. A man of his station should have better manners and ah shouldn't have to be the one to stand up to him."

George borrowed Nick's BMW, drove out the Lincoln Tunnel, and raced south on the Jersey Turnpike. He had been unable to draw down on all of his credit cards because of the daily withdrawal limitations at the ATMs in the city, so he was headed to Atlantic City. For the next three hours he wracked his brain as to how he was going to raise $8,000 in cash in less than twenty-four hours. Sam had topped out at $500. George could try to hit up another fifteen guys for $500 each, following each one to their cash machine, but everyone he knew with any money worked at City Trust and word would spread that he was desperate for cash. Not something he could afford on the back of Mark's debacle. Everyone else he knew, including Sue, lived from paycheck to paycheck.

George took the Arkansas Street exit off the Atlantic City Expressway and parked at the first casino he saw. It was Caesar's, but George was too preoccupied to notice. He used the machines off the lobby to draw down everything that was available on his Visa, MasterCard, and corporate Am Ex. He had already tapped his Diners and his personal Am Ex. He had 17 grand and no available credit. For the last two hours he had wondered how much worse he would be tortured for being 16 grand short versus 8 grand short. He decided that once Frank got into his zone, he probably didn't calibrate that closely. At any rate, it was worth a shot.

On a Monday night in mid-December, gamblers were sparse. Blue-haired ladies pulled on fewer than a third of the one-armed bandits, and stoic blackjack players leaned over their cards at the few open tables. A motley crowd cheered a reptilian-looking woman who was having a run at craps. George bellied up to a roulette table that was empty but for an elderly croupier who was half asleep. He bought eight one-thousand-dollar chips and placed them on black. A greasy looking pit boss strolled over to watch the spin. George imagined himself on the hoist at the Spa. The wheel spun and the whir sounded like Frank's asylum laugh. The ball finally landed. It was black 22. George looked at the table for a minute, stunned. Then he quickly stuffed the chips in his jacket pocket and bought a double shot of Jack Daniels at the bar. His stomach wasn't ready for it, and he puked into the bar towel. He apologized to the bartender and moved on to the cashier's window. He stopped at a liquor store on Missouri Street for a six-pack of Bud. He was acutely aware that winning the 8 grand had won him a week. Period. Somewhere in the pine barrens he sucked down the fifth beer and began to feel the tension in his muscles ease.

Dom called the following morning to say that the Nicaraguans had consented and the deal would close on Friday. George ducked out at lunch and called the British Colonial Hotel from a phone booth three blocks west.

"Great news. We're closing Friday. Will Mori have the currency?"

"If the funds are wired Friday morning, I'll have the currency Friday afternoon. Yes."

"You'll be back in New York on Saturday?"

"I'm not sure. First I've got to arrange for the boat back to Florida, now that I know the timing. I've also got some business to do in Miami."

"What business in Miami?"

"My business. None of yours."

"Bullshit, Morgan. You have to come right back to New York with our money." George's mind was racing. What if Morgan made a drug buy in Miami and it went bad. Or he used all 500 grand on the buy to leverage his investment. What if the cops brought a dog on the train—busted him on the way to New York?

"No," replied Morgan. "You got a beef, come down here and pick it up."

"I'll be at your hotel on Friday afternoon."

"Come to the bank if you want."

"I don't want to get within five miles of that bank. And if you need to leave a message at the hotel, leave it for Mr. Pink."

"Watch *Reservoir Dogs* lately?" asked Morgan.

"No. I've lived it."

Back at the office, Enrique was very happy with George's performance. Pablo and George had talked two new hedge funds into Ecuador. They bought $60 million from City Trust, creating $400,000 in trading profits for George, and their activity pushed the price up 2 points to 51, creating mark-to-market profits of $2.4 million on the $120 million inventory.

"Hey, Enrique, I was wondering if I could take a long weekend. Friday, maybe Monday too."

“No problemo, amigo. Going anywhere fun?”

“Haven’t decided yet. Probably someplace warm. I’ll call in every day.” Enrique was already back on the phone. George hit up one of his brokers for a couple of orchestra seats to *Miss Saigon* on Broadway. He’d shower Sue with attention this week before explaining that he was taking a tropical vacation without her. Now if only Sam’s $500 check would clear by Friday, he could afford a plane ticket to Nassau.

The red Impala pulled up in front of the coffee shop, and George got in front next to Kevin.

“And Frank?”

“Do I need Frank? You don’t have the vig?”

“No, I’ve got it. Just wondered if he’d been recaptured. Sent back to the loony bin.”

“No such luck for you. He disappears or I disappear, TD finds somebody else like us. Same deal for you. Maybe I should start friskin’ you, see if you don’t believe that. Ivy League boy wants to knock us off.” Kevin drank from the tall Colt 45 can between his thighs.

“That wasn’t my train of thought at all. If you frisk me, all you’ll find is this.” George handed him a thick manila envelope. “I just wanted to follow up on a conversation I had with Frank about informing you guys of my travel. I have to go out of town Friday. Back on Sunday or Monday.”

Kevin saw a patrol car in his mirror and pulled away from the curb to avoid being hassled. “This the trip to the Bahamas to get the money?”

“Yeah.”

“How did you arrange for that kind o’ dough sent to the Bahamas?” Kevin looked at him closely.

George returned his gaze. “When I get my travel details I’ll leave them on Frank's machine." They stopped at the traffic light on Third, and George opened the door. Kevin grabbed his arm hard.

"How much?" Kevin waved the manila envelope.

"Twenty-five. It's all there." George jerked his arm away and hurried down the avenue. Picturing the roulette wheel, his spine tingled. Had he hit red, he would still be in the car—headed for Frank and the Spa treatment.

14

George called Sue's office from the Nassau airport on Friday morning. He chatted with her for a few minutes, then asked her to forward the call to City Trust. That way the bank's phone records would show an incoming call from her office at Grey Global, which was a daily occurrence. A police investigation would uncover his flight, since he had to travel under his own name, but an internal bank investigation would find no evidence of him being in the Bahamas. The markets for all his deadbeat countries were strong. He had checked in, as he promised he would. He told Enrique he was in Florida. Angie transferred him to operations. Dom told him that the Nici trade had closed as promised. George thanked him as calmly as he could. Then he called the British Colonial Hotel and was informed that Morgan had checked out.

"Did he leave a message for Mr. Pink?" Holding for an answer, George tried not to panic. Morgan had a clientele, a whole sordid life in New York City, where George knew how to find him. How could he skip?

"Sorry to keep you holding, Mr. Pink. Mr. Somoza moved to the Atlantis."

George took a cab to Paradise Island. He gaped at the magnificent stucco and glass towers of the Atlantis Resort and Casino.

There was a message that Mr. Somoza would meet him in the lobby at 5:00. George strolled the splendid grounds of the four-star resort to kill time. The water park featured multiple swimming pools and hundred-foot-tall water slides cascading from Mayan-style pyramids. George zeroed in on a gorgeous woman with a rock hard body covered only by a string bikini. Brazilian, he guessed. She bent over, mooning him directly with her smoking, bare ass. Very special. He wondered if his sunglasses concealed his stare. When she straightened up she held a cherubic toddler over her shoulder. Different kind of special.

The majority of the pool and beach crowds were families. George heard them speaking in Spanish, Portuguese, Italian, German, and British English. They were thinner and fitter than the swimmers at the public pool in Bethlehem or the trailer-park lakes where he vacationed with his family as a youth. Was it the Latin and European mix or the wealth? Probably both. He wondered if he would marry a classy woman like Sue and earn enough to bring the family to the Paradise Islands of the world. Or would he get caught ripping off City Trust and vacation at the trailer parks with other ex-cons. He wondered how much he could earn playing poker for a living.

At 5:00 George reclaimed his bag from the bell desk and sat down in the lobby.

"Hello, Mr. Pink." Morgan wore a self-satisfied smiled beneath his leaden eyes. He wore a tropical-patterned shirt and white straw hat and carried a shiny metallic suitcase.

"Hello, Mr. Somoza." They shook hands solemnly.

"Your room or mine?"

"I haven't checked in."

"When did you get here?"

"No money or credit."

"We'll fix that. My room then."

They proceeded down a marble corridor lined with shops—Cartier, Gucci, Versace. Impeccably dressed ladies with ostrich-skin necks browsed happily. Immediately upon entering his room Morgan tossed the case on his luxurious king-sized bed and worked the combination locks. He handed a cotton sack to George. It contained thirty bundles of hundred-dollar bills, each labeled $10,000.

"I bought the paper at 13¼. Two and five-eighths points on $25 million is $656,250. Ten percent commission for my boy is $65,625, leaving $590,625 for us. I've been down here working this thing for a week, so my expenses exceed yours by $6,625, which I'm taking off the top. There's $292,000 here."

"$6,625 a week?"

"I live well. Plus, I've given up a lot more than that because I haven't been in New York running my business. You have."

George counted the bundles, selected a few at random, and counted the one hundred C-notes in them. Everything was in order. More like a movie than reality, he thought.

"When do we sail for Miami?"

"Whenever Lawrence feels like it."

"Lawrence?"

"Wealthy businessman from Miami. You'll meet him tonight. We're going in on his yacht. It's perfect. Pleasure craft is the best way in. Plus, Lawrence is a celebrity at the Miami Beach Marina. Nobody will hassle him. We rent a speedboat, whatever, go in ourselves, the Coast Guard will give us the business. Have to explain the currency. Or they confiscate the currency and throw us in the drink. Only problem is we're on Lawrence's schedule."

"I'm not in New York with the money on Tuesday night I'm dead."

"Lawrence said something about having business in Miami. You should be OK."

"How'd you meet this guy?"

"Guess."

"You're his supplier?" Morgan nodded. "Guy's a coke head?"

"I've never seen him use it. He likes to keep some around for his friends. Until now I've only supplied him when he was in New York. I'm the coke head." Morgan pulled out a vial and snorted from a tiny spoon. George declined. "You should be kissing my ass for setting up this transport. Couldn't be more perfect."

"Thanks, Morgan. Where do I store this money?"

"Good question. Banks are closed. Won't fit in the hotel safe-deposit boxes. You could deposit it at the hotel, get a receipt. Or at the casino—pretend you're a high roller."

The last thing George wanted was a written record. "I think I'll keep it with me. Can I borrow your case?"

"It's all yours. Combination is 9876. Let's see if we can find Lawrence." Morgan took another snort, then led George down the elevator and through a majestic corridor to the casino. No blue-haired ladies on the slots. Morgan nodded toward a middle-aged man in khakis and a blazer playing blackjack. He was nondescript except for his intense, sparkling green eyes. Two gorgeous women flanked him—a blonde in a strapless red cocktail dress slit up to her hip and a redhead in a tight black minidress with a plunging neckline. Both appeared to be in their early twenties. Lawrence was winning, and the girls were fawning shamelessly. They rubbed his back and thighs and kissed him when he won. He let them cut the deck. As his stack of one-thousand- and five-thousand-dollar chips grew larger, people began drifting over to cheer. After twenty minutes of high-stakes drama, Lawrence lost two hands in a row, the second on the dealer's blackjack, clipping his impressive stacks. He stood up with his palms in the air and coolly declared, "I'm done." He tossed the dealer a five-hundred-dollar chip and the girls each a thousand-dollar one. They kissed his lips in turn. The dealer changed Lawrence's pile into a neat stack of twenty-five-thousand-dollar chips as the casino manager looked on with his arms folded across the front of his crisp blue suit. When Lawrence approached the cashier's window with his stack, the manager waved him into the adjoining office for a private cash out. The girls followed them in excitedly.

"Wow," said George.

"By the way, I told him that you would crew across to Florida. Do you know anything about yachts?"

"No. Went deep-sea fishing with clients once this summer. Other than that it's just ferries—and canoes."

"You'll have to lie then."

"What do I have to do?"

"Unless there's a problem, you'll need to handle the lines when we cast off and dock. Maybe mix cocktails when we're underway."

"I'll hang around the marina and watch the guys with the ropes."

"Not ropes, lines. Starboard is right, port is left; fore is the front, and aft is the back."

"If you'd told me, I would have bought a book."

"You'll be fine."

Morgan approached Lawrence when he emerged from the office. "Congratulations, Lawrence. Nice run."

"Hi, Morgan. Thanks. The key is you have to know when to quit."

"This is my friend George from Wall Street. The guy who volunteered to crew for you over to Miami."

"Crew for me?"

"I asked you on Wednesday night, remember? You said it would be fine."

"Whatever. Pleased to meet you, George." They shook hands. "This is Gretchen, and this is Linda." The girls smiled amiably as they offered their hands. George liked the way Gretchen's pearl necklace curved into her cleavage.

Lawrence invited everyone to his boat for cocktails. They walked out the casino's side door, across a small lawn, and onto a brand-new, hundred-foot luxury cruiser. The deck was spotless white fiberglass trimmed with teak and shiny brass. The Stars and Stripes hung on the radio antenna above the white canopy of the flying bridge. Twenty-foot-long trolling outriggers were folded inboard and clipped down onto the corners of the teak transom. Holding their shoes in their hands, the girls ducked inside the cabin. A man who looked to be in his late thirties hopped out of the cabin wearing sailing whites and a captain's hat. His face was weatherbeaten, and the capillaries made his nose look like an urban road map. Right out of a Jimmy Buffett song, thought George.

"This is Sean, our skipper. Sean, George. You've met Morgan."

"Welcome aboard. Should I bring the cooler out, sir?"

"You bet."

"I'll help," said George, and he followed Sean into the cabin. George had never imagined a more opulent boat. A magnificent teak bar dominated one wall, and there was enough space for a full dining table and chairs, all made of varnished hardwoods. A Springfield bolt-action .30-06 was mounted on the bulkhead opposite the bar. Except for the open sights rather than a scope, it looked exactly like the rifle that George used to hunt deer in the Poconos with his uncles.

"You keep the rifle loaded?" asked George.

Sean nodded. "Shark attacks your diving party, you don't have time to load."

"Same if pirates attack, I guess."

"This ain't the South China Sea. Pirates aren't attacking this boat. Only time I ever used it was when sharks were after a big yellow fin that Lawrence was taking his time reeling in."

George helped Sean load wine, beer, soda, and ice into a white plastic cooler and carried it out to the deck. Sean followed with a silver tray filled with glasses, limes, and accessories. Linda and Gretchen were dancing barefoot. The Rolling Stones' "Brown Sugar" was blasting from huge speakers mounted above the deck. Sean opened a bottle of Pouilly-Fuissé and began pouring. Lawrence started grilling George about his job on Wall Street. His questions were incredibly insightful for someone with no related experience.

"If you'd like to invest, I can recommend a couple of hedge funds that are doing well in emerging market debt."

"Too intangible for me. I own real estate. I can understand a mall's location because I can drive there. I understand my tenants because I can shop in their stores, talk to their managers." Lawrence leapt up to embrace a lanky man about his age who had stepped onto the deck. The man's gold Rolex and diamond pinky ring clashed with his casual, tropical attire. Linda gave the man a big hug and kiss, and Sean pumped his hand. Lawrence introduced the man as Roger to George, Morgan, and Gretchen.

"How do you like my new sound system?" asked Lawrence.

"Awesome," replied Roger, as he accepted a glass of wine from Sean. The girls resumed dancing.

"Klipschorns. Cost me 40 grand, including installation."

"They sound great. What about Gretchen? Is she new in the program?" Roger was grinning from ear to ear.

"Just got her starter kit last week," replied Lawrence. "She's great so far."

"George looks puzzled," laughed Roger. "Explain to him what a starter kit is."

"You go ahead." Lawrence was amused, but not as animated as Roger.

"A starter kit consists of an upscale one-bedroom apartment in the city of her choice, in this case—"

"Miami Beach," said Lawrence.

"An American Express card with a $5,000-per-month spending limit and the use of a late-model sports car, in this case—"

"A BMW 325i convertible," interjected Gretchen with a smile, while she was dancing.

"And assorted gifts and first-class travel to wonderful places such as this," concluded Roger. Morgan made a snorting sign, and Gretchen and Linda followed him into one of the staterooms.

"What's the program?"

"Being in the program means they do whatever Lawrence

wants them to do, whenever he wants it. He asks them to be in Cannes on Friday for the film festival, they show up or they're out of the program."

"Whatever Lawrence wants?" asked George.

Roger chortled. "No S and M. I mean, Lawrence's a normal guy. Right, Lawrence?" Lawrence just grinned.

"How many girls are in the program?" asked George. "I mean, if you don't mind me asking."

Lawrence answered, "It varies. Three to six. Right now five."

"How do you meet these girls?"

"Various functions. You meet a pretty girl, ask some questions. It doesn't take long to figure out if she'd be interested in this type of arrangement."

"They hear about your program and seek you out, don't they?" asked Roger.

"Sometimes. But it's not like I advertise." Morgan and the girls returned to the deck. Linda sniffled and pinched her nose, then resumed dancing with Gretchen. Morgan grabbed a beer from the cooler.

"What I can't understand is, between your businesses and malls and everything, how you find time for these girls? Five of them?" asked Roger.

"Every man's got a hobby, right? Some guys golf. Some guys have a family—coach Little League, whatever." Lawrence drank off some wine and smiled at Roger. "My hobby, my passion, if you will, is pussy. I don't engage in any of these other activities. When I was younger I spent all my time chasing pussy. I got tired of the chasing part, so I established the program." The girls just smiled and danced. They seemed energized by the cocaine. A waiter from the hotel appeared with a tray of shrimp, crab claws, crusted tuna, and conch dumplings. Two couples in evening attire, about Lawrence and Roger's age, came aboard and accepted cocktails from Sean. Then Roger's two college-aged sons and their dates arrived and grabbed beers.

"Our reservations are at eight," said Lawrence to the girls, who had taken a break from dancing and were sipping their wine. They disappeared into a stateroom and reappeared in sexier dresses, with heavier makeup and more elegant jewelry.

"You guys are more than welcome to hang out here with Sean," said Lawrence to George and Morgan as he rose to leave with the others. Seeing a yacht entering the marina, George grabbed his metal case and walked over to watch the crew handle the docking. Then he proceeded to the lobby to check into a room.

"Your passport, please," said the pleasant Bahamian receptionist.

"I'll be paying in cash, in advance."

"I still need to see your passport, sir."

"Is that hotel policy or Bahamian law?"

"I don't know, sir. I only know that I can't check you in without seeing some kind of ID. Would you like to speak to my manager?"

"Will I get a different answer?"

"No, sir."

"I'll get my passport and come back." George had no intention of registering in his own name at the same hotel as Morgan. When he got back to Lawrence's yacht, Morgan and Sean were snorting lines off a saucer on the bar in the cabin.

"Why are you still carrying that case? I thought you were checking in?" asked Sean.

"No. What are you guys doing for dinner?" George changed the subject.

"I have to stay on the boat to get things ready for tonight," replied Sean.

"Want me to get something, bring it back to the boat?" asked George. He took their orders for takeout from a seafood restaurant in the hotel.

"You want to stay on the boat tonight?" asked Sean. "Won't cost you 500 bucks."

"Great. Thanks." George hurried away so they wouldn't notice that he didn't leave his case. He went into a stall in the casino restroom, took out $1,000 from the bundle that was marked short, then changed the combination on the locks. He got a pocketful of change from the cashier and called Frank. Luckily the answering machine picked up. After the beep, he explained that he couldn't leave a return number, since he was staying on a boat, but Frank could trace the call to Nassau if he didn't believe him. He spoke in code and disguised his voice by feigning laryngitis in case the tape ever showed up in an investigation. Then he bought three very expensive seafood dinners and brought them back to Lawrence's yacht.

"So what's up with Gretchen and Linda?" asked George. He was drinking from a freshly opened bottle of Lawrence's exquisite Pouilly-Fuissé.

"What do you mean, what's up with them?" replied Sean through a mouth full of mahimahi.

"You know, what's their deal?"

"I thought Lawrence and Roger explained their deal. The program."

"I mean, what's up with that? How do they live like that? What do they tell their parents—where the apartment and BMW come from?"

"I don't know. What do strippers tell their parents? How 'bout you, Morgan? What do your parents think that you do?" asked Sean. He was drinking a rum Collins. The three men laughed, drank, and after dinner helped ready the boat for the evening festivities. By the time Lawrence, Roger, and their guests returned, the skipper and his two crewmen were fast friends.

The rock music blasted, the liquor flowed, and Gretchen and Linda danced. Other wealthy-looking people drifted over singly, in pairs, or in small groups until the deck was packed. Everyone seemed to know Lawrence and Roger. Linda complained that she was hot and sweaty, so Roger suggested that she take a swim. She stripped, dove in the water, swam around for a minute, then climbed the aft diving ladder and dripped on the deck, totally nude, until Sean brought her a towel from the cabin. Everybody, including Lawrence and Roger, seemed amused.

George sensed that Gretchen was coming on to him, which flustered him greatly. It's not like she's Lawrence's wife, he thought, or even his girlfriend. More like a mistress. What code pertains to messing around with another man's mistress? He thought about Fielding's *Tom Jones* and the like, but he'd only read about situations where rich guys had one or two mistresses, not a program with a starter kit and whatnot. Gretchen seemed more like a concubine than a mistress. He thought about *The Arabian Nights* and flinched at the image of the eunuchs guarding the harems with scimitars. Not applicable, George decided. Gretchen was making him very horny; intentionally, he thought, but the last thing he could afford to do was lose his transportation back to the States. His quandary was solved an hour later when the party broke up and Lawrence took a girl on each arm and retired to the hotel. Gretchen winked at George over her shoulder as she left.

"Did Lawrence say when we're going back to Miami?" asked George.

"Tomorrow, if the sea lies down. Lawrence doesn't like to travel through swells over four feet," replied Sean.

"What if it doesn't lie down?"

"Then we wait. If it lasts too long, Lawrence will fly back."

"How long is too long?"

Sean shrugged. George passed out on plastic cushions in the cabin, praying for calm seas.

In the morning George struggled through a bad hangover to observe the boatmen casting off the departing yachts. About 9:00 Lawrence and the girls appeared on the deck, looking refreshed. Sean summarized the weather report from the maritime radio. Lawrence announced that they would head back to Miami, then took the girls back to the hotel for brunch. Shortly after they returned, with Roger, a uniformed Bahamian policeman came on board with a German shepherd. The dog immediately sniffed Morgan's pants pocket and started barking. The sharp-looking cop rewarded the dog with a biscuit, then led him around the cabin, including inside the staterooms, and around the deck, fore and aft. After bantering with Lawrence and Sean for a few minutes, the cop accepted a brown paper bag from Sean and took his leave.

"You know the rules, Morgan. Use it or lose it," ordered Lawrence.

"Aye, aye, sir. We'll use it up on the voyage." At that the girls squealed, popped up, and started dancing. George sidled over to Sean and quietly asked him what was going on.

"Lawrence wants to make sure that none of us are bringing contraband," he replied.

George and Morgan had no trouble casting off as Sean expertly piloted the yacht away from the dock. Morgan immediately started laying out lines of coke for the girls and himself. Lawrence and Roger shared a bottle of Pinot Grigio and talked business. George hung out on the bridge with Sean and quizzed him on the nautical aspects of the trip. Wearing a yellow bikini, Gretchen brought a couple of plates of cold lobster salad up to the bridge. She looked great, and she knew it. After lunch Lawrence led the girls into the master stateroom. Gretchen brought the wine, and Linda carried a Scarface-sized pile of coke on a saucer. Roger napped in a deck chair. After an hour the girls emerged and proceeded to sunbathe nude on the foredeck. The perfect tan of their bodies, the pristine white of the deck, and the deep blue of the Atlantic Ocean—it was like some surreal *Playboy* shoot, thought George. He was mesmerized by the way the girls' breasts bounced as the yacht skipped over the waves. Periodically the girls would prance aft to snort a line, visit with Lawrence and Roger, and change the music. As they approached the Miami Beach Marina they slipped on their bikinis and posed on either side of the bowsprit. Human ornaments. They smiled and waved at the boats heading out to sea.

"Lawrence had the girls topless on arrival until two years ago, when we got cited for public lewdness," remarked Sean.

"Far out," said George. He gaped at row after row of luxury cruisers and sailboats. He wondered how the aggregate value of the yachts compared to the GNP of some of the deadbeat countries he traded. On Sean's command, he jumped down on the dock with the bowline and secured it to a giant metal cleat. Sean told him to slacken the line to allow for a rising tide, and he complied. Back on deck, George and Morgan both thanked Lawrence and said good-bye to Roger, Gretchen, Linda, and Sean.

"I'll need your passports," said Sean to George and Morgan.

"How come?" asked George.

"Customs manifest." Morgan handed over his passport.

"Let me get mine," said George. The last thing he wanted was to have his name on a federal document next to Morgan's. He walked into the cabin, through the master stateroom, out the fore hatch, across the foredeck, and onto the pier as quickly and quietly as he could. He was almost onshore when he heard and felt the pounding of running feet on the wooden pier. He started to run, then thought better of it, stopped, and turned around to face Sean.

"What the fuck?" growled Sean, trying to sound tough.

"Where can we talk?"

"What talk? Give me your passport."

"Give me two minutes to explain."

"I've got work to do on the boat."

"I'll make it worth your while." George led Sean past a swimming pool surrounded by tables with thatched canopies and into Monty's Crab House. Sean followed him into the men's room to make sure there wasn't a back window, then retreated to a nearby table. George ducked into a stall, unlocked his metal case, pulled the remaining ten C-notes out of the short bundle, then locked the case. He sat down across from Sean and looked him in the eye.

"Look, George, I can get in a lot of trouble if the customs manifest isn't accurate." Sean spoke up to be heard over the music of the steel-drum band.

"I can't give you my passport."

"Why not?"

"Here are a thousand reasons why not." George handed him the bills under the table. Sean examined them between his legs for a second, then stuffed the wad in his pocket.

"Adios, amigo." Sean pushed past the waitress who had just arrived to take their order and hurried out the door. George ordered a double Johnnie Walker Black and soda. The happy-hour crowd was as varied as he had ever seen at a bar. Crusty mates from the fishing boats, stinking of their trade, drank eagerly with the stewards and stewardesses from the luxury craft. There were a number of wealthy middle-aged men who looked like Lawrence and Roger. Several were hitting on the locals, inviting them out to their yachts to party. George wondered if any starter kits were being proffered. He grabbed a cab in front of Monty's and got off at the Miami Amtrak station. He called Frank to report his itinerary, as required, and was surprised when the message was interrupted by Frank's voice.

"Yo."

"It's York." George disguised his voice.

"Ya sick or sumptin'?"

"Yeah. I'm on the Silver Star, arriving Penn Station at 8:05 tomorrow night."

"Silver Star?"

"Amtrak train."

"Ya got da money?"

"Yeah."

"Tamorrah night, huh? Let's see. Come t' Daisy's when ya get here. Take care o' business."

"Daisy's, the strip joint?"

"Yeah. Times Square."

"See you tomorrow night." George rang off and walked over to the newsstand. He bought a *New York Times,* an Elmore Leonard novel, and a James Lee Burke novel for the twenty-six-hour trip. He couldn't find *The Economist* or the *Financial Times.* It was a train station, not an airport. When he was boarding the train, Morgan appeared at his side.

"I thought you had business in Miami?" asked George.

"Deal didn't happen. If it had, I would have rented a car. Now, you don't have to worry about being near me."

"I still don't think that we should be seen together."

"Whatever." Morgan shrugged. After Morgan found a seat George bought three Buds and a microwaved burger at the bar car. He continued forward for three cars until he found two empty seats together. He stuck his case in front of the empty window seat and sat in the aisle seat. The beer tasted great. The burger could have been worse. He switched seats often over the next day so that no one would notice his case, but he avoided the back of the train, where he knew Morgan was sitting. They glanced at each other once in the dining car, but they never spoke.

At Penn Station, Morgan appeared next to George at the front of the taxi line.

"What the hell, Morgan?" scolded George under his breath. "We agreed to not be seen together."

"So we never speak again, huh?" asked Morgan.

"Correct. Starting right now."

"Well, it's been real." Morgan offered his hand and George shook it reluctantly. "You want to share a cab uptown?"

"Are you nuts? Take this one. I'll get the next one." Settling into the back of his cab George noticed a red Impala pulling out behind Morgan's cab. He opened the window to try to see if Kevin or Frank was in the car, but he couldn't even tell if there was a passenger. I must be paranoid, he thought. But still, if it was them, why would they be tailing Morgan? George pondered that question all the way uptown. He showered at Club 16B, transferred the money to an old gym bag, and headed out to hail a cab back to midtown.

15

George got out of the cab and entered the "gentlemen's club." There was a booth just inside the door that sold lap-dance tickets along with calendars and videos starring the house talent. The bouncer eyed George's gym bag but said nothing. George paid the $20 cover charge and surveyed the scene. A few dozen affluent-looking men in business suits sat in deep, gray easy chairs that surrounded small tables laden with cocktails. There were a couple of loners, but most were in groups of two to five. George noticed a cluster of drunk, Asian businessmen reveling in one corner. At several tables, young women in bright dresses cuddled with the men. Girls wearing G-strings were giving lap dances to some of the other transfixed patrons. At the rest of the tables the customers drank and watched the nearby dancers or one of the three stage shows. The men did not appear to be communicating with one another.

George spotted Kevin slouched at a table near the main stage. He was cradling a cocktail and staring at a raven-haired beauty who was wriggling out of a blue sequined dress. As George walked over, she slowly pushed the dress down to her ankles.

"Hey, Kevin." George had to lean close and shout to be heard over the Commodores' "Brick House," which was blasting from the speakers.

Kevin looked George over carefully, his eyes coming to rest on the gym bag.

"Is it all there?"

"Yes," George replied.

"Nice goin', partner. Let's celebrate. What're you drinkin'?"

"Shouldn't we take care of business first?"

Kevin shrugged, grabbed the gym bag, and set it by his foot. "OK. Now, what're you drinkin'?"

"I'd like to watch you and Frank count it."

"OK, 'cept Frank's busy right now. Be here in a little while."

George hesitated for a moment, then said, "OK. Let's you and I count it."

Kevin nodded. "You'll have to wait until Natasha finishes her set." he slung his eyes toward the stage. "She loves me," he said with a grin.

"Better be careful with these young Russian immigrants. Heard about a guy took a Russian hooker back to a midtown hotel. Woke up in the bathtub full of ice, minus a kidney."

"*You* be careful, not *me.*" Kevin grinned his surly wise-guy grin. It wasn't crooked like Frank's.

"You invulnerable? Superman?"

"Not invulnerable. Connected. And Natasha's not a hooker."

George suddenly thought that Kevin could be the guy who brokered the kidneys. He stifled the retort that had been forming on his lips.

Natasha was hanging upside down with her legs wrapped around a shiny fireman's pole, wearing only a G-string. As Kevin returned his attention to the stage, Natasha smiled at him. She crawled around the stage, kneeling before each patron in the front row, arching back and undulating her crotch near their faces until they slipped a bill under her G-string. She took care of business, but it was clear that she was dancing for Kevin. When the music stopped she kissed him on the lips, and he slipped a twenty under her G-string.

Kevin led George over to a nearly invisible door next to the ticket booth at the club's entrance. A fat, gray-haired man dressed in black emerged, listened to Kevin for a second, nodded, then waddled toward the bar, leaving the door open.

Kevin ushered George into the cramped office and closed the door. There was a steel desk and three matching office chairs, but not much else. Kevin casually tossed the gym bag under the desk and motioned George to sit down. A bored-looking, mostly naked waitress ducked in, delivered two drinks, and ducked out. The walls muffled the music enough that it was comfortable to talk.

"Double Johnnie Walker on the rocks work for you?"

"Fine. Thanks, Kevin."

Kevin leaned back, trying too hard to look relaxed. "I'm really impressed. Anyone can raise that kind o' cash in a month is an impressive dude, in my book."

George nodded.

"Guy's gotta know his way around. Gotta have some savvy. And balls." Kevin paused and drank off a good third of his scotch. George took a swig. He stared at Kevin and said nothing.

"Frank and I would love to work with a guy has your street smarts, your guts. You know, we can hold up our end of the deal. You need false documents, transfer money onshore—no problem. We got mules, bring anything across the border. Need to launder money—takes us a day. Got a reluctant party in the deal—we can be very persuasive. You know?"

George's eyes widened as he stared at Kevin.

Kevin sat up straight. "What I'm sayin', we'd like to be your partners. I don't know what your racket is exactly, but I'm sure that we could be very valuable. We gotta lotta resources. Lotta connections."

"You're goofin' on me, right?"

"Serious as a heart attack. You got the Wall Street connections. The legit world. We handle everything else. Match made in heaven. Whaddaya say?"

"You're shittin' me. Enough already. Let's count the money."

Kevin frowned and began bobbing his head slowly. "OK. I get it. The Ivy League boy is too good for us lowlifes. Don't wanna stoop to our level, huh?" George couldn't help but wonder if Kevin practiced his look of utter indignation in front of the mirror. Got it from a wise-guy movie. "Is that it? College boy too good for us, huh?"

"Look, Kevin, it's not like that at all. You mentioned my 'racket.' I don't have a racket. How I got the money, it's a one-time thing. Can't be repeated. Not possible."

"Can't be repeated, huh? Let's talk about that. Maybe it can be repeated with the help of partners?"

George looked into his drink, then looked into Kevin's glare and held it. Kevin's face reddened as they stared each other down for half a minute. It seemed much longer to George.

Kevin leaned forward, inches from Georges face, and snarled, "How'd you get the money, George?"

George was certain that Kevin had practiced the snarl in the mirror. "You don't really want to know," replied George, feigning calmness as best he could.

Kevin leaned even closer. "Yeah I do. I really wanna know."

George stared back. Another minute passed. Kevin asked, "So that's the way it is?"

George nodded. Kevin tossed the gym bag on the table. He reached into a desk drawer and pulled out a digital bill-counting machine. He snatched the bundles of C-notes from the bag, removed the bands, and fed the bills into the machine. Twenty-seven times the digital display read 100 and once it read 50—$275,000. As Kevin counted, the redness and anger in his face gradually faded.

"Look, George, I'm sorry I got tough with you. I really do think we could make a ton of money together. I'm really disappointed. But hey, no hard feelin's, huh?" Kevin grinned and reached out to shake hands.

"Sure. No problem." They shook hands. "I'd still like to see Frank, make sure he knows we're squared away."

"You really don't trust me, do ya?"

"I don't know you that well, Kevin."

"Maybe if you did you'd want to partner." Kevin stood up, grinned again, and slapped George on the back. He cracked the door to the ticket booth and asked about Frank. "He shoulda been here by now. Any minute. Go on out to the table while I put this away. I'll make sure you have a good time while you're here." Kevin winked.

Another double scotch arrived at the table. As soon as George finished it, another one appeared. He was starting to feel pretty good. Natasha sat down and put her arm around him. "Hi, George," she purred in a heavy Russian accent. "Come upstairs vith me for your private lap dance." Her breath was wet in his ear. She smelled of just the right mixture of sweet perfume and female sweat.

"I don't know. I don't think I can afford it."

"No vorry, big guy. Kevin takes care of everything. And it's much more intimate upstairs, you know vhat I mean."

George leaned back and looked her over. She looked like a seventeen-year-old swimsuit model. The scotch told him to go along. She took his hand and led him upstairs, to a dimly lit private room that smelled of a more flowery, less pungent perfume than Natasha's. Without a word, she shimmied out of her sequined dress and began her sultry lap dance. George was obviously aroused when she whispered, "You vant me to take my G-string off, big guy?"

"Is this a trick question?" breathed George, smiling broadly.

"Noooo," she cooed. She removed a sheer, black silk scarf from around her neck. "But I need to tie your hands so you von't touch my pussy."

"Why not?" George was still smiling ear to ear.

"If the vice cops look in, they close the club down." She slid behind his chair and clasped his hands together, but it wasn't silk that tightened on his wrists. Hard, sharp plastic bit down across his flesh. He was handcuffed. "There ve are," she shouted. In an instant, Natasha slipped out and Frank barged in. His muscles bulged beneath a tight black Gold's Gym T-shirt.

George jumped up and screamed in Frank's face, "What the fuck!"

Frank calmly picked George up by the throat and bashed him against the back wall. "Promise not t' yell and I let go." George gurgled an affirmative through the chokehold. Frank eased him into the chair. "Relax. We gotta talk. That's all." Frank leaned out of the room, brought in two drinks, and held one to George's lips. "Drink your scotch. It'll help your t'roat." Frank sipped his drink and stared blankly at George.

"Kevin didn't tell you that I paid?" rasped George.

"Sure. Paid in full. But he also says ya don't wanna be our partner."

"So you're going to choke me until I agree to partner? Are you nuts, or what?"

"No more chokin' if ya keep your voice down, like ya promised. But ya hafta tell me how ya got da money."

"Like I told Kevin, that information won't help you. It was a one-shot deal. I can't do it again. No way."

"Ya hafta tell me how ya got da money."

"No."

Frank leaned out of the room and brought in another chair. Then he pulled a pair of hawk-billed garden shears out of his back pocket. He sat down very close to George and pointed the shears at his nose. "Lemme me tell ya how it is, Georgie boy. We got your partner Morgan next door. He won't tell us how ya got da money either."

"Bullshit. I don't know anyone named Morgan."

Frank leaned out of the room and spoke to someone. A few seconds later Kevin pushed Morgan's battered face through the doorway. Morgan scowled at George. "You stupid, fuckin' cock-sucker. . . ." He growled through swollen, bloody lips as Kevin pulled him away.

"That's funny," Frank chuckled. "Morgan seems t' know ya." Then he was serious again. Deadpan. He pointed the shears at George's nose. "Lemme tell ya how it is, Georgie. I'm gonna ask ya one more time how ya got da money. If ya don't tell me, I'll cut off a finger. Then I'll go next door and ask Morgan. He don't tell me, I cut off one o' his fingers. I go back and fort' 'til your stories match or I have twenty fingers and two cocks in my bag here. I cut your cock off, ya bleed to death and it'll be over."

"Are you nuts? You think you can get away with this? You're way out of your element, man. You think I'm some kinda thug that the New York justice system doesn't care about? You mutilate me and you'll go to prison for a long, long time."

"Let's looka dis in two parts. Part one, ya *are* gonna tell me how ya got da money, 'cause you'd be crazy not to, and I know you're not crazy. I may get caught, sent to da joint, but you're a corpse with no fingers or cock. You're gonna tell. That's part one."

Frank took a drink. "Part two is, after ya get outta here, are you gonna go to da cops? Let's look at *dat* question in two parts. Part one is what happens t' me. I go t' Sing Sing, see all my buddies, tell 'em about da college-boy bankers I squeezed for 900 large. Maybe I'm wearin' your fingers on a necklace. If I got your cock on my necklace, you t'ink da faggots'll fuck wid me?" George just stared. "I don' t'ink so. Anyway, it'll all be in da papers, so everyone'll know it ain't just cell-block bullshit. It'll really help my rep in da joint. A guy's rep is very important in da joint. It'll help my rep when I get out too. You know anyone'd fuck widda guy has a finger, thumb, and cock necklace?" Frank took another drink. "I don't."

"Part two o' part two is what happens t' you if ya squeal. Morgan is a convict, so it's a cinch that you two committed a felony or t'ree to get 900 large. You go to Danbury, not as rough as Sing

Sing, but ya still get cornholed every day 'cause you're pretty and ya won't be able t' make a fist t' fight off da rapists. Plus you won't have a cock necklace to scare 'em off. And when ya get out, if ya don't die o' AIDS, you'll be an ex-con. Good-bye, Wall Street. Hello, McDonalds, car wash, landscapin' crew, whatever. Hello, poverty. Nah, not you. You're already a criminal—you'll probably stay outside da law, like Morgan. Maintain your lifestyle. Then you'll be a criminal, like me and Kevin. You won't be able to look down on us like ya do now. We'll probably partner when we get out, so why not do it now? Save a ton o' trouble?" Frank finished off his drink. "Point is, ya stand t' lose a lot more than me if ya squeal t' da cops, so I know ya won't. That's why I'm not afraid t' cut ya up. Got it, George?"

George had turned ghostly pale and was taking quick, shallow breaths. "If I tell you, how do I know you won't blackmail me forever?"

"C'mon, George, we'll be partners. Do partners blackmail each other?" Frank didn't blink. "How did ya get da money, George?"

George shook his head. Frank produced the gag from the Spa. After he gagged George, he stood him up, spread a towel under the chair, then sat him back down. He walked behind George and clamped the shears on the top knuckle of the little finger on his left hand. "Last chance, Georgie boy. Be smart an' nod your head." Frank's voice was flat now. Emotionless. George bit the plastic ball. Frank snipped off the top of his pinkie and slipped a towel into George's right hand. "Press it against da stump, stop da bleedin'." Frank knocked on the wall, dropped the bloody fingertip into a ziplock sandwich bag, and slapped it into the hand that appeared in the doorway.

The pain was excruciating. George tried to fight back the tears that rolled down his cheeks. He'd be damned if he'd lose his education, career, reputation, everything he'd strived for, to blackmail. These thugs will never break me, he swore to himself. Never.

Several minutes passed. It seemed like an hour to George. He envisioned explaining to his parents and to Heidi how he got blackmailed into a life of crime. Then Kevin walked in and Frank walked out. "Relax, partner. It's over. We showed Morgan your finger and he told us all about tradin' the Nicaragua shit. He told us about the Swiss bank that handled the money. I can't say I fully understand it, but I understand enough to know you go to prison if City Trust finds out. I'm gonna take the gag off, and you're gonna tell me the name of the Swiss bank, and the price of the trade, just so we can cross-check a couple o' facts." George just stared angrily through his tears.

"Jesus, George. You've already proven you're a tough guy. Don't be a stupid asshole. You wanna lose more fingers for no fuckin' reason? I already know the answers. I want you for a partner, the tough guy, not some crippled freak. C'mon, answer the questions and we'll get you to the hospital."

George closed his eyes and nodded. Kevin removed the gag and cut the handcuffs. "We traded the paper 13 to 16. Bank Mori, Geneva. Now give me my finger," spat George. Kevin handed him the ziplock bag, which had been filled with ice. He offered George three small white pills. George didn't move.

"C'mon, I'm not gonna poison my new partner, am I? It's Percocet, kill the pain." George's hand was throbbing. He grabbed the pills and washed them down with scotch.

"C'mon, we'll drive you to the hospital," said Kevin.

"I'm not going anywhere with you cretins. I'll take a cab."

"You might pass out in the cab."

Morgan leaned into the room. "I'll take him."

"OK, just one more thing," said Kevin. "George, you're squared with TD. He don't know nothin' about our new loan trading partnership. That's between you, me, Frank, and Morgan. Period. Is that clear?" George nodded. "OK, try New York Hospital on York. Great microsurgery department. I know a guy got his thumb cut off. They reattached the blood vessels, tendons, nerves, everything. Almost good as new. You'll feel better next week. We'll have our first partnership meeting."

"Fuck you, you degenerate, sadist asshole." George stood up, steadied himself, and walked out and down the stairs, pressing the bloody towel against his bloody hand. George and Morgan did not look at each other as they marched out to the street.

Kevin and Frank watched them go. "George shouldn't be so conspicuous with that bloody towel," observed Kevin.

Frank shrugged. "Yeah. So what's tradin' defaulted Nicaraguan debt?"

"You know, buying and selling markers owed by some shitty spic country."

"How do ya collect on a marker owed by some shitty spic country?"

"If they got an army, you gotta send in the marines. If they don't got an army, just a palace guard or whatever, you use mercenaries."

"How do ya know dis shit?" asked Frank.

"*Soldier of Fortune* magazine. C'mon, let's find Natasha, snort some more of Morgan's blow. Celebrate."

"Yeah. Celebrate 900 large."

"Fuckin' A," laughed Kevin. "Let's celebrate our new partners."

16

Morgan hailed a cab and told the driver to go to New York Hospital, emergency entrance. The young, turbaned man protested. "Hey, hey. You bleed, get ambulance. Not my cab."

George and Morgan piled in the back. The cabbie got out and stood on the curb with his arms folded.

"He'll bleed in the towel," barked Morgan. "But if you don't get going now, I'll wipe the blood all over your cab."

"Fuck you," yelled the cabbie. Then he got in and peeled out into traffic. Morgan slammed shut the payment window in the bulletproof partition.

Morgan trembled in anger, but he spoke in a low, measured voice. "Why did you tell them about me?"

George tried to match Morgan's controlled intensity. "Why did you tell them what we did? Chapter and verse."

"Don't be an ass. They weren't going to stop. We'd both be bleeding to death if I hadn't."

"Yeah, whatever. I didn't tell them anything about you. Nothing."

"Then what was Goon Frank doing at my building when I got home?"

"He must have seen you with me at Penn Station. Followed you home."

"How'd he know I was arriving at Penn Station?"

"He knew I was. Must've figured out the rest."

"You're a moron," Morgan hissed.

"You're the one who came up to me in the taxi line." George let that sink in. "Looks like he roughed you up pretty bad."

Morgan sighed. "My face will heal. He forced me into my apartment at gunpoint. He took my 300 grand split, two ounces of coke, couple of grand in cash . . . my working capital. I'm out of business. Went through all my stuff. He knows where my parents live, my parole officer. Everything about me."

They sat in silence for a minute. George rocked over the throbbing hand in his lap, and Morgan stared at him with a penetrating, unnerving intensity. "You know there's only one way to stop them."

"Yeah, what's that?" asked George.

After a long, silent stare, Morgan leaned in George's ear, mindful of the cabbie. He spoke in a quiet but forceful tone. "We have to kill them."

"You're serious, aren't you?"

"Dead serious."

George looked at his shoes and shook his head slowly. "Murder wasn't on the curriculum at Princeton. Or at Fletcher," he whispered. He raised his eyes to Morgan's. "There must be another way."

"Don't you get it? If we don't play ball, they'll torture us. If we do, they'll push us until we get caught, and I'm not getting caught again. I'd be a two-time loser. A recidivist. That means serious time. Parole at middle age. Not going to happen. We've got to stop it now."

"If you murder them, you'll do life at Attica."

"Not me. Us. And only if we get caught, which we won't if we're smart."

"Not us. I'm not a murderer. I don't have it in me."

"You're either a killer or a witness."

"What are you saying?"

"I can't have any witnesses."

"What are you saying? You're going to kill me if I don't kill them?" George was losing his cool, but he kept his voice down.

"We're in this together. You're either an accomplice or a witness. I can't have any witnesses."

"You're as crazy as they are. I'm surrounded by psychopaths. What the fuck?"

"George, you're a little fucked up right now, with the finger and all." Morgan lightened up. "When you have a chance to think clearly, you'll realize there's no other way out of this. No other way."

George squeezed his hand in the towel and rocked against the pain. He surveyed the midnight sidewalk crowd as the cab weaved through the traffic on Third Avenue. Men, women, young, old, white, black, Asian, Latino, drunk, sober, stoned. He wondered if any of them had ever killed anyone.

After a few blocks, George returned his attention to Morgan. "Did you get raped at Danbury?"

"What? No. But what the hell does that have to do with anything?"

"Frank said that I'd get raped at Danbury."

"You're not going to Danbury. This Nicaragua deal is wrapped and packed. The only loose ends are Kevin and Frank, and they're about to disappear."

"I didn't think they had rapes, you know, violence, at the white-collar prisons. I thought that stuff went on at Rikers Island, Attica. Those places."

"There's rapists at Danbury, and you're a lot cuter than me, so you probably would be a bride. Or maybe get passed around. All the more reason that we have to get rid of those thugs."

"That's what Frank said. That I'd get raped because I'm pretty."

"If there's one thing Frank knows," affirmed Morgan, "it's prisons."

The cab turned off York at the emergency entrance and

stopped behind an ambulance that was unloading a stretcher case. Morgan reached in his pocket for the fare.

"No," ordered George. "Take off. I'll handle it. Go sit in a church. Reconsider this murder idea."

"Fuck you." Morgan was fired up again. "Ask the doctor for a shot of testosterone. Get a month's supply. Your Sunday school crap will only buy you more suffering. You know what we have to do."

George slammed the car door and walked into the emergency room. A plump young woman with big, bleached-blonde hair and too much makeup occupied the admissions desk. George cleared his throat and she looked up from her *People* magazine. "Yes?"

"I cut my finger off, and I need a surgeon to sew it back on."

"Insurance card?" She yawned. George struggled to remove the card from his wallet with one hand while the receptionist took a bite of her doughnut and returned her attention to her magazine. He handed the card to her and in return was given a set of medical forms on a clipboard. "Have a seat and fill these out."

George returned with the completed forms. "Have a seat and we'll call you when the doctor is ready." George just stood there. After a minute the girl looked up, obviously annoyed that George was still there. George held up the baggie containing his iced fingertip. "I think I need this taken care of before the nerves and veins start to atrophy."

"Have a seat and we'll call you when the doctor is ready."

George sat down and looked around the waiting room. An elderly woman in a shabby pink nightgown muttered incoherently. Periodically he could make out her cursing under her breath. A handsome young Hispanic man bent over in pain grabbing his gut while a lovely Hispanic girl in a tank top and jeans tried to comfort him. George wondered if the guy's appendix was bursting. A well-dressed black family occupied a row of hard plastic seats. The two youngest children slept while the mom and dad tried to entertain the other two with a good humor that defied the hour. None were visibly distressed. Perhaps they were waiting for someone. A young, burly uniformed security guard sat by the door reading the *New York Post.*

The Percocet had dulled but not eliminated the throbbing in George's hand. After ten minutes, he stood in front of the big-haired receptionist again, but she refused to look up. "Can I talk to the nurse on duty, please?" George strained to sound polite.

"Have a seat and we'll call you when the doctor is ready." Big Hair refused to look up. George removed his finger from the baggie and placed it under his nose, puckering his lips to hold it. Big Hair ignored him . . . a test of wills. After a minute George faked a sneeze and the finger landed on her *People* magazine. Unfazed, she picked it up with the napkin from her doughnut and dropped it in a wastebasket.

"Give me my goddamn finger. I'm going back there, now!"

"Vinny." Big Hair raised her voice enough to be heard across the room but remained nonplussed.

The security guard folded his *Post,* placed it on his chair, then sauntered over to the counter. "Is there a problem here?" His voice was calm but tough.

"Just a guy who can't wait his turn," yawned Big Hair.

"I cut my finger off and I'm waiting a half hour to get it sewn back on. She threw it in the garbage." Vinny raised his eyebrows at Big Hair, who shrugged, then used the napkin to remove the fingertip from the trash and hand it to George. He held it up to Vinny and dropped it in the baggie.

"I gotta get this taken care of, Vinny."

"Maybe you should pay your debts on time. Then you wouldn't wind up in emergency rooms at midnight." George was taken aback. What did this guy know? He opened his mouth, but nothing came out.

Vinny leaned back against the counter and smiled. "Look, buddy, the stretcher case that came in right before you was multiple gunshot wounds, so they're busy back there. You could try another hospital, but you'd just have to wait all over again. Why don't you sit down and wait for your name to be called."

After another ten minutes, Big Hair directed George to a cramped room where a pleasant and efficient nurse took his blood pressure and temperature and asked him a series of questions.

"You're very lucky, Mr. Wilhelm. There's an excellent hand specialist in the building. He's on his way here now. I'm sorry that you had to wait, but only a specialist can assess a reattachment." She then escorted him into the operating room, where a minute later they were joined by a doctor.

"Hello, Mr. Wilhelm. I'm Dr. Singh and this is Nurse Ecklund. Lie down on the table with your arm stretched out this way and we'll get you numbed up so I can probe the wound."

"Can I get something in addition to the local?"

"You've been mixing alcohol and codeine. I'm afraid that further sedation is out of the question. How did this happen?"

"I was trying to slice a coconut with a machete."

Dr. Singh looked closely at the detached part of the finger. "Really. Looks like you cut it from the top and bottom. More likely a scissor cut." George said nothing. "What is the foreign substance?"

"Foreign substance?"

"There's a white powder on the finger."

"Must be sugar from the receptionist's doughnut."

Dr. Singh looked at Nurse Ecklund. "Of course. The receptionist's doughnut."

"Can you reattach the finger?" asked George.

"Give me a moment."

"This may sting," said Nurse Ecklund as she injected the local anesthetic into the stump of George's pinkie. Dr. Singh examined the detached portion through a binocular microscope while waiting for the stump to numb. Then he examined the stump, probing occasionally with what looked like a dental instrument.

"Mr. Wilhelm, your distal interphalangeal joint has been crushed. The cartilage and nerves have been totally destroyed. I can replant the fingertip, but I doubt that I can restore the functionality of the joint."

"What are the odds?"

"There's a fifty-fifty chance that some modicum of functionality can be restored. The chance of full functionality is zero."

"What good is a fingertip that doesn't function?"

"Purely cosmetic."

"What's the procedure?"

"The replantation procedure will take several hours and will require two teams of surgeons—one to prepare each end of the amputation. You'll remain in the hospital for a few days so I can monitor the fusion. Your hand will be immobilized and heavily bandaged, so you won't be using it for six to eight weeks. If there is not adequate venous supply to reconnect at the time of replantation, we may need to periodically drain the accumulated blood and for that procedure I favor the use of medical-grade leeches. And again, I cannot guarantee that you will regain functionality of the top joint."

"Leeches?" asked George. "You're kidding me, right?"

"No, I would not kid you. If I perform a revision, which means to clean it up and close the wound, you'll be out of here in a few hours. If there's no infection, you'll be sore for only another week or so.

"What do you recommend?" asked George.

"It's up to you, Mr. Wilhelm. If I close it up and it bothers you cosmetically, you can always have a plastic surgeon perform an additional revision with a skin graft to add a little length at a later date." George thought for a moment. He pictured himself confronting Frank with his hand covered in leeches.

"Close it up, please," said George.

17

George stopped at the drinking fountain on his way out of the emergency room and popped three more Percocets. While walking up York Avenue he pulled the baggie containing his fingertip out of his pocket and tossed it into a storm sewer. Back at Club 16B he chugged two beers in front of the 4:00 A.M. *SportsCenter* before crashing. He got up at ten and showered with a baggie over his bandaged hand. The pain had subsided enough that he decided to tackle it just with aspirin to keep his head clear for trading. He figured Enrique would assume he had taken a morning flight up from Florida. When he arrived at the desk, several people asked about his hand. He mumbled, "A little fishing accident. . . ." That response had worked for Captain Willard with the spooks in *Apocalypse Now.* George briefly compared himself to Colonel Kurtz's snail, "crawling, slithering, along the edge of a straight . . . razor . . . and surviving." Surviving was the key.

The market for pre-Brady loans was virtually unchanged from the prior week. One of the messages on George's desk was from Dom, whom he called back immediately.

"Good vacation?" asked Dom.

"You bet."

"Listen, George, you're not going to want to hear this, but I found out the price where Mori bought the Nici. Better brace yourself." George froze. The needles walked up his spine to the base of his neck. "Twelve." George held his hand over his mouthpiece as he gasped for breath. Several seconds passed. "George, are you still there?"

"I'll be right down," choked George. He breathed deeply to regain his composure on the way to the elevators. What if Enrique finds out? He'll certainly investigate the trade, he thought. He immediately felt sick. Dom led George to an unoccupied office near his cubicle and closed the door.

"Are you sure? Twelve?" Morgan had said 13¼. Where did 12 come from, wondered George.

"Our lawyer saw a document that he wasn't supposed to see."

"How did that happen?"

"He wouldn't say. Probably sneaked a peek when the other lawyer left the room to piss. Stuff like this happens more often than you would think. The seller was Chase—the agent."

George buried his face in his hands for a minute. When he looked up he asked, "Who else knows this?"

"Just you, me, and the lawyer, Stuart Schenfeld. I figured you didn't want it broadcast."

"Jesus, you got that right. If Enrique finds out he'll probably fire me for incompetence. I sure picked the wrong time of year to get my face ripped off. You've got to promise not to tell anyone," implored George.

"If Enrique asks me, I can't lie. But I promise not to volunteer the information. Why would I want to make you look bad?"

"I appreciate it, pal. I owe you big."

"No problem, George."

"And make sure that Schenfeld dummies up, will you please?"

"Already done. I'll stay on top of him."

"Thanks, Dom." George headed back to the desk. Morgan had taken an extra $312,500 out of the trade. George figured he had probably lied by a fraction, but the fuckin' guy had haggled over half a point when he had an extra point and change in his pocket. Then George remembered Frank bragging about squeezing the bankers for 900 large, which meant his own $275,000 plus the $600,000 that Frank had stolen from Morgan. That corroborated Dom's information. Twelve was the price. George tried to put his anger at Morgan aside so he could concentrate on the risk of Enrique learning of Chase's selling price.

Back on the desk, George went through the motions of catching up on news about the pre-Brady countries. There was a message on his desk from Ricardo, one of the loan traders at Citibank. George had met him at an Emerging Market Traders Association function, and despite the fact that they were competitors, they had stayed in touch and discussed the market periodically.

"Hey, Ricardo. I've been out of town. You called?"

"Hey, George. You were nosing around Nici week before last. I just thought I'd post you that Chase sold $25 million at 12." George's stomach turned over. "George?"

"Yeah, I'm here. Did you hear it directly from Chase?"

"No, those guys never talk to me. I got it from a hedgie who was posted by one of their sales guys."

"Any chance it's a phony post?"

"Chase is a big lender to Nici, so if they had more to go and they wanted to paint a picture, they'd post it higher than 12, wouldn't they?"

"Who was the buyer?"

"I thought you might know. Didn't you have a buyer?" George didn't reply. "All I heard was an offshore bank. My sales guys are trying to find the buyer."

"Why, do you have Nici for sale now?"

"I already told you I didn't. I just want to find the poor bastard who's buying Nici. Guy that will buy $25 million Nici—I could stuff him like a Thanksgiving turkey with my dog shit inventory."

"Is this trade widely known?"

"When I couldn't find you I called around a bit. Guys active in pre-Bradys seem to have been posted." George almost gagged. Ricardo continued. "So, you've pushed Ecuador up to 50. You loading up again or do you have buyers? George?"

"A little of both."

"Offshore or onshore?"

"A little of both."

"C'mon, George. Give me something."

"Two U.S. hedge funds have started buying. New buyers. I have to go." Enrique is certain to get posted, George thought. That worm José covers most of the hedgies—he'll post Enrique directly, if he hasn't already. Or Enrique will hear it from a dealer. He talks to everyone. What if he already knows and he's testing me to see when I will own up to being sodomized? He's got to hear it from me. It's got to be up front. Not like I'm trying to get away with something. George retreated to the men's room and splashed tap water on his face. He approached the trading desk like a condemned man straining to look brave before the gallows.

"Enrique, got a minute?"

"What's up?"

"Off the desk?"

The fear in George's eyes startled Enrique, who quickly stood and replied, "Sure."

Standing in Pablo's vacant office, George wasted no time. "The . . . my purchase of the Nici block . . . uh, we found out that Chase was the original seller at . . . uh . . . 12."

"You're shittin' me, right? We paid, what was it, 15⅞?" Enrique's tone was disbelief.

"Yes, I mean no, I'm not shitting you, and yes, we paid 15⅞," choked George. "I feel terrible . . . I uh. . . ."

"You got brokered for 4 points on $25 million by Bank Mori?" Enrique's growl was not of the human race, but perhaps of a cave-dwelling ancestor. "You got broken down shotgun style and ass fucked for a million dollars by a scummy little Swiss private bank?

You've got to be shittin' me." He face turned as red as the Peruvian flag on Pablo's wall.

George couldn't take his eyes off a bulging, throbbing blue vein in Enrique's temple. George was mute. He feared the vein would burst.

"You fucked City Trust for a million bucks?" Enrique was pounding George's sternum with his index finger, backing him across the room. "You fucked *me* for a million bucks?"

"I . . . I'm really sorry, boss. I'll make it up to you, I promise. You can take it out of my bonus. . . ."

Enrique ignored him. "Is Chase the agent?"

"Yes."

"Did it ever cross your feeble pea brain to check if the agent was a seller, or was maybe aware of any sellers? Have you learned anything at all about trading in the last year?"

"The pre-Brady market has, uh, doubled in price this year. In that context, I thought 16 was a good offering for Nici. We've been the biggest buyer of pre-Bradys this year, and I thought that if I started poking around I'd push the market up and risk losing the offering."

"You thought?" exploded Enrique. "You didn't think. You just bent over and spread your cheeks. Like I never taught you how to check a market without flagging which way you're going?"

"We've only been buyers."

"You worthless piece of shit. What kind of party do you think they had at Mori? Couple cases of Dom Pérignon? Like New Year's Eve? No, it'll be the millennium. They'll play the tape at midnight on 12/31/99 since it's the best trade they'll do in a thousand years. Out-trading City Trust for a million bucks. In the meantime they'll take the tape home at night and jerk off to it. Maybe they'll pass it around the bank. Could become the most famous aphrodisiac in the history of Switzerland." Enrique was marching around the room and pounding on Pablo's furniture.

George coughed hard to clear his throat. "Look, the markup was $969,000. Whatever portion of that you feel is inordinate, take it out of my bonus. Right off the top. I'm dead serious."

"We'll talk about your potential bonus and your potential continued employment later. Has Chase's sale at 12 been posted in the market?"

"Yes."

"Who knows that we paid 15 7/8?"

"The seller, our lawyer, and the operations guys. Nobody on the desk."

"Make sure they keep it zipped. If it gets around that I got brokered for a million bucks by Bank Mori, I will shove my fist down your throat, hook my finger around your asshole, and turn you inside out." Enrique stormed out of the office and strode toward the elevators. George hurried back to his desk and called Dom.

"Hey, Dom. I told Enrique that Chase sold Mori the Nici at 12."

"Why'd you do that?"

"I decided to come clean."

"Did you tell him I told you?"

"Didn't get a chance. He went ape shit. You can tell him if you talk to him first. Total open kimono."

"I gotta go. Here comes Enrique," said Dom.

"Grab your file on the Nici trade and follow me," ordered Enrique. Dom started to say something, but Enrique had already stormed down the hall. Dom grabbed his file and hustled after him. All of the enclosed offices were occupied, so Enrique asked an operations manager if he could borrow his for a few minutes. The older man took one look at the vein bulging from Enrique's temple and vacated immediately.

"You know about this trade?" asked Enrique.

"I'm the one who told George about Mori's cost, if that's what you mean." Dom explained the snafu with the lawyers and divulged everything else he knew about the trade. Enrique raised his eyebrows when Dom told him that it was Mori's Nassau branch and that they were acting as agent for a private client. From the stamp on the trade ticket he copied "12/6/93 2:23PM," swore Dom to secrecy, and thanked him on the way out. He took the elevator to the telecommunications floor and knocked on the manager's door.

"Hey, Enrique."

"Hey, Tony. Got another trade dispute. Need the tape from George Wilhelm's line, December sixth between 2:00 and 2:30. It's a call to or from Nassau, Bahamas, and I'll want to verify the phone number."

"It'll take about twenty minutes."

"I'll be back in twenty." Enrique returned from the bank's cafeteria with a chicken Parmesan sub and two coffees. He listened to the tape four times while he ate. Other than the accelerated closing, which Dom had told him about, nothing seemed the least bit suspicious. He dialed the number in Nassau that the telecom manager had provided.

"Mr. Blanc's office," answered a woman in the quasi-British singsong of the islands.

"Is this Bank Mori?"

"Yes it is."

"Does Mr. Blanc trade sovereign loans?"

"Mr. Blanc is the branch manager."

"Perfect. May I speak to him please?"

"Who may I say is calling?"

"Enrique Guerrero. I run emerging markets trading at City Trust in New York. I need to speak with Mr. Blanc about a large transaction that your bank did with City Trust."

"Can you hold while I see if Mr. Blanc is available?"

"Sure." Enrique wondered why this Anastasio character had called from the manager's office. Maybe he had George on the speakerphone, showing off to the other Mori traders while he raped a big New York bank. Enrique seethed at the image of a bunch of traders doing end zone dances in Blanc's Nassau office. He decided to play the tape again and listen for other traders.

Morgan's banker friend answered, "Pierre Blanc." Enrique introduced himself and explained the nature of his inquiry.

"I'm sorry, Mr. Guerrero. I can confirm the sale to you of $25 million Nicaraguan bank debt at 15⅞ on behalf of a private client. For me to say anything else would be a violation of both Swiss and Bahamian bank secrecy laws." Enrique continued to pry for a few minutes to no avail.

"Do us both a favor and look into this transaction," pleaded Enrique. "If you find anything fishy, call me back."

"Fishy, Mr. Guerrero?"

"You know what I mean."

"Hold on and my secretary will take your number. Good-bye, Mr. Guerrero." Enrique had expected neither more nor less. He had done all he could on his own. Taking the investigation further with security would effectively require him to accuse his most profitable trader of malfeasance. Gold and Peters would have to be informed. But how did George get screwed so hard? It still seemed strange. He listened to the tape again and detected no stifled laughter or other background noise. He thanked Tony and returned to the trading desk. After checking the markets and returning a few phone calls, he pulled George into Pablo's still vacant office.

"So what's that you were saying about docking your bonus for this ass fucking?" Enrique's hawk-eyed stare bore in on George.

"Ah, uh . . . what I'm saying is that the markup was $969,000. If you were going to pay me $2 million on revenues of, as of right now, $23 million, pay me $1,000,031 instead."

"Last month you were practically threatening to quit and jump to Citibank if I didn't pay you 10 percent of your P&L. Now you're giving a million back?"

"Look, boss, I recognize the magnitude of my mistake both in economic terms and in the embarrassment it's causing you . . . us

. . . the bank. I'm willing to take the pain in my bonus if you're willing to agree that it won't affect my status here or compensation going forward. Clean the slate."

"You won't feel undercompensated, start taking headhunter calls in February?"

"If the baseline number is low, I'll have a beef, but if the baseline is fair I'm asking you to whack it by $969,000."

"No tears."

"No tears."

Enrique stared at George intently. This was out of keeping with any trader he had ever met. Then again, George seemed more honest than most. "Is there anything else I need to know about this trade?"

"What do you mean?" George somehow managed to stay under control.

"Any aspect that we haven't discussed?"

"My rationale for buying Nici is the same, and I still think that we will make it profitable by recycling the spec money out of Peru and Eci when those Brady exchanges are completed. Dom took you through the counterparty and legal stuff around the closing."

Enrique leaned back in Pablo's customized, padded leather desk chair. Thanks to a bull market, 1993 was shaping up to be the most profitable year in the history of EM trading on Wall Street. Bonus expectations were running wild, and the headhunters were crawling all over his guys. There was no way that Gold was going to cut an EM bonus pool big enough to make everyone happy, and the competitors would be poaching with a vengeance. Enrique figured that having an extra $969,000 in the bonus pool to spread around the other traders, salespeople, and research analysts would go a long way toward keeping his team intact in 1994. Besides, if he found out the Nici deal was rotten he would fire George and redistribute the entire $2 million. He stood up and approached his star trader.

"OK, George, you got a deal. No tears, right?"

"No tears. Clean slate, right."

"Clean slate." They shook hands and returned to the trading desk.

George was elated. He rationalized that by giving the money back he was no longer a thief. He feared that Enrique had started an investigation of the trade, but his conscience was clean. Popping aspirin and Tylenol against the pain in his hand, he traded enthusiastically for the rest of the day. He drew energy from his anger at Morgan. After work he took two Percocets and walked uptown a few blocks to a pay phone.

"Don't go away, Morgan, I'm coming to see you," barked George.

"I've got company."

"Get rid of them. I'm on my way." George slammed down the receiver and stepped off the curb to hail a cab. When he stepped into Morgan's apartment he saw Kevin and Frank seated on the couch behind the glass table. A mirror heaped with cocaine and several Heineken bottles sat on the table.

"Hey, George, you're just in time for the first board meetin' of the Manhattan Loan Trading Company. Grab a beer, have a seat. How's the pinkie?" Kevin grinned. George just looked at him. "We're just plannin' our next score. Sit down." George took a seat. Morgan handed him a Heineken. Frank bent down and loudly snorted a huge line of coke off the mirror. Then he leaned back with his mouth wide open and his eyes watering.

Kevin resumed. "Morgan here is tellin' us that our partner in Nassau has got a case o' cold feet."

"Your boss called him today and grilled him on the Nici trade," said Morgan to George. George's eyes widened.

"You didn't know that?" asked Kevin.

"No, this is the first I've heard," replied George nervously. "But if he is investigating the Nici trade, we definitely need to lay low for awhile before we do anything else." George wondered if Enrique had called the Bahamas before or after he had promised to whack his bonus.

"Fuck layin' low," snarled Frank.

"Yeah, fuck that," agreed Kevin. "What we do, we go down to Nassau, have another board meetin', this time including Pierre. We make him understand the plan."

"Are you serious?" squealed George. Morgan grabbed George's shoulder hard to silence him.

"Great idea, Kevin. But it shouldn't be a theoretical meeting."

"Whaddaya mean?"

"I mean that George and I need to tee up a specific deal. Pierre doesn't want to play his part, then we go down to persuade him." Morgan continued to dig his fingers into George's shoulder.

"I see whatchya mean," agreed Kevin.

When Kevin leaned down to snort a line, Morgan gave George a look that said "Trust me on this."

"What shitty spic country we gonna trade next?" asked Kevin.

"That's what George and I are working on."

"How 'bout Puerto Rico? That's a shitty one," offered Frank.

"Puerto Rico is a U.S. territory," stated George.

"I knew that," crowed Kevin. "That's how come there so many PRs in New York. If it was a separate country we wouldn't have to let 'em in."

Frank was tapping out a salty-looking substance onto the mirror from a vial.

"What's that?" asked Morgan.

"Powdered meth. Like crystal, but there's no glass pipes. Ya want some?" Frank asked.

"Sure." Morgan, Frank, and Kevin each snorted the amphetamine.

"I'm goin' t' Daisy's, get some pussy. You guys comin'?" announced Frank.

"George and I will stay here, work on the next trade," answered Morgan.

"Good. You do that," said Kevin as he followed Frank out the door.

As soon as the door closed George screamed at Morgan, "You son of a bitch. You bought the Nici at 12."

"Thirteen and a quarter," replied Morgan coolly.

"Don't lie to me. I've got hard evidence. Corroborating evidence. You owe me $156,000."

"More than that," Morgan said, and moved behind his desk. "I actually bought it at 10." George lost it and charged at the desk, fists clenched. He stopped suddenly when he saw the pistol that Morgan was pointing at his head—a 9-millimeter Glock semiautomatic. George was acutely aware that Morgan had a head full of cocaine and methamphetamine.

"Your thug pals stole every cent I made, so it's irrelevant," said Morgan.

"That's your fault. I told you a dozen times we should separate, but like an idiot, you had to grab me in the cab line. They followed you from there."

"Sit down!" ordered Morgan. He motioned toward a chair with the Glock, and George sat down. "None of that is important anymore. Shut up and listen. What I did tonight was brilliant. You should kiss my ass. I got the thugs to agree to come to Nassau. I made Kevin think that it was his idea, so he won't even be suspicious."

"So?"

"The streets of New York are their turf. I got them to play an away game. And they have to fly, so they can't bring their guns."

"They're connected. They can get guns in Nassau."

"Maybe, maybe not. In any case, we take them down in Nassau."

"What's take them down? I told you I'm not into murder."

"No murder. I know cops down there. Your boy Frank has a weakness for meth. We set them up to get busted for possession."

"I notice you like the meth too," cracked George.

"You read Sun Tzu?"

"*The Art of War*?"

"Keep your friends close and your enemies closer. By the time we get to Nassau, Frank and I will be best friends. If you had half a brain you'd get with that program. They trust us a little bit and they'll be pulling hard time in a Bahamian prison. We'll be home free."

"How much hard time?"

"Possession of a controlled substance for sale? Ten years without parole down there."

"Doesn't seem long enough."

Morgan just glared at him. His look was icy with contempt.

"Can I go now?" asked George angrily. Morgan waved the Glock toward the door and George bolted. He stomped back to Club 16B in a rage. He took two more Percocets so his hand wouldn't stab him at every step, then put on his sweats. Out of habit he grabbed two rolls of nickels, then put one back on his desk. There was no way he was going to hit anyone with his left.

18

George stepped out of the cab on East 46th between 1st and 2nd and walked into Sparks Steak House. The tables were packed. It was just after 10:00 P.M. and the din of Christmas cheer was becoming a drunken racket. George had heard the Knicks game end on the cab's radio just as he pulled up, so he knew that it would be a good twenty minutes before José the Worm and his client made their way across town. As George approached the bar to see if Pablo had arrived yet, he looked over a young woman's bare shoulder and caught the eye of Miguel Ergueta, her dining partner. Ergueta ran Latin American investment banking at City Trust. He was in his midforties, moderately overweight with silver, wavy hair. He wore a black Armani suit and a bright yellow Hermes tie secured by a gold pin. Miguel nodded to beckon George to his table.

Miguel shook George's hand without rising. "This is Tiffany. Tiffany, meet George." The pale, comely woman in her early twenties offered George a hand gloved in delicate, black silk lace up to her elbow. She wore a black bra of matching lace that was visible beneath her sheer, black dress and smoked a cigarette in a long silver holder. Her chocolate eyes appeared glazed over. Picturing the photos of Miguel's wife and four children that were displayed in his office, George felt uncomfortable.

"Who are you here with?" Miguel asked in his boisterous, gravelly voice.

"I'm supposed to meet Pablo, José from sales, and Bruce Fitzgerald. They're not here yet."

"Fitzgerald from Malibu Capital Advisors?"

"The man himself."

"Have a drink with us while you wait," offered Miguel with a smile. Unable to come up with a viable excuse, George sat down and ordered a Johnnie Walker Black and water.

"What happened to your hand?" asked Tiffany.

"I caught a six-foot barricuda in Florida on Sunday. But when I tried to unhook the damn thing, it bit the top of my pinkie off." George was telling this lie to everyone. Miguel and Tiffany extended their sympathies.

"Sparks is my favorite restaurant," proclaimed Miguel.

"I prefer La Grenouille," said Tiffany.

"Fitzgerald brings us here for the wine," said George.

"It's got the finest wine list in the world," declared Miguel. "But I come here for the steaks. At those fine French places you've got to search under the garnish for your entrée. Tiffany and I worked up a helluva appetite back at my apartment." He grinned. Tiffany smiled, as if to say, "Get a load of this old guy."

George squirmed in his chair. Miguel reveled in the young trader's obvious discomfort, and Tiffany also appeared amused. "George, what are the four necessities of life for a man?" asked Miguel, suddenly assuming a philosophical demeanor. George shrugged. Miguel continued, "Food, shelter, pussy . . . ," Miguel leaned forward and locked on George's eyes dramatically, ". . . and strange pussy." Miguel leaned back and chuckled. George feigned laughter. Smiling, Tiffany finished her glass of champagne and crushed her cigarette.

"I need to powder my nose," she announced. When she cleared

her throat, Miguel handed her a vial of coke under the table. As she strutted to the ladies' room George stared through her translucent dress at her perfect ass, bare but for a nearly invisible black thong. Many heads turned, subtly and otherwise.

Miguel read George's mind. "Escort service," he explained. "Last time I got caught planking one of our associates, I had to take a four-hour sexual harassment course from the snottiest lesbian you've ever seen. Next time I'm fired." Miguel drank his martini. "You know, I was here the night Gotti's guys shot Paul Castellano out front."

"That must have been scary," said George, happy to change the subject.

"Funny thing was, business really picked up after that. My friend owns a restaurant around the corner. He told the newspapers that if he'd known it was going to be so good for business he would have dragged the body in front of his place. Famous quote."

A dignified-looking waiter in black tie served oysters on the half shell to Miguel and a lump crabmeat cocktail to Tiffany's place. She returned to the table at the same time Pablo arrived. When Miguel introduced Tiffany, Pablo did not attempt to hide his disgust. George was relieved that the small table against the wall would not accommodate a fourth chair.

At the bar, Pablo moaned, "Why do we have to eat so late?"

"Fitzgerald comes to town, he requires a Knicks game. And it's only 7:15 Pacific time."

"You're a big sports fan. Why didn't you go?"

"Fitzgerald requires court side. At $1200 a seat, Enrique's not paying for more than two."

"So why can't José also wine and dine the guy himself?"

"Next to Ralph, Bruce is the most profitable client in the EM market. Every bank on Wall Street is all over this guy. José's smart enough to know that he can't compete on his own. But if he can get Bruce to bond with trading and research . . ."

"I know, I know. So where's Enrique?"

"He took Ralph to the game." They looked over to see José and Bruce stumble into the restaurant. "Look at this. Must be the cocktail service at courtside," said George.

At the table they ordered a round of drinks. Bruce ordered a double, eighteen-year-old Macallan, straight up. The man was forty-five years old going on sixty, with receding gray hair and wrinkles that had been etched into his pink face by a permanent scowl. At six three and a sloppy two hundred seventy pounds, he looked like a tailored shower curtain in his gray Brooks Brothers suit. His starched white shirt stretched across acres of flabby chest, the sea of fabric broken only by a thin, red Pierre Cardin tie.

"So how was the game?" asked George.

"The Knicks suck," spat Bruce. Cobwebs of spittle stuck in the corners of his mouth. "Ewing was 4 for 20. Hakeem destroyed him. He put up 37 with 13 rebounds."

"You've got to give the Rockets some credit. They just tied an NBA record. Fifteen straight victories to start a season really says something," countered José.

"I tell you the Knicks suck," rebuked Bruce. "Tell your boy Ewing to lay off the pregame ganja."

Bruce grabbed the wine list from José and waved the waiter over. "We'll have a bottle of the '61 Château Lafite Rothschild." José cringed. He knew it was a $500 bottle of wine. Bruce was notorious.

"I agree that '61 was a great year for Bordeaux. How about a '61 Château Malescot?" offered José. It cost $75.

Bruce scowled at José. "When KQB Bank brings me here and I order wine, their response is, 'Make it a magnum.'"

"We'll take one '61 Lafite and one '61 Malescot," ordered José in an attempt to head Bruce off from ordering a second $500 bottle. George and Pablo just watched. The salesman always signed the check.

"So Pablo, what's your view on the market?" asked Bruce. Pablo straightened his tie and cleared his throat. Showtime.

"Mexico is the engine pulling this rally. I spoke to David Beers at S&P yesterday, and he is very enthusiastic about the House's passage of NAFTA. My guess is that S&P upgrades Mexico to investment grade in the first quarter of next year. Moody's will wait for the elections in August before doing anything, but I think everyone is pleased with Salinas's nomination of Colosio. I know Colosio from—"

"What about near-term market drivers?" Bruce interrupted.

"The Venezuelan election is clearly the most important near-term event. Given the recent blackouts, bombings, and rumors of a coup, the market is on edge."

"No shit, Sherlock," slurred Bruce.

"My view is that an election which is relatively peaceful and results in a consensus that the winner is legitimate will be a positive."

"Tell me something that I don't know, like who's going to win?" demanded Bruce.

"I think that Caldera will win."

"He's a washed-up populist. How can that be good for the market?"

"I think corruption is the primary issue and Caldera is honest. As you know, his predecessor, Perez, lived openly with his mistress and resigned in a corruption scandal. Caldera is of strong moral fiber. He attends mass every Sunday. He's been married to his wife Alicia for fifty years, has six children, ten grandchildren—"

"I don't give a rat's ass about moral fiber. Inflation is 45 percent in Venie. Populist policies will drive that higher."

"He has a reputation as a populist and a statist, but I view him as a pragmatist. He will not backtrack on economic reform and privatization. I met with him in Caracas last month."

"He's a seventy-seven-year-old dinosaur," said Bruce dismissively as he turned his attention to the waiter. "I'll have the combination baked clams and shrimp scampi appetizer and the prime sirloin, rare. Bring some hash browns, asparagus, creamed spinach, and mushroom caps for the table." George and José also ordered appetizers and steaks, while Pablo ordered only a salad. He had eaten dinner three hours earlier with his wife and three teenage children. José made sure that the City Trust employees drank the Malescot, leaving the entire bottle of Lafite for Bruce. During dinner they discussed the recent coup in Nigeria where Sani Abacha, the army general, had ousted interim president Ernest Shonekan. Malibu Capital owned $25 million Nigerian bank debt. Bruce was optimistic that an iron fist would quell the constant turmoil that had racked the country since General Babangida had voided the June elections.

"Military dictatorship is exactly what Nigeria needs right now. Democracy just doesn't work in some countries," pronounced Bruce. When the waiter cleared the entrées, Bruce ordered the 1934 Justino's Boal Madeira to drink with dessert and cigars. Knowing it was coming, José was actually relieved that his ploy with the Malescot had kept Bruce to one bottle of the Lafite.

"What's your view on Nicaragua?" George asked Bruce.

"I always try to invest in countries where there's a civil war going on." Bruce's reply was drenched in alcohol and sarcasm. "I heard you bought paper in the midteens. I thought that you were smarter than that."

George took a deep breath to gather himself. He couldn't believe that José had discovered the trade and posted Bruce. He forced himself not to glare at the worm.

"I don't think the buyer is a moron," replied George, the buyer. "I think that the Clinton administration is going to—"

Bruce saw Miguel and Tiffany making their way toward the door. He waved off George like a king waving off an annoying servant and called Miguel to the table. He did not stand when Miguel shook his hand and introduced Tiffany.

"Señor Ergueta, what is happening with that shitty toll road securitization that you underwrote? My analyst says that it may not pay the second coupon?" Bruce slurred gruffly.

"Obviously, everyone is disappointed with the level of traffic. They have recently lowered the tolls to increase the traffic."

"What kind of due diligence did you do that the second coupon could be in jeopardy?" Bruce was yelling at Miguel but staring at Tiffany.

"You read the same consultant's report that I did, Mr. Fitzgerald."

"If these bonds default, you'll be explaining your due diligence in court!" threatened Bruce. Miguel nodded and slid his hands into his pockets in a gesture intended to end the conversation.

"I want one of those," said Bruce as he leered at Tiffany.

"Pardon me?" replied Miguel.

"A woman." Bruce looked at José. Pablo leapt to his feet.

"I have to go. I'm on the early flight to São Paulo," blurted Pablo. Bruce ignored him completely.

"I have to go with Pablo," said George. Bruce didn't even hear him. They bolted without shaking hands. Miguel leaned over and whispered in Bruce's ear in a tone calculated to calm him.

"You want a blonde? Redhead? Latino?"

"Black," cried Bruce. "Black with a round, bubble black ass, but not fat. And young." Every head at the three nearest tables turned. Miguel cringed. José slid down his chair, covering his face. Tiffany started giggling.

"You want me to make a phone call?" she asked. Miguel nodded. She knocked on his wrist and he discreetly handed her the vial of coke. Dozens of eyes watched her swung her hips as if the path to the ladies' room and the phone bank were a fashion-show runway.

In the cab uptown, Pablo vented furiously. "This man is a lowlife. His boorish behavior is absolutely unacceptable. I can't take it anymore."

"Look, José is stuck with him, but you can avoid him. Enrique's a stand-up guy. Level with him. Arrange to be out of town when Bruce comes to New York," said George.

"Enrique? How can Enrique permit this type of entertainment?"

"He'll hold his nose and sign the expense report. It's legal entertainment and it's good business. We'll recoup the 4 grand in one trade. The hooker he'll never find out about. That will come out of José's pocket. Maybe Miguel will split it."

"He'll find out if I tell him," fumed Pablo.

"You think Enrique would appreciate that? You think he wants to know?"

Pablo shook his head in disgust. "Enrique's not the problem, Bruce is. If I have to move to another bank, who's the first portfolio manager they would call to check me out?"

"Ralph."

"And the second?"

"Bruce. For sure."

"Precisely. If I duck him he'll blackball me at every bank on Wall Street."

"Maybe he'll get fired?"

"Maybe he won't. I'll promise you one thing, the minute I sign my youngest daughter's last tuition check I'm going back to teaching full time. I teach a class at Columbia now and they'd be delighted to give me a chair. So would Princeton, Georgetown, and Stanford." Pablo was ranting. The taxi dropped him at 72nd and Third and headed across to York to drop George. He watched the midnight *SportsCenter* long enough to see the highlights of Olajuwon dunking on Ewing. When they went to slow motion, he swore he could see Bruce and the Worm at courtside.

19

Frank snatched his bacon cheeseburger from the waitress and had half of it in his mouth before she could even get Kevin's off the tray. They were in a booth next to the pool tables at their favorite Flatbush tavern.

"Frank, I'm worried about this guy Morgan."

"Wha'?" Frank asked, digging into his cheese fries.

"Listen to me. Don't you think it's weird you beat the shit outta the guy, rip him off 600 large, and he wants to be your buddy?" Ravenous after two hours of weight lifting and several bong hits, Frank just shoveled the remains of the burger into his mouth. Kevin continued. "Don't you think maybe he's trying to get us to trust him, get us to drop our guard? Maybe the trip to the Bahamas is a setup. We go there, we get whacked."

Frank chugged a Bud, belched loudly, and stared squarely at Kevin. "No," he said flatly.

"No, what? No, it's normal to suck up to a guy who busts your face and robs you? No, what?"

"No, da guy's not gonna try t' whack us."

"Why not? What would you do?"

"I'd whack us. But I'm not an Ivy League banker pussy."

"How do you know this guy's a pussy? Or George? George dummied up, let you cut his finger off."

"Pussy."

"And Morgan did time."

"Danbury ain't fuckin' time. They play tennis, have tea parties. They're both Ivy League pussies."

"Bet your life on it?"

"Name one Ivy Leaguer's not a pussy." Frank devoured the rest of his fries while Kevin considered his response.

"Calvin Hill, Dallas Cowboys."

"Nigger. Don't count." Frank signaled to the waitress for another round of burgers and beers. "Name a white boy."

"Ed Marinaro."

"Perfect pussy example. Big star in Ivy pussy football. Sucked in da NFL, for da Vikings, Jets."

"Doug Swift. Dolphin No-Name Defense."

"Pussy. Never took on a block, always went aroun'."

"Gary Fencik, Bears' Super Bowl defense."

"You ever seen anyt'ing more pussy than da Super Bowl pussy Shuffle? Whadda 'bout boxing? WWF? Weight liftin'? You can't name one Ivy League college boy's not a pussy."

"I still think somethin's up. Why else would Morgan be so friendly? It's crazy otherwise."

"Pussy's scared. He sucks up so I don't kick his ass again." Frank accepted another Bud from the waitress. "Makes you happy, we'll carry down there."

"How we gonna bring guns into the Bahamas? We'd have to get 'em down there," said Kevin.

"We'll call Anthony." Frank chugged half his beer. "He's connected everywhere. I'm sure he's gotta guy dere can take care o' us."

"You nuts, or what? What job in the Bahamas you gonna tell Anthony we need guns for? You got any idea what he'll do to us if he finds out we didn't cut him into the dough we took from these bankers? We're dead. We can't go to Anthony for help with this scam. Too late for that."

"Shit." Frank belched.

"We don't know nobody down there, gotta keep it secret from Anthony here. We gonna go to a strange country, get guns from a stranger? You kiddin' me?"

"You're da brains, Butch. You'll t'ink o' somethin'." Frank bit into his second bacon cheeseburger. "What kinda Porsche should I get? Carrera or 911?" he asked through a full mouth.

"How the fuck many times do I hafta tell ya? You buy somethin' big, you gotta explain to Anthony where you got the dough. Why he didn't get a taste."

"I'll tell 'im I stole da car."

"Anthony knows that even you aren't dumb enough to drive a brand-new, stolen Porsche around the city."

"Whaddaya mean, *even* I ain't dumb enough?"

"Don't mean nothin'. Look, just spend the money gradual. Live large, but not conspicuous."

"Fuck dat. Fuck Anthony."

"Yeah, fuck Anthony. Right. You wanna die, that's your decision, but Anthony finds out about the 600 large it's both our asses. We'll be upstairs at Daisy's again, but this time *we'll* be losin' the fingers. We're in this together. Don't fuck me."

"Fuck Anthony *and* fuck you. '*Even* I ain't dumb enough.' Fuck you."

"Don't start this shit." Kevin drank his beer as he considered how to deflect Frank. "I'll bet Magnum Joey's connected in the Bahamas. Guy's runnin' drugs into Miami, ya know."

"You shittin' me? You t'ink I'm dumb?" Frank pointed his thumb at his muscle-bound chest. "You wanna get whacked by Anthony, do business wit' Magnum Joey. You fuckin' nuts?"

"Not directly. I gotta guy can set it up with Joey, leave our names out of it. We use aliases in the Bahamas."

"You trust dis guy t' keep our names outta it?"

"Fitsie? Yeah, I trust him. He's married to my cousin." Kevin finished his beer. "Look, I'll take care o' the guns. What you gotta do is get a new passport."

"Yeah?"

"I gotta guy does the IRA. IRA soldiers fly Ireland to New York, buy guns and explosives, they use this guy's documents. I'll get a set for you."

"No shit?"

"No shit, but he's expensive. Ten large for the passport. Another 3 for a matching driver's license."

"What's your cut?"

"Knock it off, Frank. I'd introduce you, but this guy won't meet nobody. I gotta deal through this Irish guy."

"Thirteen large. I can buy half a pound o' coke."

"What you gotta buy is a new identity. You get stopped for a traffic violation today, cop runs your ID, you're back in the cuckoo's nest."

"Cop runs my ID t'day, I shoot 'im between da eyes."

"Whatever," said Kevin. " Just go to the Jap camera store across the street, get some pictures taken. And don't pose like a wise guy."

"You t'ink I don' know how I'm s'posed t' look on a passport? You keep callin' me stupid, I'm gonna tear off your head, shit down your fuckin' neck."

Kevin stood up and dropped a twenty on the table. "Sorry, Frank. We both know that if it wasn't for a couple of unlucky juvenile busts, you'd be a rocket scientist at NASA."

Frank lunged at Kevin, who darted outside. After two more beers Frank grabbed his gym bag and crossed the street to buy the photos. Despite his earlier protest, he grinned his crooked wiseguy grin for the photographer. Afterward he stopped at a porn shop to pick up a video for an afternoon jerk, to be followed by a nap. The sallow, stubble-faced old manager, who ordered rape films from Honk Kong specifically for Frank, pulled one from behind a box on the shelf. It was as close as he dared get to the snuff flicks that Frank asked him for. Frank shoved the video in his bag, then strode down Flatbush Avenue and turned into his street.

He was a block from his apartment, enjoying the buzz from the beer and pot, when he spotted the dark blue Plymouth. He immediately started backpedaling, and the car's engine started. Frank sprinted between two brick tenements, cut left down an alley, and ducked behind two garbage cans. Crouching, he drew his Browning from his gym bag and crossed himself. Two uniformed cops bolted from the Plymouth and sprinted past with their guns drawn. When they were out of sight, Frank stuffed his Jets jacket into his bag and ran down the intersecting alley. Trying to blend in with the other pedestrians, he crossed the avenue at the light, hurried down the side street, and again ducked between buildings and hid behind a Dumpster. After five minutes he watched as a heavy, middle-aged woman walked by carrying two bags of groceries. Frank had to get off the street, and the woman's burden suggested that she lived nearby. He followed her for a block, hanging back until she produced her keys. Then he rushed her at the door to her building and shoved his Browning in her ribs.

"We're goin' inside. Make a sound and I'll fuckin' shoot ya dead." Inside her apartment, the woman began crying and pleading in Spanish. Frank didn't understand a word.

"Shut da fuck up." When the woman continued to cry, Frank raised his gun to strike her. She put her hands up and turned her head away. Frank put one hand under her chin and gently turned it back toward him. In his other hand, he held the gun barrel to his lips.

"Shhh. Jus' be quiet. I don' wanna hurtcha."

She looked at him like she understood, but said nothing.

Frank started muttering. "I was gonna bust your melon, but ya look jus' like Sister Ivette."

The woman crossed herself. She didn't take her eyes off the gun.

"Sit down." Frank pointed the gun toward a red vinyl couch as he moved to the window. He parted the thin curtains an inch and studied the street for a minute before turning back to the traumatized woman.

"Anybody else here?"

The woman said nothing. "Ya speak English?" Frank roared.

She cringed. "My husband, he works. He come home six o'clock."

"Ya got any beer?"

"Sí." The woman rushed to the kitchen and produced a can of Old Milwaukee and a tall glass. Frank grabbed the can before she could pour.

"Have one yourself, Señora." He wanted to calm the woman down in case the cops came to the door. If they came he would shoot them in the face, as they'd probably be wearing bulletproof vests. After a half hour and three beers Frank decided that if a neighbor had called the cops, they would have been there by now. With a grunt, he plopped on the couch next to the woman. There were framed photos crowded next to the lamp on the side table. One of them was of a man about Frank's age. His hair was shaved close, and he had a pencil-thin mustache that curled down at the corners of his mouth.

"Who's dis?" Frank asked. "Your son?"

"Sí. Like you, no? But no grande." She hunched and flexed to indicate Frank's bulk. "He have trouble with la policía, run away." Nodding slightly, Frank studied her face.

"No kiddin'? What kinda trouble?"

"La policía say he steal car. I no think so."

"I'm sure you're right. Cops're always wrong. I ain't done half da stuff they said I done. He in jail?"

"No jail. He go away."

"Back t' Puerto Rico?"

"No Puerto Rico. Somos Dominicanos."

"No kiddin'? Sister Ivette was Dominican. Saint Christopher's Orphanage on Jamaica. Ya know her?" The woman shook her head. "Wha's your name?"

"Maria."

"It's unbelievable—ya look jus' like Sister Ivette. She pro'ly saved my life. Found out my foster father was beatin' da, uh, stuff outta me, brought me back t' Saint Christopher's." Frank got another beer from the refrigerator and continued. "I useta wet da bed, ya know, when I was a kid. Da other nuns whipped my butt. Sister Ivette, she'd bring me clean sheets, pray wit' me I could learn t' stop wettin' da bed." Frank went to the window to hide his emotions from Maria.

"You see her?"

"I broke outta da reformatory and went t' see her. She said da cops had been dere askin' about me. I see her again, I put her inna bad spot. She could get in trouble she don't call da cops. I don't wanna put her inna bad spot, ya know?" Frank looked out the window. The somber December dusk was just settling in.

"Why you go to jail?"

"Playgroun' fight."

"Jail for a playground fight?"

"I was kneelin' on dis kid's shoulders, poundin' his mug. When da principal pulled me off, he was almos' dead. Woke up t'ree days later."

"Why you beat this boy so much?"

"He stole da Twinkies from my lunch."

"Twinkies? You beat this boy for Twinkies?"

"Wasn't about da Twinkies. It was about who was da toughest kid." Maria regarded Frank quizzically. He turned back to the window. "See, I was always short. Still am, right? So I useta get beat up all da time. Started goin' t' da Y when I was ten, liftin' weights two, t'ree hours a day. I'm twelve I can bench 225." Frank simulated weight lifting. "I'm da toughest kid in da class. Everybody knows it 'cept Joey, da class bully. He found out da hard way. I been locked up or on da run ever since."

Maria crossed herself. Then she got up and brought Frank a fresh beer from the refrigerator. "What you do now?"

"I leave at dark. Don' worry, you won't see me no more. Could ya do me one favor?"

"OK."

"Ya see Sister Ivette, don' tell her ya seen me wit' a gun. OK?"

After dark, Frank took the subway into Manhattan. All the way in he congratulated himself for keeping his loot in his gym bag rather than his apartment, which had probably been searched. He wondered how many open warrants the cops had on him, and how they had traced him to his digs. He found Anthony at Daisy's. He was fifty, six foot two, and powerfully built under his double-breasted Armani suit. His handsome, Roman face was cleanly shaven and his silver hair was meticulously groomed. Anthony and Frank sat down in the office where Kevin had counted George's payoff.

"You did a nice job for TD and me with that Wall Street kid. Thanks," offered Anthony.

"No pro'lem. It was fun." Frank grinned crookedly.

"How you doin'? You look a little fucked up."

"I'm good. I just had a tough day, ya know. I need t' move outta my apartment."

"You need a place to stay?"

"Yeah. Some place outta da way, ya know?"

"No problem. Hang around and have a drink. I'll get you the address."

"Thanks, boss. I 'preciate it. Anyt'ing I can do for ya?"

"Actually, I'm glad you asked. I got a troublemaker, needs some attention. You interested?"

"O' course."

"See Al tomorrow, get the particulars."

"You got it, boss." They shook hands and Frank headed out to find a seat by the main stage. Feeling the weight of his gym bag, he laughed to himself. At least he had the cash for a lap dance or two, he thought. Or maybe fifteen thousand lap dances.

20

At 7:30 A.M. on the Tuesday of Frank's escape from the police, George cornered José on the fire stairs adjacent to the trading floor. Fearing that George was going to punch him, José cowered against the cinder-block wall.

"Look, George, when I posted Bruce that we bought Nici in the midteens, that was before I got posted on Chase's sale at 12. You have to believe that. It's my job to build you up with these guys, not make you look like an ass."

"How did you find out about my buy?" George asked.

"The ticket was sitting in the bin when you stepped off the desk."

"You're a snake."

"Hey, the more I know, the more effective I can be," said José.

"Who else did you post, besides Bruce? And don't lie to me."

"Only the guys who care about the real spec stuff. Bruce, Ralph, and Consuelo. Look, these are busy people. I don't think they spend a lot of time trying to figure out whether or not George Wilhelm got out-traded."

George shoved his red face within an inch of José's and pounded his scrawny chest. "From now on, you never post a trade in my sectors unless I tell you, understand?"

"Understood." José slid along the wall and out the fire door to the trading floor.

George took a couple of deep breaths. If Bruce had been posted on Chase's sale at 12, he would have given George more abuse at dinner. But what about Ralph and Consuelo; what were the odds of them putting the trade together and the odds of Enrique finding out? George felt sick just thinking about it.

Back on the trading desk, George answered his unrecorded line. "It's me. Morgan."

"Where are you calling from?"

"Phone booth. Listen, we're on for Thursday. Book the 9:00 A.M. flight to Nassau. I did Lawrence a big favor so he's letting us hang out on his boat. He won't be around."

"Saturday is Christmas."

"Kevin and Frank have already booked. If you don't show, you're dealing with them."

"How the hell could you go to them first?" snapped George.

"Cut the Emily Post crap and get some testosterone," replied Morgan. "I'll see you at LaGuardia at 8:00 on Thursday."

Considering that he had no sane alternative, George asked Enrique for the day off, booked the flight, and made a date with Sue for Wednesday night.

On Wednesday morning at 7:00 A.M., Enrique hauled George into Pablo's empty office.

"I go to the Rangers game with Ralph last night and the whole time he's goofing on me for getting raped on 25 million Nici! It was the worst night of my life." Standing in the middle of the office, Enrique waved his arms furiously. He slammed his fist down on the desk. "How the fuck did Ralph find out about it?"

"I'm really sorry about this," choked George feebly.

"Answer me!"

"Chase posted the Street on their sale, and José posted Ralph, Bruce, and Consuelo on our, I mean my, buy."

"Why did José post the trade?"

"Because he's an asshole. You should fire him."

Enrique cracked his knuckles. It was shockingly loud. "I'll have it out with him, but he's too valuable to fire. I don't know how he does it, but he's got better relationships with the hedgies than anyone on the Street."

"He does it by giving them proprietary information. And you don't even want to know the other stuff he does," offered George, but Enrique had already stormed out of the office to look for José. George prayed that the Nicaragua trade would somehow go away. He tried to avoid eye contact with Enrique as they traded, side by side, for the rest of the day.

Neither Sue nor George could get off work before six-thirty on Wednesday, so they canceled their reservation at Gallagher's. Sue was conspicuously overdressed in her striking Yves Saint Laurent dress as she drank Heineken from the bottle in the Times Square pizzeria.

"I missed you, George."

"I missed you too, Sue. I'm really glad you could see me before I head south again."

"Me too. So how come I have to go to Cincinnati on business and you get to go to Miami?" she asked.

"A lot of the money that goes into emerging markets debt was moved offshore by wealthy Latinos. It's managed by private banks in Switzerland, the Bahamas, Bermuda, et cetera. A lot of these banks have branches in Miami." George sucked down his Rolling Rock. "The entrepreneurs borrowed it in the '70s, the heyday, moved it offshore when the local economies collapsed, and now they reinvest in the Bradys and loans at deep discounts through these banks. The round-trip of flight capital. The big commercial banks take the pain."

"Thank you for the economics lesson, Professor IMF. When are you going to take me on one of these boondoggles?"

"Don't worry, darling. It's all business."

"I'm not worried at all. After I finish with you tonight you won't have the strength to even look at a South Beach bimbo."

"Can you order oysters as a topping here?"

As soon as the lights went out at the theater, Sue was stroking the inside of George's thigh. Back at her apartment she was good to her word.

George hustled to the gate ten minutes before departure. Despite his efforts to leave Sue's apartment on time, she had not taken no for an answer that morning. She never did. Disregarding the agent's insistence that they board, Kevin, Frank, and Morgan waited impatiently at the gate. Kevin wore a tourist disguise—a flowered Hawaiian shirt, Bermuda shorts, and straw hat. Frank wore his black Gold's Gym T-shirt, black jeans, sheer black socks, and black alligator loafers. Morgan and George were both prepped out in khakis, polo shirts, and Top-Siders. The gate attendants stared, trying to discern the connection as the unlikely group boarded the plane together.

Kevin had arrived at the gate early and switched seats so he could sit with George and Frank with Morgan. George was trying to read the *Wall Street Journal* when Kevin leaned over and whispered, "So this Colombia trade? It's locked and loaded?"

"Panama," replied George. Having rehearsed carefully with Morgan, he wasn't about to get tripped up.

"That's right, Panama. All set?"

"I'm in touch with a seller and I'm authorized to buy," George lied.

"What price?"

"Seller's at 33. I can probably pay 35 without arousing suspicion."

"So all we need is this guy Pierre to step up, correct?"

"Correct."

"I don't understand why you can't just use another guy?"

George covered his mouth and whispered, "If you know another banker that will clear this type of trade and kickback in cash currency, we'll use him. This is the only guy we know." Kevin shrugged.

"On dis trip my name is Tim," Frank told Morgan between gulps of vodka.

"George and I use aliases in Nassau too. I'm Anastasio and he's Mr. Pink."

"Mr. Pink from *Reservoir Dogs*? Dat's great! As long as he's not Mr. Orange. What an awesome fuckin' movie."

"Movie was bogus," replied Morgan. Frank glared at him as if he'd been personally insulted.

"Whaddaya mean, bogus?"

"The shoot-out at the warehouse. It was bogus."

"Whaddaya mean?"

"OK. Who kills Nice Guy Eddie?"

"Ummm . . ." Frank rubbed his chin. "Mr. White?"

"No. Mr. White was pointing his gun at Joe, Joe was pointing his gun at Mr. Orange, and Eddie was pointing his gun at Mr. White. Nobody had the drop on Nice Guy Eddie. Check it out. Totally bogus." Frank stared at Morgan like a child who had just been told there is no Santa Claus. After a few minutes he chugged the rest of his vodka and held his empty glass up to the flight attendant.

"Why don'tcha have a drink wit' me, Blondie?"

"Sorry, I can't sit down, or drink alcohol."

"Ya can sit on my face."

The woman planted her fists on her shapely hips and said, "Tell it to the police in Nassau."

Kevin heard the commotion brewing behind him. "Shut up, Tim. Sorry, miss. He'll be OK." Kevin switched seats with Morgan so he could monitor Frank for the rest of the flight.

"Why you always gotta act like a degenerate? I can't take you anywhere," said Kevin.

"I'm a degenerate, playin' aroun' wit' a stewardess? Am I da guy fucks his boss's wife?"

"I can't believe you're on this shit again."

"I never fucked another man's wife. That's a fuckin' Commandment! Mortal sin."

"What about all the deadbeats you fucked up? What about the junkie you whacked in Queens?"

"I never fucked wit' anyone didn't have it comin'. An eye for an eye anna toot' for a toot'," said Frank.

"Yeah? What about 'Turn the other cheek'? The word of Christ."

"What about 'Render unto Caesar what is Caesar's'? The word of Christ. Saint Paul was a tax collector for Caesar, ya know."

"You think Saint Paul hoisted guys up, laid hot iron on their dicks?" asked Kevin.

"Caesar was a tough boss, so Saint Paul did what he hadda do. No different 'n me."

"Yeah, right. Saint fuckin' Frank." Kevin shook his head.

To no one's surprise, the Bahamian customs agent selected Frank for a body search. Kevin looked relieved when his partner emerged from the windowless room grinning. When Morgan started to tell the cab driver to take them to the Atlantis, Kevin interrupted and handed up an address on a scrap of paper. The cab drove instead to a coral-colored tavern in a dilapidated section of Freeport.

"Drive a block down this street and wait there," ordered Kevin. Five minutes later, he and Frank strode out of the tavern and returned to the taxi. Frank took his seat beside the driver and Kevin squeezed in the back with George and Morgan. When the driver was refocused on the road, Kevin pulled up his Hawaiian shirt to reveal a snub-nosed .38 in his belt. Grinning over the back of the front seat, Frank hoisted his gym bag and patted it happily. George and Morgan both tried to act nonplussed.

At the Atlantis, George and Morgan walked briskly down the corridors to stay a few steps ahead of the thugs, as if they didn't know them. At Kevin's insistence, Frank stopped at one of the shops and bought a loose-fitting tropical shirt that would conceal his pistol in his belt. Afterward the men hurried past the other stores, through the nearly deserted casino, and across the lawn to Lawrence's yacht. Sean was swilling rum in a deck chair.

"Sean, you remember George. This is Kevin and Tim. Guys, this is Sean, our captain," said Morgan.

"How ya doin'?" said Kevin.

"'Ya doin'," grunted Frank.

"Welcome aboard. You guys want a drink?" greeted Sean.

"I've got to make some phone calls at the hotel. Make yourselves comfortable," announced Morgan. When he returned, the four men were kicking back with their cocktails. Morgan whispered in Sean's ear, causing him to drain his rum glass and saunter off the boat and into the casino.

"OK, here's where we are," Morgan told the other three. "Pierre has left for his weekend place on Harbour Island, which is about four hours away by boat, northeast of here. It's perfect because it's secluded. We'll head over there tomorrow and persuade him to see things our way."

"Why don't we go there now?" asked Kevin.

"Not enough daylight left today. The harbor at Dunmore Town on Harbour Island is a little tricky, so you want to port during the day. Don't say anything to Sean yet—I still have to work this out with him."

"Whadda we do 'til then?" asked Frank.

"I'm going to rest up for tonight. Hey, it's Thursday night in Nassau. The bars'll be swimming with horny divorcées looking for tropical adventure."

"I'll give 'em a tropical fuckin' adventure!" Frank grinned as he grabbed his crotch. Kevin still seemed suspicious. In order to avoid cross-examination, Morgan disappeared into a stateroom. George drank scotch with Kevin and Frank until Sean returned, then he left the boat and went for a walk through the hotel. As he watched the young moms hovering over their kids, he wondered what kind of mother Sue would be. Definitely not something to worry about until he made it back in one piece, he decided.

Returning to the yacht at dusk, George found that the party had moved to the second deck, around the hot tub. Kevin, Frank, and Sean were blotto. Morgan, who seemed sober, was cooking fish on the countertop grill. After a raucous meal, which included a game of fish-head dodge ball, everyone headed across the lawn toward the casino. When Sean fell on the grass, Kevin and Frank picked him up by his armpits, all three cackling with laughter. They stopped at the craps table and bought chips. Morgan gave the cocktail waitress a twenty-five-dollar chip on the sly and instructed her to keep mai tais flowing for Kevin and Frank. After an hour at the five-dollar blackjack table, George started wondering when the party was going to move into Freeport. He pulled Morgan away from the craps.

"Don't we have to go into town? Don't we have stuff to do around the bust?"

"Tomorrow. Like I said, my friend is a cop on Harbour Island. Everything happens tomorrow in Dunmore Town." George studied Morgan's eyes. If he wasn't telling the truth, he was a damn good liar. "Don't worry," Morgan continued. "I've got everything under control." George took Morgan's drink from him and sniffed it. It was straight cranberry juice.

At 2:00 A.M., Frank and Kevin stumbled back to the boat, leaning heavily on each other. Sean had returned earlier and was passed out on the cushioned bench in the cabin. Kevin grabbed the shark rifle off its rack, followed Frank into the master stateroom, and leaned the .30-06 against the teak dresser.

"Keep your piece handy, case the college boys try somethin'," slurred Kevin.

"Ivy League pussies. Fuck 'em." Frank passed out on the bed. Kevin weaved back into the main cabin and sat down at the dining table with Morgan and George. He pulled his .38 and alternated his aim between each man's nose.

"OK, Ivy League banker boys, what's goin' on?" Morgan and George just stared at him. "I know, you guys think you're better than us, me and Frank. You think we don't see you pretend you don't know us around the hotel, casino? You know what? I don't give a shit. But let me tell you something. When it comes to the rough stuff, you guys can't carry our jockstraps. We're fuckin' professionals. Let me tell you what's gonna happen. If this thing tomorrow doesn't go smooth as a baby's ass, Sean over there is gonna take us to a deserted beach, where Frank and me are gonna stake you out in the sand and slit your guts open. 'Cept we're not gonna rip your guts out, we're gonna hold the slits open with sticks and prop your heads up so you can watch the crabs crawl inside, eat you alive. You pass out, we revive you with seawater. Maybe keep your eyes open with toothpicks, like in *Clockwork Orange*. Whaddaya think of that?" Morgan and George continued to stare at him. "So I smell anything fishy tomorrow—anything at all—you fuckin' pussies'll wish you'd never been born. Understand?" Morgan and George nodded. Kevin lurched back into his stateroom, bolted the door behind him, and fell asleep holding his revolver against his sternum. George vomited in the head. When he returned to the cabin, Morgan had retired to his stateroom. George knocked on the door until Morgan opened it a crack.

"What? I'm going to bed." George shouldered the door open

and shoved past Morgan. They stood in the middle of the room, glaring at each other.

"Keep it down. These walls are thin," whispered Morgan as he closed the door.

"What are we doing here? Kevin's so suspicious, we're not going to trap him," George hissed in Morgan's ear. "What's the plan?"

"Just leave it to me, George."

"Not good enough. You heard what the guy's going to do to us if tomorrow doesn't go right. Now what the fuck are we doing?" George sprayed Morgan's ear with saliva as he hissed.

"OK, OK. I obviously understand that these guys are not going to stick their necks out. Here's what's happening. The seas are going to turn rough tomorrow afternoon, so there's no way that we'll be taking the boat back here. My cop buddy's got a hatch key. While we're at Pierre's he plants the drugs in their bags. We make Pierre fly us back to Nassau in his Cessna. My buddy nails them with the drugs and guns at the Dunmore airfield." George stepped back and stared into Morgan's eyes. It sounded too clean and easy.

"Why is this cop doing this?" George leaned forward to whisper.

"Guess."

"Tell me."

"Combination of cash, drugs, and favors. We'll negotiate the details later. Listen, tomorrow's going to be the most important day of your life. Better get some sleep."

Morgan's face gave nothing away. George went back to his stateroom, but his nerves were too frayed for sleep. He wondered why Morgan had only just now told him he had bribed the cop. It was out of character for Morgan not to put George on the hook for his share.

21

At daybreak Morgan shook Sean awake. "C'mon, man, we're going fishing."

"What time is it?" asked Sean, wincing against the pain of his hangover.

"It's time to go fishing. C'mon." Morgan dragged Sean out onto the aft deck. After rubbing his eyes for a time, Sean noted the flags atop the masts of the sailboats.

"Too rough to fish. Must be blowin' thirty-five knots."

"We'll fish the leeward shores. No problem. Do us a favor, grab us some breakfast, juice and bagels should do, and some bait. Couple pounds of frozen mullet for trolling."

"Fuck me," moaned Sean.

"Here, you can keep the change." Morgan handed him a hundred-dollar bill.

"Just a minute." Sean washed four aspirins down with Gatorade. Carrying the half-full bottle, he struggled onto shore and hobbled into the hotel. Morgan immediately flipped on the fans to ventilate the bilge. He pulled a hand-printed note out of his pocket and taped it to a piling on the dock.

Sean,
Got tired of waiting so we decided to troll with the lures. Given your lack of enthusiasm for the trip I didn't think you'd mind.

—Morgan

Morgan raced up to the bridge, checked to make sure the throttles were in neutral, and started the twin diesels. He slid back down the ladder, cast off the mooring lines, scrambled back to the bridge, and began maneuvering the yacht away from her berth.

Sean was selecting bagels at the coffee shop when he looked out the window and saw Lawrence's yacht heading out. Ignoring the splitting pain in his head, he sprinted outside and onto the dock on the starboard side of the narrow exit from the marina. With a loping start he jumped three feet onto the aft deck of the yacht. Morgan did not see Sean until he was beside him on the bridge.

"What the fuck do you think you're doing?"

"Going fishing. You didn't seem like you wanted to go so I figured I'd do you a favor, leave you at the hotel."

"Are you crazy? This is a four-million-dollar yacht! You know what Lawrence would do to me if something happened to it and I'm not on board? You think he lets *anyone* pilot this yacht?"

"Relax, will you? Lawrence told me that I could use the boat. He said nothing about you needing to be on board. And I'm a Power Squadron certified pilot."

"Don't do this again unless I hear directly from Lawrence that it's OK." Sean was still steaming. "Give me the fucking helm."

"No problemo, amigo." Morgan eased down into the cabin and started scrounging around for some breakfast. After twenty minutes the yacht cleared the breakwater and started slamming over six-foot swells. That brought George out of his stateroom.

"Aspirin's in the cabinet above the bar. Gatorade's in the fridge," offered Morgan.

"I'm not that bad. Any coffee?"

"Nope."

"Seas going to be like this all the way to Harbour Island?"

"Yep. Don't mention Harbour Island to Sean yet. He thinks we're going fishing." George threw Morgan a quizzical look over his shoulder as he climbed onto the deck. When he climbed back down to the cabin he heard loud, retching sounds coming from the master stateroom. After a few minutes Kevin stumbled out and steadied himself with both hands on the edge of the dining table. The front of his flowered shirt was covered with vomit. Frank literally crawled through the door and remained on his knees, gagging.

"The cabin is the worse place for you guys. You'll feel much better on deck. Try to stand up and look at the horizon," instructed Morgan from the galley. Kevin staggered up the ladder and onto the deck. Frank gathered himself for a minute, rose slowly, and followed Kevin. Chuckling a bit but still feeling queasy, George opened a can of peaches. Morgan marched up on deck.

Kevin and Frank were draped over the transom, puking in the ocean. Standing behind them, feet apart, Morgan drew a Sig Saur automatic from his belt. He held the barrel inches from the back of Kevin's head and fired once. Morgan immediately turned the gun on Frank, but the muscle man sprang at him before he could shoot. Frank chopped Morgan's gun hand with his left fist as he drove his head up into the taller man's mouth, busting all his front teeth. Morgan flew backward and landed unconscious. Frank pulled a Remington automatic from his belt and straddled Morgan's hips. Although wobbling from seasickness and bleeding heavily from the tooth wounds in his forehead, he wiped the blood from his eyes and found his balance long enough to pump three 9-millimeter slugs into Morgan's chest.

At the sound of the first shot, George had grabbed the .30-06 from the master stateroom. Working the bolt action quickly, he chambered a round and flicked off the safety as he moved to the deck ladder, but he stumbled backward when the engines shifted to neutral. When he recovered his balance, Frank was standing over Morgan's corpse. Sean slid down from the bridge onto the deck and froze in his tracks. Still wiping blood from his eyes, Frank shot at Sean but missed as the yacht rolled in the swells.

Standing at the bottom of the ladder, George fought a panic attack. He could barely breath. He raised the rifle and shot Frank through the chest. The 220-grain bullet exploded his heart and knocked his body over the transom and into the sea. George set the rifle down, climbed up to the deck, and picked up Morgan's pistol. He sat down on the fiberglass bench and held the automatic on his lap. With one eye on Sean he vomited on the deck.

Sean stood trembling, his trousers stained with urine. The yacht had broached and was wallowing dangerously in the big waves.

"Let's discuss this on the bridge," ordered George. Sean scrambled back up to the bridge, followed by George. He put the engines in gear and steered to windward as George surveyed the ocean. With the seas this high there were no other boats in sight—only a cruise ship in the distance. "Go back for Frank's body," commanded George. Glancing at the pistol that George held at his side, Sean nodded and began a wide 180. George scanned the sea silently while he gathered his thoughts.

"OK, number one, I had no idea that Morgan intended to start this. I didn't even know that he was armed. I am not his accomplice." George's tone was authoritative and surprisingly controlled. "Number two, we are going to sink these bodies, and you and I are the only people who are ever going to know what happened out here. Is that clear?"

"Cover it up? Why? Why can't we tell the police?" squealed Sean. "You killed Frank to save my life. That's justifiable homicide in any country."

"I can't tell you my reasons for not going to the police. I would if I could. Your reason is that I saved your life and you owe me. Good enough?"

"Sure, but won't there be an investigation when these guys turn up missing?"

"Good question, but the answer is no. Not in Nassau. Morgan came down here to commit murder. Do you think he told anyone? Lawrence is not going to launch an investigation if he never hears from Morgan again, and I'm pretty sure that their families don't have Thanksgiving together in Connecticut, if you know what I mean." Sean was nodding. "Morgan and I both paid for our plane tickets in cash, so there will be no credit-card records. No trail. Got it?"

"What about Kevin and Tim, Frank, whatever his name is?"

"These guys are . . . were mobsters. They also came down to commit a crime. The important thing is that they didn't tell their people about this caper because they didn't want to share the profits. They don't use credit cards either."

"Are you sure they didn't tell anyone? How do you know?"

"Morgan figured it out because Frank was a stupid drunkard and drug addict. He's also criminally insane."

"Look!" Sean interrupted, pointing at a roiling, red disturbance off the starboard bow. As he steered closer, they saw four large sharks attacking Frank's body. Jaws locked on, they wagged their heads savagely and rolled over and over to twist and tear the muscular flesh from the corpse. Sean approached the macabre scene and stared in silence.

"Jesus. That didn't take long," observed George. Sean nodded. "Listen, if it will make you feel any better, Frank was the lowest of the low. He tortured and murdered people for a living. Now, are you with me or not?"

"I guess so." Sean nodded tentatively.

"Don't give me 'I guess so.' I just saved your life."

"All right. I'm with you. All this never happened."

"Good. Now get upwind so we'll drift to the body. When I get the gaff in him, you'll have to come down and help me lift him on deck."

"For Chrissake, there won't be anything left of him in a few minutes. What are you doing?" protested Sean.

"You think a chewed-up human carcass won't start an investigation? If the slug is still in his chest, it could be traced to the rifle, to this boat. Now where's the gaff?"

"Locker underneath the starboard seat cushions." George slid down the ladder to the aft deck and grabbed the eight-foot aluminum shaft with a three-inch hook at the business end. Leaning over the transom, he was terrified by the primal ferocity of the sharks in their feeding frenzy. He took two deep breaths against his fear, hooked Frank underneath his jaw, and jerked upward until the gaff hook protruded from his mouth. Steadying himself on the rolling deck with his right hand, and holding the gaff handle with his left, he beckoned Sean with his head. The skipper idled the engines and came down the ladder to assist George.

"OK, grab hold. We'll lift on the count of three."

"You want to lift those sharks on deck?" asked Sean.

"They won't let go?" George asked. Sean shook his head.

"Hold this," ordered George. Sean held the gaff while George retrieved the .30-06 from the cabin. Before raising it he scanned the ocean for other boats. Seeing none, he shot the biggest shark in the eye and it released its grip immediately. George operated the bolt action and shot the second largest shark in the eye, but it kept its jaws locked on Frank's thigh. He shot it a second time, this time between the eyes, and it flopped away. He quickly shot the remaining two sharks, flipped the safety on, laid the rifle on the seat cushions, and joined Sean on the gaff. On the count of three both men released their holds on the transom, put all hands on the gaff handle, and heaved with all their strength. The yacht rolled and they slipped and fell backward on the bloody deck. Frank's shredded corpse landed on Sean's feet, followed by a five-foot shark that had clamped onto the body. The shark thrashed wildly on the deck between the two fallen men. George quickly moved across the deck, but Sean was momentarily stuck under Frank's corpse. The shark's razorlike teeth caught his duck pants and tore them apart. Screaming loudly, Sean threw off Frank's body and scurried up the ladder. When the shark bounced against the transom, George dashed for the ladder and joined Sean on the bridge.

"Let's get the fuck away from here. But not back to shore. Not yet," ordered George. Sean put the twin diesels in gear and headed northeast with his torn pants flapping in the wind. George watched the shark flop around below him, splashing blood all over the deck and flinging it high against the cabin walls with its tail. Over several minutes it gradually slowed down. When it stopped moving, George darted past it and, leaving his bloody shoes at the top of the ladder to the cabin, retrieved a sheaf of nautical charts from a cabinet. After checking the shark for signs of life again, he delivered the charts to Sean on the bridge.

"Find the deepest water and avoid shipwrecks or anywhere else where people might be diving. Where's the tool kit?"

"Same storage space where you found the gaff," replied Sean.

"Thanks." George returned to the aft deck, removed the gaff from Frank's jaw, and hooked the shark through the gills. It didn't move. George lifted it over the side and shoved it under the water to unhook the gaff. Much of the flesh had been torn from Frank's arms, legs, and buttocks, but his torso was relatively intact. George used the gaff to turn him over, hoping to find an exit wound so he wouldn't have to dig the 30-caliber bullet out of his chest. He found it. Next he scrambled to the fore deck, untied the lines from the anchor chains, and carried both anchors back to the aft deck. He wrapped one of the chains tightly around the necks of the three bodies and used wire from the tool kit to fasten the links together. He stopped once to vomit over the transom. Then he removed the dead men's cash and casino chips and tossed them on the bed in Sean's stateroom. After stuffing all of their other possessions, including their wallets, into their travel bags, he wired the bags to the second anchor chain. The entire process took forty-five minutes.

"Are we in the deepest water yet?" George shouted to the bridge.

"Yes," replied Sean.

"Come down here." Sean set the automatic pilot and climbed down the ladder to the deck. He tried to avert his eyes from the carnage. "Anything that would link the anchors to this boat? Serial numbers or whatever?"

Sean examined the anchors carefully. "Thirty-five-pound Danforths. Buy 'em at any marine supply store."

"Any chance the bodies will bloat up with air, drag the anchor to the surface?" asked George.

"How would I know?" Sean shrugged. George sliced each body open from sternum to pubic bone with a fishing knife. Then he the set the anchor on the top of the transom.

"Give me a hand," ordered George. They lifted the bodies over the transom and watched them disappear beneath the yacht's wake. "I'll drop the other anchor after a couple of miles. Where's the cleaning kit and ammunition for the rifle?"

"Sliding wood cabinet above the gun rack."

"Will Lawrence notice the missing shells?"

"Lawrence? Are you kidding?" Sean returned to the bridge. George cleaned and reloaded the .30-06. He carefully wiped his fingerprints off the rifle, cleaning kit, ammo box, and the shells that he loaded. He policed the cabin meticulously to make sure there were no signs of the dead men. He found one spent .30-06 shell in the cabin and another five on the deck, along with five 9-millimeter shells. He threw them all in the ocean along with Morgan's Sig Saur. Finally, he threw the anchor with the overnight bags attached into the sea. He spent the rest of the trip back to the marina cleaning blood and bits of teeth, skull, and brain off the deck, cabin wall, and transom. As they approached the marina he scrubbed the blood off his shoes and hands and changed the bandage on his left pinky. As soon as they docked Sean screwed a high-pressure nozzle on the marina's hose and they spent another half hour scrubbing. Just two guys cleaning up fish blood.

After George showered and packed, he sat Sean down in the cabin and looked him squarely in the eye. "All of their cash and chips are in your stateroom. About 30 grand. That should cover the anchors and fuel."

"Thanks, George."

"There's one more thing you need to know. If you should unwisely change your mind and tell someone about this, I'm going to go straight to the cops and tell them all about how you were the mule in a drug deal gone bad. It will be your word against mine, and I guarantee you those corpses won't end up on my record. I apologize if this offends you, but you have to ask yourself if a Bahamian jury is going to believe a drunken sailor or a star Wall Street trader."

"No offense taken, star Wall Street trader. But that's the thing. I mean, I know what Morgan did for a living. But you? What the fuck?"

"Exactly. What the fuck? Exactly right." George stood up. "We'll never see each other or speak again. Merry Christmas, Sean."

"Yeah, right. Merry Christmas." They shook hands and George left for the airport.

From the departure area, George called his mom to apologize because he was going to be late. She was disappointed he would miss the caroling, but happy he would wake up at home on Christmas morning. He then called Sue's mom's house and left a Merry Christmas message on the machine. He drank two double Johnnie Walker Blacks while waiting for his plane. He recalled Morgan's obsession with "no witnesses." Had Morgan been planning to shoot him next? George was staring into his second double of the flight when he decided that Morgan had definitely intended to kill him.

22

City Trust management communicated bonuses to employees on Wednesday, January 5. The bonus pool was based on earnings estimates for the year ending December 31st. Because of the limited offices on the trading floor, most of the trading and sales managers took space on adjacent floors for the day. Everyone on the trading floor studied the faces of the young professionals as they emerged from the stairwells. Having just learned their rewards for a year's work, very few were able to conceal their emotions. George cursed under his breath when he saw José breeze onto the floor with a smile on his face. Shortly thereafter, Angie, Enrique's assistant, motioned for George to head upstairs.

"Sit down, George," said Enrique from behind an immaculate, cherry desk. George smiled when he saw Philip Gold sitting in the corner because he knew that Gold only sat in on seven-figure bonus conversations.

"As you know, you're compensated based on the bank's financial results, the fixed income department's financial results, the EM trading business's financial results, and your individual performance." Enrique was reading from a script provided by human resources. "The bank's earnings are not public yet, but Street consensus is for net income of one and a half billion dollars, up 15 percent from last year. Fixed income will earn about $550 million, up 20 percent. Net revenue for EM trading is roughly $105 million, up 40 percent." Enrique looked up from his cheat sheet and met George's intense stare with his own. "George, your performance was outstanding. Your knowledge of the pre-Brady market, work ethic, and professionalism have made City Trust the number one trader of pre-Bradys. Most importantly, your trading ledger is up $23 million for the year."

"Twenty-four," interjected George.

"You've got Nici marked at cost. I marked it down for comp purposes due to illiquidity." Enrique stared at him. "Hopefully, you'll make it back next year."

"Understood."

"Your compensation last year is not relevant, since it was a stub period. Your total compensation for 1993 is $1,850,000, consisting of your salary of $70,000 and a bonus of $1,780,000." Enrique looked at George to gauge his reaction, which was amazement. "60 percent of your bonus, or $1,068,000, will be in cash, and 40 percent, or $712,000, will consist of restricted stock." Enrique was reading again. "This package describes the terms of your restricted stock units, as well as the details of tax withholding on your cash component. You will receive your bonus check on February 1st. If you disclose your compensation to anyone, your employment may be terminated and your bonus revoked." Enrique looked up from his script and smiled. He stood up and handed George a manila envelope. "Congratulations, George." Enrique grabbed George's hand and pumped it twice, squeezing his knuckles painfully.

"Well done, George. Congratulations." Gold walked over and shook George's hand with more customary pressure.

George was speechless. He mumbled his thanks and floated out of the room, giddy but confused. He wondered what the hell had happened to the $969,000 hit that he had agreed to take for the Nici fiasco. He stopped in the stairwell, took a couple of deep breaths, assumed a poker face, and returned to his desk.

"Hey, Angie," George whispered, leaning over her back. "Do you think you could get me a reservation for two at one of the four-star restaurants tonight?"

"For you and Sue?" Angie winked.

"Yeah. I'd really appreciate it."

"Shouldn't be a problem." Angie's relationships at the upscale restaurants were incredible. Enrique's tipping habits were legendary among maitre d's. She booked George at La Côte Basque at 8:00. George called Sue and she enthusiastically accepted the date. George had wanted to bolt at 5:00 sharp to avoid the bonus-day gossip and to allow time to run the reservoir before dinner. He desperately needed the therapy, but his curiosity overwhelmed him. What had happened to the $969,000 hit? He leafed through an economic research report from the World Bank while he waited for his boss.

At 5:15 Enrique emerged from the stairwell and George popped out of his chair. Nodding to him, Enrique scanned the trading floor to find an empty office. The big hitters had all been paid in closed offices, but the glass offices were all occupied by midlevel managers paying the grunts and secretaries. Enrique motioned for George to stand against a pillar with him. When George opened his mouth, Enrique raised his palms to indicate that he understood the question.

"It's very simple." Like a catcher conferring with his pitcher on the mound, Enrique held his hand over his mouth to foil the lip-readers. He knew that there were dozens of eyes on him, trying to glean bonus gossip from their conversation. "I went into Gold with the lower number that we talked about and he grilled me on why I was paying you only 5 percent of your P&L. He thought that I was trying to take advantage of you because you're a rookie from the ivory tower and he didn't approve. I had three choices. I could either tell him about Nici, make up some other reason why you're not entitled to normal trader compensation, some kind of fuckin' defect, or jack up the lower number. I chose the latter. You know what that means?"

"What?"

"Means you owe me." Enrique had a predatory look in his eyes. George was transfixed.

"I owe you big time. Thanks, Enrique. Thank you very much."

"Be cool," said Enrique, sensing that George was about to shake his hand again. On bonus day, public displays of joy or gratitude were just as taboo as public displays of disappointment.

The restaurant had sunny murals of the Basque port of St. Jean de Luz painted on the walls. On the way to their table, Sue scanned the crowd for celebrities.

"Too early for the rich and famous," offered George. "Maybe as we leave." Having been tactfully told by Sue that his light navy blazer didn't cut it in the winter, he wore a pin-striped Brooks Brothers suit. He would buy a nice winter blazer when his bonus check cleared. The waiter spoke with such a heavy French accent that George could barely understand him. He ordered a bottle of Chassagne-Montrachet '88 because he had observed Enrique doing so with Ralph at Chanterelle. It cost $58, double what he'd ever spent on a bottle of wine away from the City Trust entertainment account, but he figured he'd be rich in six weeks, so what the hell.

"Here's to your bonus, George." Sue raised her glass to toast. "Are you going to tell me the number?"

"It's a lot more than I thought. Enough to take you on a first-class tropical vacation at the resort of your choice."

"How about the Bahamas?" Sue replied. George choked on his wine. He was coughing in his napkin when the waiter rushed over.

"Monsieur, monsieur. Are you all right?"

George nodded and waved the Frenchman off. Sue looked puzzled.

"Something wrong with the Bahamas?" she asked.

"Uh, no. I heard the weather's a little dicey in February. Maybe someplace farther south. How 'bout Jamaica? You know, Jamaica is for lovers."

"So you're not telling me the number?"

"I got a letter from my mom. She missed you at Christmas in Bethlehem."

"That's sweet. Tell her that I would've loved to have been there, but after missing my mom on Thanksgiving I really needed to see her at Christmas."

"She'll appreciate that, of course. I mean, you would want your kids to visit you on Christmas, right?"

"I don't have any kids."

"Well . . . uh . . . you want some . . . uh . . . don't you?"

Considering George's anxiety in asking the question, she decided to toy with him. "Where are you going with this, George?"

"Don't normal people talk about the future, you know, their aspirations, whatever, without going somewhere?"

"Don't close friends discuss their salaries, whatever?"

"Mademoiselle?" The waiter interrupted.

"I'll have the escargots to start, and the monkfish with truffles and Madeira sauce, please."

"Très bien. Et monsieur?"

"I'll have the house smoked salmon and the beef Bordelaise, please, medium rare."

"Très bien." The waiter filled their glasses with a flourish before retreating. Sue smiled at George over the rim of her glass.

"If I didn't want to maximize my reproductive success, I'd be genetically defective, right?"

"Jesus, Sue." George looked hurt. Sue watched the wine that she swirled in her glass for a moment, then met George's eyes and smiled softly.

"Does three constitute reproductive success for the modern human female?" Sue took a long drink of her Burgundy. "Of course, I'll reserve the right to reassess after each one."

"Of course."

"So, is three considered reproductive success for the modern human male?"

"Absolutely. Excellent number. Fifty percent increase in the gene pool." They clinked glasses and drank.

"So, George, how can I help you celebrate your bonus if I don't know what it is?"

"Look, once the bonus number is communicated, it's owed. The exception is if the bank finds out that you told. They can revoke your bonus, even fire you."

"Who am I going to tell?"

"If you told Missy and she told Nick and Nick told Sam and Sam told someone at work and it got back to Enrique . . ."

"I won't tell anyone. I promise." She zipped her lips. George leaned more than halfway across the table and whispered.

"One and three-quarter million."

"Oh my god," Sue shrieked. Everyone in the restaurant looked at Sue. Oblivious, she leaned across the table and kissed George firmly on the lips. "Congratulations, I mean, that's awesome. Really awesome," she beamed.

Blushing, George whispered, "Only 60 percent is in cash. Forty percent is restricted City Trust stock that vests over five years. After withholding tax it's only 600 large in actual cash." Sue started laughing in her napkin to avoid spitting out snail. "What's so funny?"

"*Only* 600 *large*. You sound like a gangster." George rolled his eyes. Sue finished her glass. "Why don't you order a red with your beef and I'll finish the Montrachet? I think you can afford it." Enrique always ordered a Château Margaux when clients had beef at Smith & Wollensky or the Palm, so George did the same. When the meal ended they had settled on St. Bart's for their February getaway. George remembered to slip the maitre d' a twenty on the way out, as Angie had instructed.

They were all over each other in the cab back to Club 16B. George tried to remember if he'd ever seen Sue so happy and playful. They were both tipsy, and clearly preoccupied. Neither of them noticed the teenager who followed them out of the elevator. When George opened his apartment door the boy roughly shoved both him and Sue inside and slammed the door behind them. When George turned around he was pointing a pistol at his nose.

"Where's my brother?" the boy demanded. His eyes were glassy and his gun hand shook.

"I, I have no idea who you're talking about." George backed into the living room in a panic. The boy followed, keeping the Glock inches from George's nose.

"You came back from Nassau and Kevin didn't. Now where the fuck is he?"

"I don't know who you're talking about." George backed down the hall into the living room. Ignoring Sue, who stepped into the hall closet, the boy followed, keeping the pistol in George's face.

"Yes you do, George. You fucking Ivy League pussy. I'm gonna to count to five, then I'm going to blow your fuckin' pussy brains out. One, two, three . . ."

Inside the closet, Sue had quietly pulled the three-iron out of Nick's golf bag. Opening the door carefully, she snuck up behind the trembling hood and at the count of five swung and hit his ear. He collapsed, bleeding heavily on the rug.

"Oh my god. Did I kill him?" George knelt down and felt his pulse.

"No, you just knocked him out." George pulled off his tie and bound the youth's wrists tightly behind his back. He ran into the bathroom, threw up in the toilet, rinsed his mouth, and returned to the living room with gauze and tape. Sue was still standing over the unconscious boy, holding the three-iron.

"Here, see if you can stop the bleeding. And don't touch the gun."

"Shouldn't we call 911?"

"In a minute." George knew his suitemates were supposed to be traveling on business, but he checked their bedrooms to make sure. "Listen, Sue. Please listen carefully. We're going to tell the police that this was an attempted robbery, OK?"

"What? What is going on, George?" Sue looked up from dressing the wound. "Do you know this kid? His brother?"

"No time to explain now. We've got to call the police, and we've got to tell them that this was a robbery."

"This is too weird. What's going on?"

"I'll explain later. This was a robbery, OK?"

"You want me to lie to the police?"

"Trust me, Sue. This is a bad kid. I'm sure the cops will be happy to believe that it was a robbery. You have to trust me, Sue."

"I trust you, George, but you have to trust me. You have to promise to explain what the hell this is all about!"

"I promise. Now we have to call this in before the kid's blood coagulates. It was a robbery, right?"

"Yes. It was a robbery," conceded Sue. George called 911.

"Everything happened just as it happened except for what he said. He said, 'Give me all your money or I'll blow your fuckin' brains out.' Can you repeat that?"

"Give me all your money or I'll blow your fuckin' brains out," repeated Sue.

The uniformed patrolmen were young and courteous. George described the incident to a handsome Latino while his redheaded partner administered first aid. After finishing his note taking, the Latino carefully deposited the Glock in a plastic evidence bag. He also placed plastic bags over the handle and the head of the three-iron. When the paramedics arrived, the redhead handcuffed the barely conscious boy and handed George his tie.

"Will both of you come down to the station, please? We need

to get official statements." In the back of the squad car, George and Sue held hands in silence. Activity at the 19th Precinct was subdued, with only the usual drunks being routinely processed. After twenty minutes a detective with a face like a tenderized ham stepped into the room.

"Will you follow me, Miss Collier?" he asked in gravelly Brooklynese.

"Of course." Sue followed Detective Riley to a dingy little room containing a metal table with a tape recorder on it and two metal chairs. Sue repeated the story that George had given the patrolman, interrupted with clarifying questions only twice.

"Have you ever seen the assailant before, Miss Collier?"

"No."

"Any idea why he picked on you and Mr. Wilhelm?"

"No."

"OK. Thank you." The detective led Sue back to the waiting room and repeated the process with George. Afterward they sat in the waiting room for an hour until the detective brought in two clipboards with their typewritten statements. They read them quickly and signed.

"The kid's name is Brian Murphy. He's got an ugly rap sheet. Dangerous kid—he had a round in the chamber of that automatic," the detective rasped. "I'll be shocked if this case makes it to trial. He'll probably cop a plea and serve his time."

"How many years?" asked George.

"Depends on the judge. Like I said, he's a dangerous kid. This will be his first adult conviction, but two of his juvenile convictions were violent. I'd guess five years hard time." He handed each of them his business card. "Call me if you need to leave town for more than a couple of days. Do you need a ride home?" George and Sue shook their heads. They walked through a thick, silent snowfall, across the East Side to Club 16B, under other circumstances a romantic stroll. Once inside, Sue put her back to the door.

"George, what the hell is going on!"

"You'd be much happier not knowing."

"George, I just committed perjury for you and now you are going to tell me the truth!"

George had never seen her so angry. He went to the kitchen for a bottle of Johnnie Walker Black, a bottle of soda water, and two glasses of ice. He drank with purpose as he told her about the gambling and the meetings with TD.

"How could you? How could you bet more than you could afford to lose?"

"I knew that I could afford to lose it on February 1st. What I didn't understand was that TD wasn't going to wait." He explained about the vig and described the trip to the Spa.

"How did those creeps get a Polaroid of me?" shrieked Sue.

"They said from a private detective. Believe me, I was horrified." George told her about the Nicaragua scam and his stint as Lawrence's crewman. Sue listened dumbfounded until he described the torture at Daisy's.

"Jesus Christ, George."

"Have you heard enough? Can I stop now?"

"Not on your life. Tell it all the way to the thing tonight."

"My god," she said when he was finished. "I mean . . . my god."

"Morgan was sure that the thugs had not mentioned their trip to any other mobsters, because they wanted to keep all of the money—not share it with their bosses." Tears were now rolling down his cheeks. "What happened tonight makes me think that he was right. If the mob were involved they would have sent a professional, not some cracked-out kid. Tonight was definitely personal. I think we're safe, at least until the kid gets out of prison." Sue started to cry also. "Look Sue, I know that I made horrible mistakes. When they took me to the garage and showed me your picture, I was desperate. I got the money the only way I could think of. I tried to give it back to the bank, but they wouldn't take it. If I'd had any idea that people were going to die, or that you were going to get sucked into it . . ." He trailed off. "I mean, my God, I deserve a lot worse than a severed finger." They held each other tightly and quietly. After a half hour there were no more tears.

23

George called Detective Riley on Thursday and Friday, claiming that he was concerned that Brian would try to avenge Sue's blow to his head. He was relieved to hear that Brian could not make bail and would be charged as an adult with multiple felonies. George called the Bethlehem Savings and Loan and arranged to pay off the $37,000 balance that would be outstanding on his parents' home mortgage on February 1st. He also spoke to Mr. Vandermeer, the manager of the Bethlehem Sears and his former Little League coach, about the appliances that he would buy for Greta. He promised to mail George a catalogue. Ducking out at lunchtime on Friday, he met with a Manhattan travel agent who promised to look into Caribbean cruises that catered to invalids. He let Sue handle their bookings for St. Barts.

Sue and George spent every night together that week. On Sunday morning George sat on the couch in 16B, flipping between the NFL pregame shows with the remote. Sue lay with her head on his lap, rubbing gently and waiting for signs of life there. When Missy and Nick returned from brunch, Sue rubbed less obtrusively.

"Hey, George, what do you think of the Giants today?" asked Nick.

"What's the spread?" asked George.

"Seven," replied Nick.

"Strahan and Jumbo are out, Collins is limping, and Daluiso lost five pounds with the flu. With the Giants this banged up, seven is a major overlay, even at the Meadowlands. I'll take the Vikings plus the points. Are you calling now?"

Sue stood up and punched George squarely in the nose.

"Ouch!" George pinched his nose to keep the blood off of his shirt.

"Lean your head back. I'll get some cotton." Sue disappeared into the bathroom.

"Mercy, George. What was that all about?" asked Missy.

"What can I say? Sue really hates it when I go against the Giants."

ACKNOWLEDGMENTS

I would like to thank Lehman Brothers, my employer, for granting me the flexibility to write this book.

I must thank my best friend, Ted Brandt, and my other good friends who gave me the feedback that shaped this novel and the encouragement that kept me going: Owen and Jennifer Williams, Jim Mullin, Stuart Cauff, Terry Dunne, Andy Szabo, Don McNicol, John Bernlohr, and Jeff McAnallen.

Thanks also go to Arturo Porzecanski and Ken Hoffman for providing information on Latin loans; and to Gary Evans for teaching me pre-Brady arbitrage.

I thank my family for their support and input: wife Sallie; sons Fred, Jamie, and Bill; and Sallie's parents, Jamie and Audrey McConnell.

Last but not least, I thank my editors, Starling Lawrence and Tom Mayer, and my copy editor, Elizabeth Pierson, for their superb work on the manuscript.